MW01154423

Cygnus Rising

Cygnus Space Opera
Book 1

A Tale in the Free Trader Universe

By Craig Martelle

ISBN 10: 1537773364
ISBN 13: 978-1537773360
ASIN: B01LZINJEP

Cover art created by Christian Bentulan
CoversbyChristian.com
Background image on the cover provided courtesy of
NASA from a picture taken by the Hubble Telescope

Editing services provided by Mia Darien
miadarien.com

Other Books by Craig Martelle

Free Trader Series

- ➤ Book 1 – The Free Trader of Warren Deep (February 2016)
- ➤ Book 2 – The Free Trader of Planet Vii (March 2016)
- ➤ Book 3 – Adventures on RV Traveler (April 2016)
- ➤ Book 4 – Battle for the Amazon (August 2016)
- ➤ Book 5 – Free the North! (September 2016)
- ➤ Book 6 – Free Trader on the High Seas (October 2016)
- ➤ Book 7 – Southern Discontent (January 2017)

Cygnus Space Opera – set in the Free Trader Universe

- ➤ Book 1 – Cygnus Rising (Sep 2016)
- ➤ Book 2 – Cygnus Expanding (2017)

End Times Alaska Trilogy, a Winlock Press publication

- ➤ Book 1: Endure (June 2016)
- ➤ Book 2: Run (July 2016)
- ➤ Book 3: Return (August 2016)
- ➤ Book 4: Fury (December 2016)

Rick Banik Thriller Series

People Raged and the Sky Was on Fire (May 2016)

Short Story Contributions to Anthologies

- ➤ Earth Prime Anthology, Volume 1 (Stephen Lee & James M. Ward)
- ➤ Apocalyptic Space Short Story Collection (Stephen Lee & James M. Ward)
- ➤ Lunar Resorts Anthology, Volume 2 (Stephen Lee & James M. Ward)
- ➤ Inanna's Circle Game, Volume 2 (edited by Kat Lind)
- ➤ The Expanding Universe, Volume 1 (edited by Craig Martelle)(Dec 2016)

Craig Martelle

Aletha

Table of Contents

Acknowledgments

I love the space opera genre and want to thank those who've written books where I've read the whole series – David Weber, Raymond Weil, Mark E. Cooper, Joshua Dalzelle, N.D. Webb, Jonathan P. Brazee, Edgar Rice Burroughs with his John Carter series, and even Gene Roddenberry with Star Trek. Inspiration can come from anywhere and everywhere, but in the end, the thing that matters most is the relationships between the characters. Thousands of years in the future, people will still get upset by misspoken words and unkind acts. How will they respond? Those are the tales that are timeless. And that is what I try to do in every one of my books, as well as include a variety of intelligent species, because you suspect that your cat would murder you in your sleep, if he could only master the can-opener.

After becoming a full-time author, I've found kindred spirits in the publishing world. A few have been very kind to allow the use of their names as we memorialize each other in print. I fear that Craig Martelle has died hideous deaths in the books of my fellows. I'm far less bloodthirsty, but sometimes, characters get hurt… Shout out to Kat Lind, J.L. Hendricks, and Michael Anderle, all of whom sport a namesake in this book. Michael writes the wildly popular Kurtherian Gambit series. Jenn writes the Eclipse of the Warrior Paranormal Romance series, and Kat writes mostly non-fiction, but she's slowly coming over to the dark side with the rest of us fiction geeks☺.

I want to thank some readers by name as they are the ones who we look to when we're feeling a little down. Diane Velasquez and her sister Dorene Johnson are powerhouse readers, ready for anything I throw at them and always willing to give feedback. Andrew Mackay and Joe Jackson also helped me with a pre-read of this book, just to make sure that it hit the right notes and you can thank Andrew for the inclusion of the Line & Block org chart. I like his suggestion to add visibility to the loose structure that the SES embraces. Norman Meredith and Chris Rolfe dive into anything new for me as well and they are very kind and fully supportive. My goal went from publishing a book, to writing better books, to not letting people like these down. I endeavor to get better with each new title in telling a good story with believable characters doing things that matter.

NOTE: For those who've read the Free Trader series, we have changed the capitalization in Cygnus Space Opera from what you've seen to a more standard English. We hope you enjoy the story.

Humans and the Intelligent Creatures

Intelligent creatures are capitalized – Rabbits, Wolfoids, Hawkoids,

The Hillcats
Mixial – Tandry's bonded 'cat, a small, long-haired calico
Lutheann – bonded with Cain, all white
Carnesto – bonded with Ellie, all black

The Humans
Cain – Great-great-grandson of Free Traders Braden & Micah
Aletha – Cain's true love who wants to stay home
Ellie – Cain's classmate at Space School
Tandry – classmate at Space School
DI Katlind – Discipline Instructor at Space School
SI Hendricks – Space Instructor on the RV Traveler
Lieutenant Simonds – class escort on the RV Traveler
Dr. Johns – clone of the Cygnus VI survivor. In charge of the space program
Captain Rand – captain of the Cygnus-12 Deep Space Exploration ship

The Hawkoid
Chirit – Crew member on Cygnus-12, Sensor Operator

The Tortoid
Daksha – Third Master of the Tortoise Consortium, son of Aadi, Commander of the Cygnus-12 exploration mission

The Lizard Men (Amazonians)
Peekaless – nicknamed "Pickles," classmate at Space School
Rastor – Lieutenant, legacy crew member from the Cygnus-12,

The Rabbits
Brisbois – called "Briz," technical genius, classmate at Space School
Allard & Beauchene – gardeners assigned to the Cygnus-12

The Wolfoids
Black Leaper – called "Stinky," team leader of the Space School class
Lieutenant Strider – Engineer aboard the Cygnus-12

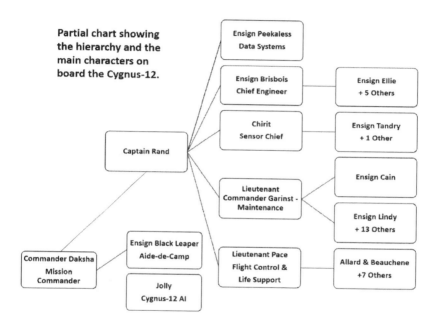

Partial chart showing the hierarchy and the main characters on board the Cygnus-12.

Ensign Peekaless
Data Systems

Ensign Brisbois
Chief Engineer

Ensign Ellie
+ 5 Others

Chirit
Sensor Chief

Ensign Tandry
+ 1 Other

Captain Rand

Ensign Cain

Lieutenant
Commander Garinst -
Maintenance

Ensign Lindy
+ 13 Others

Ensign Black Leaper
Aide-de-Camp

Commander Daksha
Mission
Commander

Lieutenant Pace
Flight Control &
Life Support

Allard & Beauchene
+7 Others

Jolly
Cygnus-12 AI

Fire!

Flames shot through the open hatch. Cain yelled, "Engineering's on fire!" The klaxons continued to scream, echoing down the corridor away from him. He sensed, more than heard, the anguished cry.

The hatch was open. The automated fire suppression system had failed.

He ripped open the damage control panel and pulled the tank out. He threw it hastily over his shoulder, reached behind him with a well-practiced maneuver to start the flow of air, and wrapped the dangling mask across his face. He draped the fire hood over his head as he ran. He didn't have time to put on the whole outfit. People he knew were dying.

He hit the flames of the doorway at a dead run. The intense heat scorched his bare forearms as he passed, and he yelled into his mask as he slid to a stop in the middle of the space, looking for survivors. A Rabbit lay under a terminal, an ugly scorch mark cut across his white fur, leaving blackened hair around burned pink flesh. The Rabbit moved–Briz was alive.

Cain slid him out from under the melting terminal. The Rabbit was dense and blocky, half Cain's height but the same weight. Cain pulled an equipment cover off the back of a chair, wrapping it around the Rabbit's head and over as much of his body as he could, then he hefted him up, trying to avoid the injury. Cain lumbered toward the hatch, ducked his head, held his breath, and jumped through the flames. He deposited the Rabbit in the passageway and raced back into engineering. Ellie was in there somewhere.

He should have been alarmed that the flames didn't seem to hurt as much this time. The next victim was a Wolfoid, horribly torn apart from the force of an exploded containment vessel. He saw something odd about the way the Wolfoid's body, bigger than a human's, was laying on the floor.

A pink-fleshed hand snaked out from underneath the gray fur. Without remorse, Cain heaved the Wolfoid's shattered body to the side. Ellie was dazed, but seemed to be okay. The Wolfoid must have taken the full force of the rupture, protecting her. Cain's breath caught as he looked at her golden blond hair, the ends curled and brittle from the heat that had passed over her.

He pulled her to him as blue lights started to flash, signaling the imminent flooding of argon gas into the compartment. He kneeled, rolling her from a sitting position to over his shoulder. He stood without much effort. She wasn't heavy and laid easily over his shoulder as he hurried for the hatch. The flames had died down somewhat, but he still ran through, hoping speed would keep them safe. Once through, he stopped, took off his hood and breathed deeply of the better air in the corridor. The hatch to engineering closed.

The klaxons stopped as someone helped Ellie from his shoulder, and he looked at the closed hatch. Anyone still in the space would be denied oxygen, just like the fire. The argon gas was supposed to be flushed in a matter of seconds, but it would be too late. He was surprised he didn't know how many people worked in that space. Three? Four?

"Holy Rising Star, Cain! You shouldn't have gone in there. Why the hell would you do something like that?" the captain's words were harsh, but his eyes were grateful. As the older man looked at the two survivors in the corridor, he added, "But I'm glad you did, son. Looks like you saved two lives, irreplaceable lives."

The two Hillcats waiting for Cain and Ellie in the corridor couldn't have agreed more. Carnesto yowled in pain as Ellie came to her senses. The burns on her lower body attacked her with waves of agony. He put a furry paw on her head to help her through the worst of it.

Why had Cain taken such risk knowing what his death would do to his 'cat, to his family? He'd had no choice. It was who he'd always wanted to be. It was who he was. He'd spent his short life trying to live up to one man, the Space Exploration Service Captain who showed him how a hero acts.

Six Months Ago

He didn't know how it started, and he didn't care. When smoke poured down the school's hallway, he'd taken Aletha's hand, and they ran from the building. Others streamed out after them.

Tears poured down Aletha's face as they watched flames gut the building where they'd met, where they'd learned about life.

A man passing by stopped his vehicle and ran toward the school, yelling, asking if everyone was out.

No one knew. He pulled his shirt over his mouth and nose, wrapped his light jacket around one arm, and bolted through the open main door.

He was only gone a few heartbeats before two people stumbled out. The man followed, dragging another person, who he deposited on the lawn before going back into the building. He returned twice more with others. The fourth time he entered the building, it collapsed around him. Six people lived because of that man. He didn't know them. He'd risked everything for strangers.

He was a captain in the new Space Exploration Service with a promising career ahead. Cain wondered why the man had thrown it all away. He'd asked, but only his father had an idea.

"It's what your ancestors did. Free Trader Braden gave up everything to make our world what it is today." Cain was confused. He'd always thought Braden was the richest man ever.

"That's the modern story, son, and that was toward the end of his life. He and his wife probably had more scars than any other people in our history. He risked his life, over and over, without thought of reward, simply because it was the right thing to do," his father finished. "We come from a proud bloodline. Maybe we need to talk more about what that means."

"I agree, but not now. I need time to think," Cain said softly. He left their home and walked toward the river, deliberately taking a direction away from Aletha's home.

I cowered outside while people were dying, he thought, condemning himself. *When it became dangerous, I ran. Aletha deserves a better man than that, a man like the* captain.

Without asking anyone's advice or permission, he'd gone to the recruiter's office the next day and signed up. And there he sat, waiting for transportation to take him to the space center for his initial training. He'd sent Aletha a short message, telling her that he was leaving.

Cain sat in the recruiter's office, still smelling of smoke from yesterday's fire.

He expected Aletha to race to the recruiter's office for a teary farewell. She didn't come. Her only reply was even shorter than his note. "If that's what you think you have to do," was all it said. His ham-handed attempt at controlling her had fallen flat yet again. She made him a better man every day, but he didn't deserve her. This time, he wouldn't have a chance to apologize. The transport was there and they were collecting communicators as the recruits boarded. He looked at his blankly as he handed it over and climbed the steps, leaving his old life, and Aletha, far behind.

The Obstacle Course

Cain's assigned bunkmate was a Wolfoid named Black Leaper. There was no idle chatter so they didn't get the chance to talk. The Wolfoid had the lower bunk because Cain volunteered to climb the small ladder to the upper bed. The Wolfoid would learn over time, because ladders were prevalent throughout the ships in the space fleet. Cain didn't want his bunkmate to have a harder time than he knew they all would already have.

Training was about preparing one's mind to deal with the stress of space. The instructors believed that meant abusing the bodies of all recruits, regardless of fur, feathers, or skin. Everyone was equally accepted and the instructors had no favorites. They treated all recruits like trash, ready to be jettisoned from the nearest airlock.

Mostly.

In the millennia leading to present day, only humans had operated spaceships. The designs had been focused solely on human physiology. That was starting to change, but non-humans continued to be at a disadvantage. Cain couldn't understand why things were still antiquated and arrayed against the other intelligent species.

He wanted no part of that, so Leaper got the lower bunk. Someone quipped about him sleeping on the floor, which led to Cain tripping the person on their first formation run and "accidentally" stepping on her as he ran past. She got the point, but Cain learned quickly that it wasn't good to have enemies.

The next day, they were negotiating the obstacle course, directed to use teamwork to navigate pits, traps, walls, and other barriers. When Cain first looked at it, he wasn't sure which creatures would best be able to run the entire course. As it turned out, it took all of them.

Cain ran toward the wall and the slim blond held out her hand for him to grab as he vaulted upward. With an extra kick from the wall, he gained the height he needed to reach the outstretched hand, which she pulled away at the last instant. He grasped at empty air as he started to fall backwards, catching a boot on the wall and landing flat on his back. Black Leaper was there in an instant to pick him up so they could run at the wall together.

A voice from beyond reverberated across the obstacle course. "RECRUIT! I saw that. Get down here!" A stocky woman with a crewcut stormed across the muddy ground of the obstacle course. Her uniform remained immaculate. Cain stepped back. He thought it was something he did. Leaper thought it was something he had done.

They were both wrong. She stopped next to the two recruits, sneered at both of them and with a dismissive wave, encouraged them to run away, around the wall to the next obstacle. They didn't hesitate as they bolted for the rope swing across a sludge-filled pond.

"GET DOWN HERE!" Spittle flew from her mouth as she screamed at the young woman who'd pulled her hand away and let Cain fall.

She ran down the ramp on the back side of the wall and stood at attention while the Discipline Instructor, the DI, berated her and her entire lineage all the way back to the RV Traveler, the colonization ship that brought all intelligent life to Cygnus Seven, or Vii as they called it. When she finished, she took a deep breath.

"Are you ever going to let your teammates down again, Recruit?" the DI asked in a calm voice.

"No, Master DI!" the young woman shouted.

The DI was unpersuaded. "Why would you do that?" she asked in a low voice, serious about the question.

"Master DI, the recruit doesn't know!" the young woman belted out her already well-practiced response to anything she supposedly did wrong.

"Cut the crap, Ellie," the DI said conversationally. "You did that for a reason. Did he do something to you?" The young woman's hesitation gave the DI her answer. "Tell me, what did he do?"

The integration of the training was a newer standard and some men were having difficulty seeing women as equals. It was a holdover from the days before Braden and Micah, the old days, the dark male-dominated days.

Finally, Ellie found her voice. "He tripped me in our formation run, then stepped on me."

"On purpose?" the DI pressed.

"Yes, Master DI. On purpose."

The DI thought about it. "Why do you think he'd do that?" The DI didn't mind a certain amount of horseplay, but she wouldn't tolerate open combat between the recruits as some were extremely deadly, like the Wolfoids who, to this day, killed game without the use of weapons.

"I suggested the Wolfoid should sleep on the ground instead of the bottom bunk," Ellie whispered, ashamed to hear it from her own mouth.

"I would have stepped on you, too. I suggest what's-his-face tried to teach you a lesson and I'm glad he did. He's your new recruit team leader. No, the Wolfoid, he's your new team leader. And don't even think thoughts like that again. At some point in time, you will need to count on every single creature here, and they will have to count on you. If they can't, you're out of the program, and you'll be a ground crew refueling shuttle rockets and cleaning out the john. You get me, Recruit?" the DI said in a dangerous voice.

"Yes, Master DI!"

The DI made Ellie climb the wall again, but there was no one on top to pull her up, which meant that for the remainder of the time allocated to the obstacle course, she would run at the wall and make futile attempts to kick off high enough to reach the ledge on her own.

The DI stalked around the obstacle to find Cain and Leaper swimming through the mud, having failed to correctly use the rope to swing across the obstacle. She waved to one of her fellow DIs, nodding toward the two in the pit.

"The human made it. The Wolfoid slipped. The human swung back to help. He almost had him, hanging onto the rope with one hand while trying to pull the Wolfoid out of the muck with his other. So close." The other DI laughed as he walked back to his post.

"YOU TWO KNUCKLEHEADS! HERE, NOW!" the short DI bellowed, stabbing a finger toward the ground in front of her. Cain and Leaper stopped. They were almost to the other side. She could see them trying to figure if they should fight their way back through the mud or run around the obstacle, which was supposed to be taboo, although they'd already done it once. Seeing their confusion between the standing order and her current order, she decided to elucidate. "Get out and run around," she stated, trying not to laugh.

Recruits. Breaking them down was the easy part, but building them back up to think for themselves while still working as a team was tricky. Many figured it out, a few did not. This was the breaking down phase, two days into the ninety-day training cycle, followed by an additional ninety-days of specialization training. She expected them to be confused, but at least they were giving it their all. She watched them scramble out of the pit. The Wolfoid dropped to all fours and raced ahead, but slowed, letting the human catch up. Whether it was for mutual support as neither wanted to face the DI alone, or simply the two had quickly become a team, she didn't know. It didn't matter, either. The end result was the same.

Black Leaper and Cain arrived together and stood upright. The Wolfoid towered over the short DI while standing a head taller than Cain. He wore a collar with a vocalization device, a small unit that translated his thought voice into out-loud speech. The devices captured some of the emotional nuances of the speaker depending on how long the creature had worn it. In this case, Leaper had just received it so most statements sounded monotone.

"Recruit Black Leaper reporting as ordered, Master DI," the slightly mechanical voice relayed. Leaper didn't like the sound of it. He'd invest in a quality unit when he graduated.

"Recruit Cain reporting as ordered," Cain said softly, trying to project the same volume as Leaper.

"At ease, recruits. Why do you think I called you over here?" she asked almost conversationally. Cain and Leaper froze, not wanting to move and draw the attention of the DI although she looked from one to the other and back again.

"Never mind. You, Black Leaper, you are the team leader for this mob. You'll have five recruits that you are responsible for. This one will help you. Your job is to make this group tight, work as one unit. You think you can do that?"

"Yes, Master DI," Leaper responded, his mechanical voice not reflecting the full measure of his excitement, but his head bobbed slightly as he realized the honor he was just given. It usually took weeks for a team leader to be designated.

"I'll probably have to fire you tomorrow, but for now, you're it." She leaned forward and sniffed, then coughed. "Get your stinky asses over that wall!" She pointed back toward the obstacle they'd previously run around, thinking they were free and clear of it. Cain tried not to roll his eyes as they both dashed away before she could change her mind and fire Leaper sooner than tomorrow.

Leaper barked and Cain gave a hearty "yeehaw" as they ran to get into position to vault the wall.

"You first, Stinky," Cain joked. The Wolfoid yipped, not sure if he liked the nickname, but knowing full well that from that point forward, he'd never be called anything else.

Leaper ran and true to his name, kicked off the wall, sailing high, but his push-off kept him out of reach of the top. He landed gracefully in the sand pit. "I need to push off farther out, away from the wall." Cain rain forward and got on all fours, making himself into a springboard. Leaper ran away from the wall, made a sharp turn without slowing down, and ran back, hitting Cain at full speed.

Cain withstood the onslaught, vowing to never do that again as Leaper sailed high enough to land on the top of the obstacle on his four paws. It took a great deal to impress the DI and in her two years at the school, she'd never seen anyone do what Leaper had just done on his second try.

The human stood, a little slowly, then jogged to a position where he could take a run at the wall. He stopped, gauged the distance, licked a finger and held it up to the wind, then sprinted forward. He hit the wall with his left foot to push himself higher, reaching for the top. Leaper hung his front paws down the wall where Cain grasped one, barely. They stayed where they were, in limbo. Leaper was ready to fall and Cain hung on by his fingertips.

He looked up at Leaper's face as the Wolfoid showed his fangs, struggling to find a better perch. With a push from below, Cain bounced upward. Leaper scrambled back and kept pulling until Cain was on the top. They both looked down to see Ellie wiping the sand of Cain's shoes from her hands.

"Somebody has to keep their eyes on you two," she said with a smile, before looking quickly at the DI standing on a hill not far away. She bolted before the DI could give her a tongue-lashing for running around the obstacles to get back to the wall. Ellie ran for the rope swing, enjoying the exercise. She vaulted, caught the rope, and easily swung to the other side, hitting the ground without breaking stride. Leaper and Cain both watched, before running down the back ramp of the wall obstacle to build speed for their second attempt at clearing the pit.

First Classes at Space School

The entire morning consisted of physical labor, from the formation runs to the obstacle course, to individual calisthenics designed to get the most from each and every recruit, whether Wolfoid, Rabbit, Hawkoid, Amazonian, Hillcat, Aurochs, and even Tortoid. There weren't any Tortoids in Cain's group, but there were instructors from each of the intelligent species.

Cain and his twenty-five classmates had been assigned to class Beta 37 for the second quarter's class of the year 137. One hundred and thirty-seven years had passed since President Micah assumed leadership on Vii and helped to turn Vii into a peaceful society of coexistence and intellectual expansion. The intelligent species of Vii were considered to be its people, to be one humanity encompassing all those with any trace of human DNA, which was what the scientists had spliced into the creatures that later evolved into the intelligent species.

Lunch at Space School was magnificent. Cain was fed well throughout his life, but he'd never seen a spread like they offered at the school. There was something for all of the intelligent species, including live beetles and raw meat. Of all the things they trained at the school, dealing with starvation wasn't one of them. The instructors knew that the recruits would burn the calories, so they gave them as much as they could eat in the fifteen minutes allotted.

Which was more than enough for both Cain and Leaper. Ellie only managed to eat half her food before they were rushed from the dining hall, and the other two members of Leaper's team were equally challenged in finishing their meals. An older woman called Tandry, and her bonded Hillcat Mixial, looked forlornly at the food being wasted as she passed her tray to the scullery. She took too long getting the food, but next time, she'd grab faster and eat more. She left the dining hall hungry.

Mixial was nonplussed. She'd eat when she was hungry, to include hunting game in the local woods if the mood took her. The Hillcats only attended Space School with their bonded humans, never by themselves.

They mostly went to the classes, but weren't responsible for anything. They were, after all, 'cats.

The last member of the team was a Rabbit called Brisbois, a dainty male who joined because he was a technical whiz. If one wanted a career in math and physics, there was no better place than the Space Exploration Service. Most everything on Vii was managed by Artificial Intelligence. To get into the Cygnus VI Research and Development Center, the off-planet station, he had to establish himself. Serving was the best way to do that. Plus he was one of the very few Rabbits who didn't enjoy gardening and that accounted for why he was smaller than his siblings. At least that was what his brothers and sisters told him.

They ran from the dining hall as five teams of five, plus a total of seven 'cats trotting leisurely alongside the group. The DI shooed the 'cats out of the way as she tried to claim her spot alongside the formation. She wondered if the recruits were working surreptitiously with their 'cats to get in her way, slow her down. It would not have been the first time recruits conspired with their 'cats against the DI and it wouldn't be the last.

The DI sprinted out in front of the formation and yelled over her shoulder that the recruits needed to catch up. The Wolfoids and Rabbits hopped awkwardly as they stayed upright. Dropping to all fours would have made the race irrelevant, but they needed to arrive in their five-person teams. The lone Amazonian rocked as he ran, bouncing into others from his team as he struggled to keep up.

No one was happy, just as the DI meant things to be. This lightened her mood considerably so she slowed down to let the formation tighten up. It wouldn't do to look like a ragtag mob when they arrived at the classrooms. It wouldn't do at all.

She slowed them to a march so the recruits could catch their breath and walk in like they owned the place. She'd never graduated all twenty-five before, but in this group, she saw no one as the weak link. If she stayed out in front and cut short any issues, like the minor prejudice against the Wolfoid, before they could fester, then she might be able to reach her goal. Only one other DI had graduated all twenty-five. She wanted to be the next one to do it. She had no control over whether the recruits stayed or went, that was up to third parties who observed the various phases of training. All she could do was teach them to be better as a team than alone, while letting their individuality help them to be better versions of themselves.

The DI had high hopes.

She dismissed the group and had them walk smartly in a single file into the great building outside the space center. Only a short subway ride away was the New Sanctuary oasis and the New Command Center, which was the heart and soul of all operations in the Cygnus system.

The recruits started in one of the satellite buildings and throughout training and follow-on classification school, they'd move into better and higher tech rooms to help facilitate turning them into experts in the fields they were best suited for.

The first week of classes were all introductory or history-related. What was the Space Exploration Service all about; how did it come to be; what were its goals; what was its future; and most importantly, how the useless recruits in that room could blossom into contributing members of the SES.

Each instructor built up the class's hopes, followed quickly by the DI dashing them as she took the stage between classes.

DI Katlind stood tall, seemingly much taller than her actual short stature called for as she looked down on the recruits from the stage where the lecturers briefed. She looked at each of the new faces, ascertaining who was listening and who was sleeping with their eyes open like Tortoids and Rabbits could do. Satisfied that she had their attention, she drilled them on the key lessons from the day.

"What do you live for?" she shouted.

"The ship! Our purpose is to serve the ship. The ship is life," they repeated, mostly in unison. It took seven more times before the DI was satisfied with the volume of the recruits' response and the accuracy of the words.

"You!" She pointed at Leaper, who sat upright, like a dog, on a padded cushion with a small writing desk. "What does that mean?"

"The ship must always come first. Without it, no one can live in space. The ship is life," Leaper spoke passionately, judging by how his shaggy brown head bounced and his mouth worked as he "talked." The mechanical voice was getting better, but still more monotone than not.

"You!" She pointed to Cain, sitting at a human-style desk next to Leaper. The question caught him off guard as he expected her to pick someone from the other side of the room.

He stood, buying himself time to think of his version of the answer. "We are all expendable to save the ship. You can't have people without the ship, but you can have a ship without people." Katlind harumphed, but didn't counter his point.

"You! Get that out of your mouth. Why would we go to space if it's just going to kill us?" the DI asked, pointing to the Amazonian who'd been studiously chewing an old-fashioned wood pencil. The Lizard Man stood, as Cain had done. His vocalization device seemed to be well-worn. He could have been young or old, no one besides Amazonians could tell how old they were by looking at them or trying to read any of their facial expressions.

He started slowly, clearly articulating the words that were amplified by the device's speaker at his throat. "Humanity braved space millennia ago to bring us all here. We took a break to find ourselves and what we wanted from this life," he stated as if a professor addressing a class, using kind language to describe a horrific civil war. "Then President Micah and her mate Braden united all the people—fur, feathers, or skin—and made them equal. She challenged them to be better. We return to the stars to find others from Earth, fellow humans, learn from them, expand our knowledge, expand our understanding of the universe," the Amazonian finished, waiting to be allowed to return to his seat.

He wore the skin suit that allowed him to live and work in the same environments as the others. It shimmered lightly as it was powered, holding the moisture within as it was soaked daily. The skin of the Amazonians was meant to be constantly wet, and their flesh dried out quickly in conditions other than that of the Amazonian rainforest. The suits had been designed by previous generations as the Amazonians ended their war and ventured beyond the confines of their homeland.

DI Katlind slowly walked from the stage, never taking her eyes from the Amazonian. The other recruits froze in place, fearing to move and draw unwanted attention to themselves.

"What gives, Pickles? You sound like a professor," she said with a sneer.

"It's Peekaless, Master DI," the Amazonian said, instantly regretting correcting the DI.

"ON YOUR FACES!" she bellowed, surprised that only two desks were overturned as the recruits dove into the pushup position. She walked around them, happy to see the quick response from her unit, although she'd never let them know that. "You two look way too comfortable. Crouch!" she directed Leaper and Brisbois.

The Rabbit and Wolfoid half-crouched into a position that was comparably uncomfortable to the position that the humans maintained.

"Okay, Pickles, where were we?" the DI continued, indifferent to the groans and gasps from the recruits around her. "Crouch!" she directed the second Wolfoid in the class as he tried to hide behind a larger human.

"Recruit Peekaless was an instructor of history at Bliss High School, Master DI," the Amazonian said flatly, despite the fact that his vocalization device was sufficiently trained to show a broad range of intonation.

Bliss was in the southern hemisphere of the main continent on Planet Cygnus VII. It sat on the northern border between the Amazon rainforest and the Plains of Propiscius. It had a deep history of conflict between the humans and the Lizard Men of the Amazon as well as reconciliation and collaboration. The school was built and run to further the close cooperation between the Amazonians and their human brothers. It maintained an equal balance of instructors between the two species.

"Why did you sign up, Pickles? the DI asked, intentionally mispronouncing the recruit's name.

"Tired of teaching history, Master DI. It's time to make some history. My people have yet to make a difference with the SES," he said with greater feeling.

"And you won't either if you don't improve your running speed. DOWN!" she bellowed. The recruits dropped and hovered just above the floor. "Listen up, all of you. From now on, if I hear the words "my people," you had better be referring to your fellow members of the Space Exploration Service. I don't give a crap if you have fur, feathers, skin, a Hillcat, or a tortoise shell. The SES exists as one team and we have one mission. We serve the ship. UP!" The recruits completed their pushup, some more quickly than others. Some groaned through it.

"By all that's holy, it was only one pushup!" the DI bellowed, smiling inwardly. She was already proud of the group. Twenty-five of twenty-five and here she had herself a history tutor to make sure no one failed those tests. "On your feet! Straighten these desks and get ready for the next class." She made a show of storming out of the room. The instructor in the hallway, a cow Aurochs, much larger than their water buffalo cousins, snickered and bobbed her massive head, having seen the show before. Katlind scratched the neck of her friend.

"It's a good bunch, but if you hold back, try to make it easy on them, you and I will have words!"

"Of course, Master DI. I would expect no less…" The device around the Aurochs neck interpreted the words as a breathy whisper in a laughing tone. Katlind had never been able to master the mindlink, so she stayed in the spoken world, but that hadn't held her back. She tried to understand all creatures, great and small, regardless if she could speak directly with them or not.

The cow opened the door with a firm head butt and strode forward, around the hastily rearranged desks and onto a stage that groaned unhappily beneath her weight. Someone's 'cat ran to her and rubbed its body against her foreleg. The recruits stifled giggles. She tried to nose him away, but he maneuvered expertly away from her as her head was twisted upside down trying to chase him off. "Go away, you pesky little beast! Oops." She realized that she'd spoken aloud. Without further ado, she launched into a lecture on the geography of Vii, looking like she was dancing as she attempted to shoo the 'cat away with her massive hooves.

The Routine

Physical activity from breakfast through lunch. Classes all afternoon. Then more physical activity. Cain started to think that the SES was about making everyone strong enough to carry a spaceship on their backs. Cain lost weight right away, but then started to gain it back in the form of muscle. He'd always been lean, had never been a physical slouch, but he soon realized what it meant to have a workout routine. If he'd only done this when he was back in school, he would have been something.

Something for Aletha to look at, although she looked at him anyway. He thought of her often as they trained. It helped take his mind off the pain and monotony. He'd lose track as they counted pushups or during other calisthenics as he daydreamed of the day he'd be able to return to her. When they finally received mail, he was surprised at the letter he received from her. It was snippets of everyday life in Greentree, the village to the east of Bliss where they both lived. Nothing much changed. She had signed the note, "love, Aletha." That gave him some hope, but it wasn't the warm and inviting letter he'd hoped for.

He overthought it, talked with Leaper, twisted it, and finally determined that he'd lost her. He was crushed. In his own mind, he'd failed with grim finality. He awoke in the middle of the night and climbed down from his bunk, stepping on Leaper's paw and earning a pained yip from the sleeping Wolfoid.

Cain hid in a bathroom stall. *I'll do great things and she'll want me back*, he reasoned. *No, she won't. She probably thinks I won't come home to Greentree and she won't leave. That's what it is. It's not me at all. She can't leave home and I'm an adventurer like my great-great-grandfather! I'm too much for her!* Cain shook his head. That sounded like ego and not intellect. *Aletha!* he cried. *What do you want me to do? Just tell me and I'll do it. I don't want you to leave me, and I'm too stupid to know what to do to win you back.* He put his head in his hands and sobbed.

"Who's in here?" a feminine voice whispered loudly.

Cain sniffled and tried to collect himself. He pulled the door open. Ellie stood there with her hands on her hips, looking like she was going to chew on him. He waved her off and tried to get past her, but she softened instantly and pulled him into a tight hug.

"What's wrong? You're not going to quit, are you?" she asked as she pushed him to arm's length to look him over.

"No," he replied. "It's complicated."

She narrowed her eyes as she looked into his. "It's a girl, isn't it? What's her name?" This was the first day they'd received mail, in the old written form, not electronic like most people used.

"Aletha," he stammered, surprised at how easily he was found out. "Am I that transparent?" He wiped his nose on his arm.

"You're a man and you're crushed, so it all adds up. You are walking through the training like it's no big deal so I knew it couldn't be that. So, don't quit. Get over her, if that's it, and move on. She's the one missing out, not you," Ellie finished and excused herself, taking the stall that Cain had just vacated. He splashed water on his face, but his eyes were still red and puffy.

He gave up and went back to his bunk, where he lay until the morning wake up call, a racket guaranteed to wake the dead. Brisbois cringed and covered his ears, but always half a heartbeat too late. Rabbits were sensitive to sound. Cain was surprised that he hadn't taken to sleeping with earplugs. Briz, as they called him, probably had heard Cain crying in the bathroom stall. Cain wouldn't make eye contact with the Rabbit, but realized quickly that he was pretty rough in the morning. He'd learn later that Briz was an odd one among his kind in that he preferred sleeping during the day and working at night.

After Ellie's short chat, Cain's attitude improved immensely. She didn't ask him to talk about his feelings or any of that, just said how it was from her perspective. He appreciated that. And she also never took her hand away when they needed it to help each other through the obstacle course. That was probably due more so to the DI's influence, but Cain wanted to think it was because the five individuals were becoming a good team.

They discovered that Pickles was a good teacher and wouldn't let any of them fail. Briz also ensured that they understood their basic math and physics, while he worked the instructors for material related to astrophysics.

By the fourth and last week of the basic recruit-level courses, Briz had already surpassed the instructors in the area of astrophysics and spatial relation math.

The latest clone of the eminent Dr. Johns took the subway from New Sanctuary to the space center where he looked forward to meeting the young prodigy.

Briz was beyond excited and couldn't stop hopping up and down.

"Relax, Briz! This is what you've wanted all along, isn't it? Someone to notice you and put you into Research and Development? R&D for you, buddy, but whatever you do, don't think of us lowly creatures back here, duking it out with nature, trying to understand coefficients of friction and all that." Cain playfully poked the Rabbit in the ribs. Briz wrinkled his nose and flapped his ears before he started hopping again.

"It is my pleasure to have known you when you were one of the little people," Leaper said, still working on his vocalization device to teach it to reflect the tone of voice he intended. It fell flat yet again, sounding monotone and weak.

"I appreciate your sentiments, but there's nothing to say I'm going anywhere or that I'll even accept if they do offer me something," Briz said as he bounced. The Rabbit's device appropriately reflected his excitement.

"Stop it! You better accept if they offer you something. That's why you came here in the first place, isn't it?" Cain asked, shaking his head. "You don't deserve to be an insulbrick like us." The insulbrick was a critical component on a ship as it was insulation plastered into an unintended penetration in the steel plates of a spaceship. Sometimes seams came apart for no reason, other times a small meteor blasted through. In either or both cases, insulbrick sealed the breach, just like the recruits. Their bodies were forfeit for the greater good of the ship.

Save the ship, because the ship was life.

As it turned out, Dr. Johns suggested Briz wrap up that "training business" and report to the New Command Center where he'd begin immediately working with the group designing the next generation of interdimensional space engine.

"I just don't know, Dr. Johns. I have to say that I'm honored that you'd come all this way and a month ago, this is exactly what I wanted. But I really like what I'm doing now and who I'm doing it with. Will you wait for me while I finish my first term with the SES?" Briz pleaded, his device adding the appropriate level of sincerity and hope in the voice that was uniquely the Rabbit's.

Dr. Johns reached out an aging hand to caress the Rabbit's soft, fuzzy head, tickling his ears. The Rabbits and Wolfoids used touch as a way to communicate and convey emotions. To them it was natural that there always seemed to be contact with the humans. It wasn't demeaning in any way. "We can wait, Briz. I've been waiting for you for three generations. If I have to wait a little bit longer, I'll be okay. I think you have the spark of genius that we need to make the new engine work. We are so close, but none of us can see what's holding us back. Fresh blood! A fresh mind! An outsider's view. If we move some of the key research here, could you look at it for us? Help us, please."

Briz was taken aback. He knew that he had a gift and he'd always been encouraged by his parents, but felt more of an outcast from Rabbits than one who would have someone as distinguished as the eminent Dr. Johns beg to work with them. Briz felt afraid.

"What if I don't live up to your expectations?" Briz asked before thinking.

The elder scientist laughed easily in a dry, croaking way. "No matter what you give us or what you see, it is more than we have now. I'm afraid to admit it, but we haven't had a breakthrough in many years. We are so close, but so far away. We are adrift in interstellar space, looking for anything to guide us to that next star," the old man said, more matter-of-factly than pleading. He looked sincere and with a final scratch behind Briz's ears, excused himself so he could coordinate the pack-up and movement of key research to the Space School.

The staff was pinging. They didn't have any empty classroom for scientists to occupy, but when the Dr. Johns (or his twelfth cloned iteration) made a request, people complied as if it was a mandate from the president herself.

Briz was hopping too, as he had the best of both worlds. He was a recruit some of the time and an exalted professor for the rest. His co-workers on the engine research only thought of him as their boy wonder, even though he maintained that he had yet to contribute anything because their calculations were far beyond him. He didn't understand metallurgy and he knew that would be a significant factor in the fuel containment, flow, intermix, and recovery. So he started staying up at night, reading everything the R&D team gave him.

The group was in its fifth week of training, having survived the physical breakdown and rebuilding of their bodies. They were on to greater things, like an introduction to the spaceships where they'd spend an entire month studying damage control and practicing damage control methods. One month of nothing but learning how to react, because the ship was life. And then if they were assigned to a ship, they'd spend the majority of their remaining shipboard lives practicing for emergencies.

The last morning of the fifth week was the second morning after a sleepless night for Briz. The group jogged to the dining hall where they'd inhale their breakfast, then head to the spaceship mockup where they'd run around in circles carrying great hoses and misshapen chunks of insulbrick. Briz was staggering while in formation, so his teammates gave him a hand. With Team Leader Stinky on one side and Cain on the other, they managed to haul the Rabbit to a place where he could get an industrial-sized serving of coffee and fresh greens.

Once DI Katlind saw the extent to which the team was trying to hide the Rabbit's exhaustion, she decided a change to the routine was in order.

After plowing through their chow and coffee with a minute or two to spare, they casually walked out of the dining hall and formed up in the roadway outside. The team leaders were now responsible for bringing their teams to the school, so once they had everyone, they lined up behind the lead, two by two, and ran quickly to their next event.

They took one step when a voice boomed, echoing between the buildings of the space center. "STOP!" The recruits looked around and saw the DI glaring at them. They ran into each other as Black Leaper stopped more quickly than the others. Tandry's 'cat bolted to the side and hid behind a tree.

After Stinky's team collected itself and faced the DI, she walked up to them, slowly and deliberately.

"Obstacle course," she said so softly that they almost didn't hear it. They stood, a group of five recruits, eyes fixed on their Discipline Instructor widening as the delay in their response sent her into one of her well-practiced conniptions. "I SAID, OBSTACLE COURSE!" It was complete with spittle. Cain could have sworn he saw her eyes glowing red.

Tandry screamed and the group ran like a herd of stampeding Aurochs, away from the manicured grounds and toward the mud and wood construction known as the obstacle course. DI Katlind jogged at a measured pace after them. She knew they'd wait, and she knew they'd have their bodies locked at the position of attention, too. It was a good group.

She heard a meow and a purr. Looking down, Recruit Tandry's 'cat was running alongside.

'So, you think this is a good group?' Mixial asked using her thought voice. The DI was surprised, having rarely conversed over a mindlink. It gave her a terrible headache as she wasn't gifted with the ability to speak using a thought voice.

"What are you doing in my head, you mangy little cretin?" she replied, counting on her DI persona to hide her discomfort in such conversations.

'The same thing I do in everyone's head, talk to them like an adult,' Mixial answered, giving the DI a taste of her own sarcasm. *'What do you have in mind, and how can I help?'*

"Okay, 'cat. I don't do this a whole lot, but from what I understand, you already know what I have in mind and have an idea of what you want to do. Let's skip the charades and get to it. So tell me…" the DI enunciated clearly. She was running, but breathing normally. She could run like that for hours if need be.

'I think you must have been a Hillcat in a previous life, but did something wrong and that's why you are doing penance within your human shell. Here's what I'm thinking, which, if you weren't being punished for a past transgression, you'd already know…'

The DI arrived at the obstacle course slightly after Stinky and his team. She had a big smile on her face as the 'cat assumed a position next to her. Tandry glared at Mixial, but the 'cat only yawned, showing its fangs, smacking its 'cat lips, and looking away, seemingly disinterested.

"Traitor," Tandry said out loud to receive a loving caress to her mind from her bonded 'cat. She chuckled, until she saw an unhappy glare magically appear on DI Katlind's face.

"Would you look at this place?" the DI belted out, not expecting the recruits to look anywhere other than front and center. "I don't know what slobs were here last, but we need to clean this place up. You have one hour to rake, wipe, and straighten. TURN TO!" she ended with yelled order to begin. The recruits looked at each other and back at the DI, who pointed to a small shed just inside the tree line. They bolted for it, finding everything they needed to do the work.

Stinky ran up the back ramp of the wall to look over the obstacle course and determine priorities for work. The others joined him with rakes and shovels when they saw what he was doing. There were six obstacles, starting with the wall. Next was the mud pit, then the meandering balance beam, the over-under fencing, the inverted V climb, and finally the rope climb. The approach and departures from the rope swing over the mud pit were a mess, so Cain and Ellie took that as one project, while the other three raced to the next four obstacles. As they finished, they'd move to the fifth and sixth obstacles. The rope climb looked to be in good shape, so if they didn't make it there in the time allotted, they reasoned that it would probably be okay.

Then again, they needed to make it there in time. The worst part was when they realized that their group was the last one on the obstacle course. "It was us," Stinky said, his vocalization device carrying the appropriate amount of humility and shame. They looked at each other briefly before running off to their assigned jobs.

The DI found a seat in the shade and watched. She knew the recruits were well aware of the time so she didn't bother tracking it herself. She got bored quickly so she started walking around, looking at nothing in particular, which greatly energized the recruits who had already been working feverishly.

It always did. She tried not to laugh.

She saw her partner in crime, the Hillcat Mixial, sneaking toward the old observation tower. It had already been replaced by a new, high-tech version, but sentimentality kept the school from tearing down the old one. The 'cat disappeared up the tower steps.

Cain was first to finish his task and he ran to the fifth obstacle and started raking the approach like a madman while time seemed to skip ahead. Stinky joined him, then Ellie bounced past them to the rope climb. Tandry joined Stinky as time was about to expire. They raced to the finish, declaring it satisfactory although knowing that they could have done a better job with one more thorough pass.

The four of them stood at attention, before Stinky realized that Briz was nowhere to be seen. His rake was lying in the dirt between the balance beams. He dropped to all fours and raced at Wolfoid speed to the obstacle.

Before he made it, a cry echoed across the entire obstacle course.

"FIRE!" DI Katlind yelled. Flames licked at the bottom of the old observation tower. At the top, Mixial and Briz stood, waving their arms frantically. Smoke started to billow skyward.

"Save the ship!" Cain yelled as the recruits ran toward the tower. The flames enveloped the stairs, preventing a climb up or down. Tandry used her shovel to throw dirt on the quickly spreading flames. The others beat at the flames with their rakes. DI Katlind yelled for Ellie. The shed contained a hose and pump. Together they manhandled the heavy contraption to the mud pit and dropped one hose in the water. Cain and Stinky joined them to race for the tower with a hose fighting to pump muddy water. They attacked the fire climbing the steps, but they were already too far gone for anyone to use the steps to escape. The stairs were burned through. Then the recruits kept the fire from the four legs of the structure, wetting them extensively to make sure the tower didn't come down.

A platform in the middle burned and they arced clear water over it. Ellie had moved the hose closer to the inlet that fed the mud pit, which greatly improved the water pressure. Soon, the flames were beat back, then extinguished. Two of the four platforms were gone and most of the stairway to the top. Briz's white fur was sooty from the smoke, but he waved tentatively to show that he was okay. Mixial was unimpressed by it all and told them that she was hungry.

The group of recruits looked at the structure and tried to devise a plan to rescue their teammate. They looked at DI Katlind and for the first time, they noticed that she'd gotten muddy. She had waded into the mud pit to ensure the collection nozzle was clear before they started the pump.

"What are you looking at?" she bellowed at the recruits, who looked quickly away.

Black Leaper turned to face the DI and stood at attention. "Master DI, if you have any suggestions, the recruits would greatly appreciate your continuing assistance in rescuing our teammate." The other recruits looked shocked. No one asked the DI for help unless that person wanted extra calisthenics, derision, and physical pain.

"The rope on the last obstacle has a quick disconnect at the top. See it? Hurry up now, they're waiting on you." All four scrambled to the last obstacle and two started climbing at once. The DI shook her head. Ellie was the quickest climber so she continued while Cain dropped into the sand. She was at the top in no time. With one arm wrapped around the rope and her foot firmly twisted in, she reached with her free hand for the other, but the quick connect was too far away. Cain and Tandry grabbed the bottom of Ellie's rope and helped her swing until she caught the next one over. She worked the quick connect, but the tension was too great and she couldn't undo the hasp. Stinky grabbed the rope and started leaping, snapping the rope to send a wave upward. When Ellie saw what he was doing, she waited and with a wrist flick, the clasp unsnapped and the heavy rope headed downward, where surprised recruits ran for cover.

The DI laughed to herself. All thrust and no vector, as the flyer types would say. At least they had spirit.

They each secured a section of the rope and dragged it to the tower. Then they looked at each other. How would they get the rope to the top? They looked at the DI and she only dipped her head in dismay, twirling her finger which meant, "hurry up."

"Talk to me," Stinky said to the group as he looked upward.

"We have a big heavy rope that we can't throw to them. We only have to throw it as far as the lowest safe step and that's still too far. If they could grab it with something, then they could pull it up. So we have to get the rope to that point there." Cain pointed as he talked. "And they can pull it to a point where they can secure it. What can they grab it with?" They collectively shook their heads, then started looking around, close, then farther, then to the trees.

There was a thin rope that detailed the outer boundary of the obstacle course. Ellie and Tandry ran for it.

"We're going to throw a rope to you, and then you can pull the climbing rope the rest of the way," Cain yelled. Stinky's speaker still hadn't reached a point where he could yell properly. Briz waved. The 'cat looked at them through narrowed eyes, willing them to pick up the pace. When Mixial presented the plan to DI Katlind, she hadn't foreseen being trapped at the top of a rickety old observation tower. She expected they'd be down by now, although she was surprised at how quickly the fire had burned. It was never her intent to die trying to teach the team a lesson. It was fun, just until it wasn't.

With the thin cord in hand, they tied a heavy stick to one end, the climbing rope to the other, and twirled the end to build up speed, slinging it skyward at the last moment. That didn't go as planned and resulted in more scattering recruits. On the fourth try, the stick sailed to the top flight of steps and stuck. Although Briz was stocky, the climbing rope was heavy and he struggled greatly to pull it up the stairs. He only moved it a few feet before deciding he would have to anchor it there. He used the other rope to wrap around a support beam and tie it to itself, then hooked the climbing rope's quick connect hasp and was ready to attempt the climb. A Rabbit's hands were small, with dainty fingers instead of paws, while his back feet were huge and semi rounded. With the strength of his back legs, he held the rope between his big feet, and with a Hillcat wrapped around his head, he hugged the rope to him as he slowly slid down. He used his shoulder to push away from the charred ruins of each of the lower levels.

The recruits yelled encouragement until he was close enough to drop the rest of the way. Mixial jumped first, landing on her feet and then bolting for the trees before Tandry could pull her into a hug. Within a few heartbeats, they heard the scream of a Hillcat killing a squirrel. Briz winced, not understanding how the 'cat could be such a barbarian when the dining hall had the freshest vegetables, grown in a field nearby, tended by his kin and the ever present development units, the bots that did the routine maintenance and field tending in New Sanctuary.

Tandry smiled, happy that her 'cat was safe, but suspected something had gone on between Mixial and the DI. She'd prod her friend later, see if the 'cat would be forthcoming with the whole truth or just enough to keep Tandry wondering.

"Bring it in," the DI told the recruits.

"Yes, Master DI," they yelled as they took a knee in a semi-circle around the DI.

"The best lessons aren't planned," she started. "What do you think you learned today?"

The recruits looked at each other. Stinky raised his half-hand/half-paw. The DI pointed to him. "By saving the ship, it gave us time to save the people." She nodded and encouraged him to continue. "No one alone could have saved them. It took all of us, including you, Master DI. And for me, know where your people are at all times. I lost track of Briz and because of that, we could have lost him."

"Yes and no," the DI told them in a normal speaking voice. The recruits leaned closer, understanding that this was a test that they had passed. The DI had to reinforce the lessons before the best of it was lost, although they wouldn't forget. It was an emotional high with an adrenaline surge. Even if it was staged, it was more realistic than anything they'd gone through with the mockup ship. They believed that Briz and Mixial were in danger. And they weren't paralyzed with fear. That was an important lesson that they had learned about themselves.

"You could berate yourself all day long for not knowing where your people were, but did you give him a mission, with clear follow-on orders for when he completed the first task?" Stinky nodded. He had. "And you worked, too. You didn't sit back and watch your people, showing them that you didn't trust them. No! You all agreed on what needed to be done and you were doing it, including you, Recruit Black Leaper. You have to trust your people to do what they committed to do. You have to take responsibility for your own actions. In this case, Recruit Brisbois climbed the tower because I told him to. No one did anything wrong, and there is no reason to have a lack of trust in any of your teammates." She looked them over, one by one, ready to complete the day's lesson.

"Recruit Brisbois," she said, pointing to him. His ears perked up and his nose twitched. "Recruit Brisbois hasn't been sleeping, has he?" No one moved.

"No need to answer. I know he hasn't. I saw all of you carry him on the run, help him. So when you turned him loose to work, expecting him to do as you did, was that a fair expectation?" Stinky bowed his head. "That's the hardest lesson of all. But he was doing fine. He rose to the occasion and was keeping up with you. I have to admit, before the 'cat tells on me, that I'm proud of you. If any of you insulbricks ever repeat that, I'll deny it and call you every name I can think of. Do we understand each other?"

"Yes, Master DI!" the recruits belted out in unison.

"Now get your nasty butts back to the barracks and clean up. Chow at noon and I'll see you in the classrooms for the afternoon sessions." She stalked off without waiting for the recruits, hoping that no one saw her in her current state. DIs were never supposed to be covered in mud. She also had to report a fire that nearly destroyed the old observation tower. She honestly had no idea how the fire started. The fact that she planned it and agreed to it would be found nowhere in her report.

The recruits ran fast, in their usual formation, to the barracks, where they each grabbed an individual shower, stripped and washed. Wrapped in towels, they returned to their bunk cubicles for that half-wall of privacy.

They dressed in clean uniforms, which were simply a coverall that was the multi-purpose uniform worn aboard an SES spaceship.

They bodily dumped Briz into his bunk, taking the book away that he tried to sneak out. At least he'd get a couple hours sleep. When they checked in on him a few heartbeats later, he was out cold. They expected the rest of the recruits were still in their morning damage control classes.

"Did I hear that right? I think my Wolfoid ears are playing tricks on me. The DI said she was proud of us?" Stinky said, starting a full replay of the morning's events.

"We got something no one else did," Tandry added. "Thanks to Mixial!" She beamed at her Hillcat, who was curled up on her bunk, sleeping off her recent meal.

"So, what would we do differently?" Cain prodded. The others shrugged. "I'd know everything that was available to us without having to search. Where's the damage control, the DC equipment. When you don't have any time to think, that's not the time to start thinking of what you should have done…"

Space

What's Space School without a taste of space? It was the group's thirteenth week, and they were exploring the effects of zero-g on fluid dynamics. Specifically, they learned how toilets worked in space. They paid attention too, as nothing would ruin your day quicker than having a sewage leak within the self-contained biosphere of a spaceship.

That was also the week that new recruits arrived, meaning that Stinky, Cain, and the rest of class Beta 37 weren't the most junior people at Space School.

They also got to go to space. There were two different ways to get into space: by the matter transfer system tying New Sanctuary to the Resettlement Vessel Traveler in orbit around Planet Vii or by shuttle. The recruits would use the former system.

The shuttle was triangular-shaped with two Scramjets, engines that could transition seamlessly between subsonic, supersonic, and hypersonic flight speeds and two small rocket boosters for exoatmospheric thrust and maneuvers. Two larger, reusable rockets pushed the shuttle high into the atmosphere before the other engines helped it achieve escape velocity and travel beyond the pull of gravity. It was a pretty simple concept with millennia-old technology.

Having one ship that both landed on a planet and traveled through space was not only impractical for the ship's construction, the logistics support would require a second ship stationed in orbit to refuel it. It was easier to use two ships, a shuttle system for the stress of flying within a planet's atmosphere and spaceships for travel in space. The shuttles provided travel back and forth between the planet and the RV Traveler, which had transitioned into a fully functional and self-sustaining space station.

The Space Exploration Service had three types of ships: shuttles, intra-system ships, and deep space vessels. The shuttles and the intra-system ships used conventional means of propulsion, rockets and thrusters to maneuver within the Cygnus star system. The deep space vessels used the engines designed by the Cygnus VI engineering team over a period of four-hundred years following the civil war and reestablishment of civilization on Vii.

The ISE, called ice, was the interdimensional space engine. It linked two points in the universe, sending the ship from one point to the other without actual motion. The space collapsed between the points and the ship vibrated from one location to the next. The ISE-driven ships were ungainly looking beasts, rounded to facilitate a spherical vortex which engulfed the spaceship, moving it without moving. The round nature of the ships also made sense for the rotation necessary to act as artificial gravity. The people of Vii needed it for long-term health. They'd never found a way around gravity or inertia and that was what made the ISE the greatest invention of all time.

They wouldn't spend a thousand years accelerating and another thousand decelerating, a process that did not turn the human body into a jelly on the aft bulkheads.

The ISE was fueled by dark matter and operated within a dark matter environment, which meant that all travel started and ended within interstellar space, no closer than the edge of a solar system. The trip from the Cygnus star system to other points in the galaxy took only an instant, but then travel to planets within a solar system were long, deliberate affairs. Some of the exploration missions took years, simply because of the time it took to travel within a system's heliosphere using the shuttles carried by the deep space exploration vessels.

The SES had been formed a hundred years ago, when they still called a year a cycle of the seasons. From space they came, to space they returned, better than they ever were. The people of the Cygnus system were determined to find other life, maybe even return to Earth as they explored the known galaxy. Humanity would not be denied.

And they had the company of the intelligent species humans created centuries past, who evolved and became equals, partners in the journey to a better place. They were all the people of Cygnus VII.

From the ashes of their past, Cygnus was rising.

Welcome to the RV Traveler

As part of their visit to the RV Traveler, the Space School explained the philosophy behind the ship's construction. It was built in two huge main sections called cores. Each of those was cylindrical, with five decks that rotated around a central axis. This rotating five-deck unit was contained within an external shell. The shell, made up of the cryo-storage units and other equipment necessary for interstellar travel, protected the internal sections of the ship. When in deep freeze, the humans survived best in zero-gravity. When awake, life happened in the rotating sections.

The rotation was necessary to keep both humans and animals from losing the ability to survive in a planet's gravity.

Both fore and aft five-deck sections were over ten kilometers long. Each deck, floor to ceiling, was nine hundred meters. With the last deck being open, five kilometers side to side, without a ceiling.

The aft section's decks were designated 6 through 10. The outermost cylinder of the aft core, Deck 10, was the Livestock Level. That deck provided some of the meat and meat products for the crew. Most of the animals had long ago been transplanted to the surface after the ship arrived at Cygnus VII. For the resettlement, they used surface landing ships, which were then dismantled to build Sanctuary, which was subsequently destroyed during the war.

New shuttles had been built in the past century and all creatures could readily travel back and forth from Vii to the Traveler. The reestablishment of a fully functioning Livestock Level came with the designation of the Resettlement Vessel Traveler as Space Station Traveler, with full staffing and support for the growing fleet of spaceships.

DI Katlind's responsibilities were focused on the continual disciplinary development of all recruits, but she exercised the greatest influence over the first twelve weeks of their lives at Space School. She stayed with the new recruits in class Charlie 37, while two teams from Beta 37 came under the watchful eye of Space Instructor Hendricks.

The no-nonsense Hendricks had been raised in a fishing town on the Eastern Ocean. He traded life on one ship for a different life on a different ship. He wore a perpetual scowl. The class's Hillcats shied away from him, although they considered him mostly harmless. SI Hendricks knew ships and was terminally miffed at having gotten removed from service on an active spaceship to become an instructor, although from a career standpoint, the senior leadership insisted that the quality of the instructors was far more important than having a single quality engineer on board a ship. They selfishly wanted a spaceship filled with quality engineers, which took quality training in a long pipeline.

SI Hendricks looked over the two teams, scowling further. The only one he was impressed with was the Rabbit. Second was the Lizard Man. He was in a constant struggle with the other instructors at Space School because he maintained that academics and technical knowledge were far superior to any physical ability or general knowledge. The SES needed smart people who understood every single aspect of how the ship operated. He'd lectured a class on fluid dynamics in a zero-gravity environment when one of the recruits said, "ewww" after he mentioned sewage. He wanted to run away screaming. Children! He loved spaceships and everything about them, even the sewage process system. Only Briz shared his love of the technical elements required to make a ship move through space.

The recruits were excited. Two teams today and in two days, two more teams would join them. The computer system was limited to transferring twelve people at a time and sometimes it took up to two days to make the transfer. The technology was centuries old, but no one had figured out how to improve on it. So they used it as it was, within the system's constraints, planning around the limitations it imposed. No more than twelve at a time traveled.

SI Hendricks shepherded the teams through the underground tunnels beneath New Sanctuary, in the bowels of what was the New Command Center, having been named by the AI called Holly nearly two centuries earlier when the computer, with nothing more than a single bot and its own vast store of knowledge, relocated from the ruins of Sanctuary, the capital city of Cygnus VII destroyed during the civil war. Holly established the New Command Center, which served to usher in a whole new era. They even started the year count anew because of it.

The teams meandered in the hallways and corridors, around machinery and in odd rooms, until SI Hendricks took the opportunity to gnaw on both the team leaders, Black Leaper and a human called Patesh. The SI had authority and sometimes lauded it over the recruits, but only when out of sight from Space School. It was his way of getting back at the powers that be. He was not well liked.

By anyone.

Stinky and Patesh rallied their people to tighten up and close the gaps. They could get a tour after graduation. Until then, they were on the school's time.

The matter transfer chamber was tucked away to the side on the factory level beneath the New Command Center. Its door was a section of wall that moved aside to allow the travelers inside. Each would get their own reclining chair to sit in, as the technology required separation of all the travelers. The room was exact in its dimensions, down to a micron so the computer system could deal with fewer unknowns during the transfer process.

The SI wanted to bring another instructor along to watch over the group because he selfishly wanted to pick Briz's brain, but he couldn't because of Tandry's Hillcat. It was standing policy to never separate a recruit from their 'cat. The matter transfer system required every living creature to occupy its own recliner in the chamber, so the 'cat took up the remaining empty spot. This soured Hendricks' mood further.

They climbed into their chairs, received the briefing from the Artificial Intelligence, from Holly himself, and stayed still as the room began to shimmer. They kept their thoughts to themselves as darkness descended. None of the recruits had traveled using the matter transfer technology before. None of them had ever been to space either. Usually, the SI had one who'd been to the Traveler, even if it was only on vacation with their parents or on a school trip.

The travelers disappeared into a dreamless sleep as the process worked, flawlessly, as always.

The twelve people opened their eyes, seemingly only a few heartbeats after the process started, but it had been a day and a half according to Vii time. SI Hendricks wanted to be first up, he'd done this dozens of times and it was old hat. He swung his feet over the side, put his head between his knees, and yacked up his breakfast of toast and jam, as he'd done every time previously. The recruits stayed where they were, the queasiness threatened to do to them what they'd just seen from the SI, a seasoned veteran of space.

No one wanted to be the first to move, so Mixial tentatively stretched and jumped to the floor, freezing in place as she tried to acclimate herself to the ship's spin. It made her feel like she was falling sideways, just enough to be annoying. She walked with a lean, making a wide arc around the SI's puke, and headed for the panel that slid open to reveal a well-lit space beyond. The SI stood tall and told the recruits to get moving, secretly hoping every one of them would spew their guts out. He was already disappointed that the 'cat hadn't hacked up at least a hairball.

The recruits had been well briefed and moved with glacial slowness. Tandy leaned over, in slow motion, and said goodbye to her breakfast of granola and berries. The bile crept up the back of Cain's throat and his mouth started the telltale watering of imminence, but he refused. He was Braden and Micah's great-great grandson. He had their genes and showing weakness on the ship that they opened for all the people of Vii was something he refused to do. He closed his eyes and took deep breaths, thinking of other things, like which chairs they sat in as they traveled.

The eminent Hillcat Prince Axial De'atesh had also occupied one of those chairs. Legends suggest he never puked, although Cain's grandfather, when he was still alive, told the family that the Golden Warrior, as they called him, never hesitated to share his discomfort through a good pile of spew, strategically placed.

Cain coughed once and up it came, despite his best efforts to hold back the flood. The Wolfoid slid off his chair and onto the floor, feeling the spin of the ship. He stood, front feet on the floor and back legs still on the chair, before carefully moving one paw at a time until he was standing, albeit on all fours.

"This feels funny. The ship is spinning," Stinky articulated clearly through his vocalization device. The others started to gag. The smell in the matter transfer chamber overwhelmed them and they lost it. The good news with puking was that they felt moderately functional afterwards. They eventually worked their way out, wiping their boots on a special pad outside the door for that purpose.

"The usual, Hermes," SI Hendricks said loudly to a man who appeared in the doorway with a second being that Cain recognized as an Android.

He'd looked forward to meeting one, although his family had a long history of mistrusting Androids.

A small maintenance bot rolled in smoothly behind them and started cleaning the matter transfer chamber before the next group's transfer process started. The recruits put it out of their heads since the nausea passed once they were in the engineering section. SI Hendricks pulled them together in a semi-circle to give them their shipboard safety briefing.

"Never interfere with the vines you see in this section and that you may encounter elsewhere on the ship. We've finally been able to reverse their growth, but it'll take centuries for them to completely shrivel. In the interim, we work around them." The SI pointed to the odd green growth on the forward bulkhead. People of various sorts worked by the vines, but a guardrail kept the alien growth from the ship's other inhabitants.

"My great-great-grandparents cut through them with their blasters some one hundred and thirty-six years ago, right there," Cain said excitedly as he tried to see the scars, but the vines had repaired themselves and no sign of the battle remained. "And the vine gave Master Aadi's shell a vicious slash," he added in his storyteller voice.

"We're all aware of who your great-great-grandparents are, Recruit Cain. They caused a great deal of damage to this ship and thanks to Holly and the Androids' superhuman efforts to save it, we're able to use it today to explore space," the SI said sarcastically.

Cain was instantly furious. Ellie grabbed his arm to hold him back. Stinky bumped against him and worked his way in front. Mixial hissed and jumped into Tandry's arms. Briz didn't hear anything the SI was saying. The Rabbit looked at the workstations, the hints of equipment behind the aft bulkhead, the sounds of the ship in operation, the curvature of the deck, the rotation. He closed his eyes and breathed it all in. He was home.

The SI saw the anger in Cain's eyes and the others as they moved to protect him. Maybe DI Katlind was right about how tight the team had become. They seemed to know each other innately, what their next actions would be. The Rabbit looked to be in heaven.

"All of that is behind us. Let's continue with the briefing to keep us all out of trouble, and then let's begin the ship's tour. For the purposes of this visit, we will remain in the aft section, studying the life support systems and how they work to ensure a fully functioning environment for space travel. The RV Traveler has been in space for more than four thousand years and yet it still functions. How is that possible? That's what we're going to study over the next two weeks that we're here. At a special request, we'll visit Decks 8, 9, and 10 as some of your ancestors started your existence there. Moving on…" SI Hendricks started walking away as he talked.

Cain fumed. *If it hadn't been for my ancestors, none of this would be possible. Holly and the Androids! Neither of them could have done anything without Braden and Micah, you pompous ass!* he thought to himself. He ground his teeth. Ellie held his hand as they walked to help keep him calm, but all that did was send his emotions surging, until she pulled him roughly to the side.

"You need to get yourself under control! Your thoughts are projecting everywhere and I have to say, I'm a little disgusted with what you are thinking about me!" She threw his hand down and stormed away.

Cain stood confused as the two teams continued walking. Stinky looked at him and waved at him to catch up. The Wolfoid worked his way into the back of the group. With Briz attached to the hip of the SI, Hendricks wouldn't notice anything else. The two were talking as if they were old drinking buddies.

'So, what's up? It looks like you're having a bad day,' Black Leaper said in his thought voice. Cain was gifted with the mindlink, but sometimes he lost control when his emotions raged. At this point, he was well out of control.

The SI makes me mad. My girlfriend back home leaves me, and now Ellie is starting to turn me on,' Cain shared over their mindlink, leaving the details unspoken.

'Yeah, we've talked about Aletha before. I don't think she left you,' the Wolfoid said as they strolled in the back of the group, not listening to what the SI was saying. *'I think she's letting you take your man journey, find yourself and all that. What does she want?'*

'Stay home,' Cain replied quickly. She'd never said anything of the sort, but her actions and Cain's impression told him that had to be the case. He was convinced of the truth and far too proud simply to ask her and have an adult conversation about their future. He continued thinking to himself as he descended into a dark pit of his own making, *Why doesn't she want to travel with me, see the stars?*

'You're doing it again, Cain,' Stinky interrupted the human's errant broadcast over the mindlink. *'By the way, what kind of thoughts were you having that Ellie found so distasteful?'* the Wolfoid prompted his human friend.

'Sorry. I was thinking about her butt and what it would be like to caress it and give it a squeeze. That's all, I swear!'

'Why would you look at her butt?' Stinky asked, perplexed by the vision.

'Why wouldn't you? Have you seen it? It's impossible not to look at. Don't tell me you don't look at Wolfoid butts?' Cain replied, defending his happy vision of Ellie.

'No. Why would I?' Cain shrugged. *'It's the smell, my man. That tells you everything you need to know about everyone. You don't sniff them?'* The Wolfoid smiled, baring his fangs as good thoughts raced through his mind. He took a few quick steps to catch back up to the group.

'That's crazy! Why would I sniff the women? Look at this nose,' Cain countered, showing Stinky his profile before chuckling out loud, drawing a harsh look from both Tandy and Ellie.

'It's clear why you walk around in such a daze. You can't smell what's going on. And your eyes don't see much either. Can you imagine sitting around checking out Wolfoid butts? Me neither,' Stinky finished.

Cain retreated into his own mind as he watched SI Hendricks talk about something or other.

Cain shook his head. He had to get his mind wrapped around what he wanted. Why was he thinking about Ellie? Why was he so quick to think poorly of Aletha? Why had the SI tried to goad him? *'It's how we work in space. We have to put the distractions behind us. The ship is life, right?'*

'The ship is life, my friend. Now let's learn a little something. I'd hate to waste this trip watching you wallow in self-pity,' the Wolfoid replied.

'I'm going to grow a braid,' Cain threw out.

'Of course you are...'

Damage Control

Before being assigned their bunks, they had to successfully demonstrate the ability to don and clear their self-breathing apparatus and find their damage control station. Everyone on the ship was assigned one, even if they were only there briefly as they transferred from one ship to another. The colony ship was so large that crew, inhabitants, and visitors would be assigned new DC stations as they traveled, because movement over such long distances would be counterproductive in an emergency.

They were assigned to one in engineering. The locker was well stocked with all the gear they'd used in training. It helped them to be more comfortable while also grounding them. The Traveler was a massive construction, making them feel like they weren't even on a ship. But Damage Control, the practice with the DC locker, and the serious tone of the SI convinced them that this wasn't anything trivial.

They put the gear on and off four times before SI Hendricks was satisfied with the timing. Satisfied was a loose term, because he never changed his perpetual scowl except when he was talking with Briz, so the recruits devised a plan where Briz would keep the Space Instructor occupied while the others disappeared for some exploration. Their first day on ship wasn't supposed to be a full training day anyway. They wouldn't get into the real training until after the other teams arrived.

The recruits were familiar with the layout of the RV Traveler, because they'd studied it before they transferred aboard. They knew the bulkhead designations and how the ship was arranged. They'd walked through the three-dimensional maps provided in their virtual reality training at Space School. It made them feel more at home, although nothing could have prepared them for the spinning of the ship's decks. They felt like they were walking sideways. Briz seemed right at home instantly, while Mixial was the most upset. She sulked constantly, which put Tandry in a bad mood. Stinky shook it off. He had too much to worry about with the other four in various states of disarray.

The klaxons rang through the engine compartment. The recruits were conditioned to think of them as a drill, although they immediately took action, heading for the DC locker. SI Hendricks intercepted them. He had a wild look in his eye.

And half his arm was missing. The recruits stared at it dumbly. There was no blood, as the wound had been cauterized by whatever did the damage. He mouthed words, but nothing came out. He reached his good arm for them and spasmed, arching his back to breaking as he opened his mouth and spit blood.

Seven of the recruits panicked and ran. Cain and Black Leaper moved forward to catch the SI, while Briz remained frozen in place, mouth open and nose twitching furiously. He didn't blink as he stood transfixed.

Behind the SI and walking calmly toward them was an Android, its laser tool exposed as it fired again into the body of the man they held. Without checking, they knew their instructor was dead. His back had been peppered by short blasts from the work laser. The Android approached. A shiver went through Cain's body as its artificial eyes locked on his. The arm slowly rose, the laser taking aim…

Cain remembered the stories his great-grandparents had shared in their final days, stories of duplicity and distrust. For all their lives, Braden and Micah refused to trust the Androids, despite Holly's continual assurances that he was one hundred percent in control. Braden lost two fingers because of an Android-fired work laser. Braden and Micah had killed a great number of the humanoid robots, counter to what Holly asked. In the years since, Holly and the inhabitants had created new Androids to fill necessary positions. The activity within the Traveler to make it functional as a space station demanded a huge, active crew. Holly solved the problem through building more Androids, adding to the fifty percent on board from the generation built on Earth, four millennia prior. These were the ones that Braden and Micah feared.

It was an Android from that generation that seemed to be coming after Cain.

"No!" Cain screamed at the approaching enemy. He ducked his head behind the SI's body as he started pushing the corpse in front of him. Stinky caught on and helped. If they tried to run away, the Android would shoot them in the back as it had done to the SI. Cain and Stinky rammed the man's body into the Android.

They felt like they'd run into a wall. The thing was locked to the deck plate using its magnetic grappling ability. Its aim was thrown off and the laser scorched a metal panel in the corridor behind them. Stinky leapt over the falling body and clamped his Wolfoid jaws onto the arm that was firing.

Cain dodged around the Android and ripped open the DC locker where he knew there were tools. He grabbed a flat pry bar and turned, swinging for the Android's head. The bar clanged, ripping a great chunk of artificial flesh off the thing's metal skull. Stinky fought an epic battle in front, fighting to keep the creature from getting a grip with its free hand, because with the Android's powered grip, it could easily snap the Wolfoid's neck.

The Android changed tactics and swung the arm that Stinky was latched onto toward the wall. The Wolfoid bounced once and hung on. Cain hit him again, this time behind the knee, thinking it would be a weaker spot. The leg bent awkwardly, but the Android remained upright.

The second time the Wolfoid bounced off the wall, he let go and crumpled to the deck. Cain turned his swing into an overhead chop and hit the arm with the laser right at the wrist joint. The thing's hand snapped and the laser became useless. The Android reached for him with its other hand, but its damaged knee made it take a step and drag a leg. Another step, another drag.

Cain pulled an insulbrick discharger from the locker and fired it as the Android loomed over him. The insulbrick discharged wet and sticky, then started to harden. The Android's movements slowed. Cain sat on the floor, trying to catch his breath, thinking what else was at his command to fight the thing should it break free. His friend was down. Briz stood in the corridor, motionless, staring at the body of SI Hendricks.

The Android's eyes glared at Cain as it tried to fight against the hardening insulbrick. Cain raged. He stood and swung the pry bar repeatedly until the Android's face was bashed in. One last hit sparked the circuitry, killing it as it lost power. The magnetic grip failed and it toppled, falling against the wall of the corridor, a mass of insulbrick with an Android partially contained inside.

Cain dropped the pry bar and worked his way around the Android until he was kneeling next to Black Leaper. "Stinky! Talk to me," he pleaded. He could see the Wolfoid's chest expanding with each breath. He felt the pulse in his neck. Cain tenderly scratched his friend behind his ears, while cradling his head in his lap. The Wolfoid's eyes fluttered and blinked open.

He twisted around to see the Android, covered in insulbrick and leaning against the wall.

'I guess we won,' he said over the mindlink.

"Something like that, and we couldn't have done it without you. I can't believe you hung on to that thing's arm for that long."

'It's a gift, my man. You won't tell anyone that you're cradling my head and scratching my ears, will you? It's kind of embarrassing,' Stinky said, picking up strength.

'Makes you want to dream of Wolfoid butts instead, doesn't it?' Cain countered.

'Even that would be better, yes,' Stinky answered as he struggled to stand, first on all fours, then on his back feet. With a foreleg over Cain's shoulder, the two of them walked slowly to Briz. His mouth was no longer open and his nose twitched slower, but he stared. Cain and Stinky blocked his view with their bodies.

"Briz! Briz! Can you help me with Stinky? I think we need to get back where there are some people. Find the others, make sure everyone is okay."

To answer his question, two crewmembers ran toward them, while their teammates peered around the corner. The 'cat hissed beside them. The human crew slowed as they approached. One tapped his temple and his eyes unfocused in the telltale sign of a person using their neural implant to communicate directly with the Artificial Intelligence called Holly. The man pointed to Cain and directed him to a screen pad at the end of the corridor.

Cain shook his head and pointed to Briz. The other man grabbed the Rabbit roughly and shook him. Cain and Black Leaper jumped to their friend's aid. Even though the Wolfoid was still shaky, he took one of Briz's arms and together, they turned him away from the SI's corpse and led him down the corridor. He walked mechanically, hopping every third step as Cain and Stinky supported their friend between them.

Cain stopped at the screen pad and tapped it with a finger for activation. Holly's face appeared.

"Cain! I am so happy you are well. Your great-great grandparents would never forgive me if I allowed to be hurt," the AI said with a smile.

"It was close, Holly. The Android looked at me, malevolence in its eyes. I think it was targeting me. It didn't care about Stinky, I mean Black Leaper, only me. It killed SI Hendricks to get at me," Cain said passionately.

"I can assure you, Master Cain, that it did not. You sound so very much like Braden and you look a little like him, too. I see him in you, especially your paranoia toward the Androids. Did they pass that on to you in their genes? I wonder…"

"You can assure me whatever you want, Holly, but you're wrong. Can you look at their subroutines and see if there is a latent program triggered by someone of Braden's bloodline?" Cain asked, happy that he'd taken some classes in computer programming while in school. He was horrible at writing code, but understood enough to ask smart questions. Humans generally didn't write any programs. Holly and his offshoots took care of all that under the watchful eye of the Council of Elders.

"I have already started that review. I have dispatched Androids to your location to recover the malfunctioning unit. Please be aware that they are coming and as I had to plead with your ancestors, I beg of you, please do not destroy these. They are of the new models so if there were latent code, which I doubt, it definitely would not be found in the new Androids. Please don't kill them." Cain was surprised at how realistic Holly's pleading tone was. His family had the greatest reverence for the AI, but Cain could sympathize with Braden. All it took was one time when an Android tried to kill him, and that was it. No more trust. Ever.

"I also want to convey my heartfelt apologies over the loss of your Space Instructor. SI Hendricks was specially gifted in understanding ship systems. The two crew members will recover his body and take him to the infirmary. His wishes for being buried in space will be carried out after the remaining recruits from your class have arrived. The crew will take care of everything. I have asked the ship's captain to send someone to provide oversight for your group until you can return to earth in two weeks' time."

"We're staying up here?" Briz interjected, finally speaking. Cain gripped the Rabbit's shoulder, happy that he was no longer catatonic.

"Yes. Your training will continue without pause. Space is a dangerous place. It won't do to be afraid. What matters is how you react to the danger. From what I've seen on the video capture of that corridor, you, Cain, and Black Leaper conducted yourselves exceptionally well, better than could possibly be expected of any recruit and probably most in the active SES,"

Holly finished with a nod of his computer-designed head.

"It's not all that, Holly. I was just trying to save my own skin," Cain whispered. He looked around him. Besides Stinky and Briz, no one else was near. "Please don't tell anyone that we used the SI's body as a shield." Holly nodded. Cain slowly reached a hand to the pad and turned it off with a soft touch. Briz was back to staring. His nose wasn't twitching at all. A crew member had joined the others and was holding them beyond the door at the end of the corridor, on the catwalk overlooking engineering.

This corridor was supposed to take them to their berthing almost a kilometer away at the access to Deck 10, the Livestock Level. But it was now closed as the humans and Androids worked. Cain turned and glared at the new Androids who were attempting to clear the insulbrick from their fellow. The human crew members had put SI Hendricks on a stretcher and were carrying him to the elevator located next to the DC locker. They disappeared into it, leaving only the Androids. Cain swore one looked at him. He dodged out the door, happy when it closed behind him.

The crewmember who'd assumed the role as their guide looked at Briz, then Stinky, and finally at Cain.

"I've been working here for three years and never seen anything like that. I can't imagine what happened, what set the Android off." Cain looked away, over the railing, at nothing in particular. "You were the ones who stopped it," the man added, pointing to Cain and Stinky.

Stinky read the man's name badge, Lieutenant Simonds. "Yes, Lieutenant," he responded, using the rank that crew members wore when on aboard an SES spaceship. The SES had adopted the ranks used aboard the Traveler in the time of the ancients. And they had created their ranks from Earth's waterborne navies. A ship was a ship, they reasoned.

Cain remained distracted. The lieutenant touched him on the shoulder. Cain spun on the balls of his feet, fists raised, before quickly dropping them.

"Yes," was all he would say.

"Would you have any idea why it broke down like that?" the man asked, as if he knew Cain had an opinion. He looked closely at Cain as the recruit narrowed his eyes and clenched his jaw. "Do you?" he pressed.

"It was after me, because of what my great-great-grandparents did to the Androids. They've held a grudge for one hundred, thirty-six years against my family. Once they saw me, it triggered their repressed hatred. Holly couldn't control them then. He can't control them now. Just keep the Androids away from me and we'll be fine," Cain said firmly, daring anyone to disagree with him as he looked from face to face.

"Braden and Micah?" he asked. Cain nodded once. "Their distrust of Androids is legendary. I assure you that…" Lieutenant Simonds started to say how the Androids were perfectly safe, but that wasn't quite true. He had no other explanation, so couldn't discount the recruit's theory. He remained skeptical but didn't want to argue in front of the others. He was thinking of the word "unprecedented," but the attack was not. It had only been a while since the last one was made on the recruit's ancestors.

"Let's find you some different quarters and have the medical team stop by for a talk. No one should have to see what you've seen, but sometimes, space tries to reclaim its dominance over humanity."

"Have you ever seen anyone die?" Ellie asked, finally finding her voice. The others leaned in close.

The lieutenant shook his head tersely. He unfocused his eyes as he accessed his neural implant. The recruits waited, wondering where he'd gone. After a few heartbeats, he blinked and nodded to the group. "Follow me. You've been reassigned to the guest quarters in the next radial. Medical is on their way and will meet us there."

He started walking briskly, which forestalled any out loud conversations.

'Briz? Talk to me. Are you okay?' Cain probed over the mindlink, trying to feel his friend's thoughts, trying to will his friend back to the real world.

'Come back to us, Briz. We're here for you, ready to help in any way we can,' Stinky added.

"It killed SI Hendricks," the Rabbit said aloud. "It killed him!" Briz stopped walking and turned. Cain and Leaper each put a hand on his small, fuzzy shoulders, leaning in close.

"And nothing we can do now will change that. We need to save the ship, Briz. They're counting on us to learn everything there is to learn about the ship so these bastards can't sneak up on us again. And with that, we can save this ship and the others in the SES. They're counting on us, Briz," Cain lied.

"Are they?" Briz asked, turning toward the human and looking deep into his eyes. "Someday they will, Cain. Yes, you're right. Someday they will count on us not only to know what to do, but then to do it. Like you did. You saved our lives, Cain." Briz reached his small Rabbit hand up to touch Cain's cheek. Tandy and Ellie appeared, their hands rested next to Cain's and Leaper's on Briz's shoulders.

The lieutenant stopped and looked at the team, Black Leaper's team. His team at Space School had already been tight, having been challenged with life or death at the obstacle course, learning how they could work together to persevere. This was different, but the same. They had to learn their way through tragedy after they made it into space, except for the lieutenant, trapped on the space station where only the mundane happened. The real explorers docked their spaceships briefly at the Traveler, where many of their families lived, before heading back into space. That wasn't Simonds. SI Hendricks was the first death he'd seen since he'd joined the SES.

Without tragedy, no one can know how close they can get. Leaper's team lived it, survived it, and was preparing to move on. Simonds would call whoever he needed to, to encourage them not to break up this team.

Ever.

Peace of Mind

Their quarters waited for them as well as a full medical staff, which consisted of two 'cats, two Hawkoids, a Tortoid, a Rabbit, and an elderly human, all accompanied by two special medical bots. The recruits were shown their rooms then quickly returned to the common area of the eighty-four room billeting section. Leaper's team went first, each paired up with a professional to talk about what they'd seen.

Leaper looked at Cain. *'Whatever you do, don't think about Ellie's butt,'* the Wolfoid said in his thought voice as he turned and cordially greeted one of the 'cats. Cain spluttered and started to laugh. The others looked at him as if he'd lost his mind. The Tortoid and human approached him and looked him over.

"I'm Doctor Kanter and this is an observer who asked to be present, Master Daksha, Third Master of the Tortoise Consortium. Please be seated and be at peace. We are here to help you," she said in a soothing tone that Cain found grating. He surprised himself by how quickly he'd gotten over the incident. He was angry that their SI had been killed, but the perpetrator had been stopped. Cain found it too gratifying thinking back to pounding the life from the thing's head. He was exhilarated and that scared him.

Maybe he did need to talk with these people.

'I see,' the Tortoid said, clearly listening to Cain's errant thoughts. Cain cocked an eyebrow, encouraging the Tortoid to continue. *'I don't think you have anything to worry about. Your prejudice is based on the facts of your family's life. The Androids have only reinforced your reasons to hate them. The actions of one are the actions of all as they are linked through common software, my young recruit. Did you know that my father was abused by the Androids?'*

"You are one of Master Aadi's children? How could you work with them after what they did to your father?" Cain asked.

'Through force of will, young human. It is difficult and I try not to blame the actions of one on all, but that generation of Androids had glitches and a certain amount of

autonomy that no modern programming has been able to wipe from their memory cores. Some things seem hard-wired, but the Android attack on Aadi was to get to Braden and Micah. They were the target, so no hard feelings between Tortoids and the Androids. Only you and your family, I'm afraid.'

"I think we need to assure Recruit Cain that nothing of the sort is going on. One malfunctioning Android and that's all. There was no personal targeting. This Android did not come after you. If it had, you'd be dead and not SI Hendricks!" Both Master Daksha and Cain looked at Doctor Kanter.

"Okay," Cain said coldly.

'Come with me, Master Human,' the Tortoid said as he floated higher and started swimming toward the kitchen. Doctor Kanter watched them go, scowling. *'Besides beating the Android to a pulp, is anything else bothering you?'*

Cain didn't answer, but his mind raced.

'Aletha. We all have our own Aletha out there, Master Cain, but life goes on. Do not let it pass you by. Do not miss an opportunity again, or try to make something that is not,' Daksha advised mysteriously.

"I don't understand," Cain finally replied.

'So like your great-great-grandfather. He would say the same things to my father, Master Aadi. You will understand in time. For now, nod like I'm giving you the full business. More vigorously. There you go.' Master Daksha blinked rapidly and bobbed his head as he laughed in the Tortoid way. And they continued to talk about the people and what space travel meant for those who settled Cygnus VII so long ago. Cain had met Tortoids before, but never had such an in-depth conversation. He saw why he'd been raised with a strict mandate to listen to and trust Tortoids.

Briz was getting the full attention of Doctor Kanter and her 'cat companion. The Hillcat sat on a tabletop next to the Rabbit and stared deeply into his eyes. Briz sat stiffly, his big back feet dangling from the chair, looking comical if they didn't know the internal turmoil threatening to drag him into the pit of despair. The doctor talked in her soft voice while the 'cat worked directly in Briz's mind. Cain watched surreptitiously, as did the others on the team, while the Rabbit's features softened and he nodded. He blinked and looked around, making eye contact with each of his teammates, tipping his chin at them in recognition. His ears wiggled as he started to take in the other conversations around him.

The relief was palpable. The others quickly came to grip with their own concerns, but follow-ups were scheduled for every day that Class Beta 37 was to be on board the spaceship. The medical team shook hands all around, while Doctor Kanter pursed her lips, looking unhappily at Cain and Daksha. Her 'cat ran toward the young recruit and jumped. Cain caught him and pulled him to his chest, scratching behind his ears and then quickly taking his hand away before one of those sharp claws left a scratch down his arm. A number of razor-thin scars already crisscrossed both of Cain's arms. He was well acquainted with 'cats.

'I see that you are fine, surprisingly. Usually, human minds are less resilient. She thinks you need more attention.' The 'cat nodded toward Doctor Kanter. *'I think a 'cat needs to watch over you, otherwise you'll constantly be in trouble. Yes. I shall arrange that. Now let me down, you miscreant,'* the 'cat told him. Cain immediately released the 'cat, letting him drop gracefully to the deck.

When the medical staff left, the others spent their time talking about the incident. Everyone took a turn expressing their support for Briz. He retreated to his room and closed the door quickly. The others drifted to their own rooms, bringing up the touch pads to browse what the ship had to offer for entertainment or education. Cain retired to his room and stretched out on his bed.

Cain heard a soft tap on his door. He opened it, finding Ellie standing outside. She looked to make sure no one was watching as she pushed Cain into his room. The door closed automatically behind her. Cain backed up until he was against the wall, confused. She continued, pressing her body against his as he had nowhere else to go. She guided his hand around her, where he cupped her butt and squeezed. He closed his eyes, enjoying the moment.

When she kissed him, his mind exploded and he became lost within his own pounding heart.

Ship Training

When Cain awoke, he was alone, wondering if it had all been a dream. He usually folded his clothes, but found them thrown on the floor, crumpled. His recruit uniform. He shook it out until the fabric straightened, but it still looked like he slept in it. He hoped the steam from the showers would smooth things out further. He wanted to make a good impression on the crewmembers they would be meeting and training with.

He was in a great mood, humming to himself as he headed for the shower. Ellie was walking through the common area on her way to the head, too. Cain walked straight up to her with a big smile on his face, leaning in casually to kiss her. She made a fist and punched him in the mouth. He covered his face with both hands, once again confused as only a young man could be.

"That was a once in a lifetime deal. I knew you couldn't control your thoughts, and I still made a fool of myself!" she exclaimed in a breathy whisper.

"But, didn't you enjoy yourself?" Cain stammered.

"Yes! But that's beside the point." She stormed off. Cain decided to eat breakfast and catch a shower later. He heard the snuffling of a Wolfoid laughing. Black Leaper's muzzle stuck out around the corner. The area was clear, and he walked up to his friend.

'So, how did it feel?' Stinky asked.

"What!?" Cain asked, surprised at the straight forward question. Of course it felt incredible, but he knew he wasn't supposed to discuss that right here, in the open.

'Her butt, of course,' Stinky answered, cocking his head one way, then the other as he tried to understand the human's instant dismay.

"Oh that, yes, of course, that's what you meant," said through a forced laugh. "Wonderful. As expected, firm, round, and all that. What do you say we get some breakfast?" Cain asked as he sucked the blood from his lip.

'Everyone knows,' Stinky said abruptly. Cain froze in his tracks, understanding why Ellie was so angry.

"Projecting?" Cain asked tentatively.

'Oh, yeah,' Stinky said as Cain hung his head. *'You can fight an Android with your bare hands and you walk away, but here you stand, bleeding and flustered because of a woman. Bah! Just sniff and when you know, you know. You humans... So, what's for breakfast?'*

Cain watched his friend order a hearty salad, then a second one. Cain went with an omelet, something he savored when he could get it. After devouring it, he ordered a brownie and a fruit smoothie. He studiously found something interesting on the other side of the kitchen as Ellie stalked past on her way back to her room. When she was gone, he raced for the shower, hoping to straighten out his uniform and his brain before the first training session—introduction to the main decks of the Traveler starting with the Livestock Level.

The two teams gathered in the entry area of their berthing and waited for Lieutenant Simonds. No one talked. Ellie kept Tandry between her and Cain so they could avoid looking at each other. Briz kept to himself, but it seemed like he had reconciled his mind with their loss from the day prior. The 'cat had worked its magic on him and cleared his angst. Finally, Stinky couldn't take it anymore. He pulled the other four members of his team into a side hallway, looking at each of them while Mixial remained elsewhere.

"Please, I'm asking that we find a way to get back to being the tight team we were yesterday. How did we feel when Briz was in such pain? We cared about him, nothing about ourselves." Leaper hesitated, trying to shape what he'd say next. "Please. I ask that you two make peace and join us as our teammates, as our friends. We are close, some closer than others, and it's all okay. In the end, the only thing that matters is that we save the ship." Leaper ran out of things to say and walked slowly from the group back to where the other team waited.

Ellie was ashamed of herself, accusing Cain of things that she felt about herself. Cain cursed himself for not talking with Ellie about what their way ahead looked like. Tandry slapped them both on the arm and excused herself from standing between the two of them. Briz understood the ways of love. He was a Rabbit, after all. He casually strolled away.

Cain's mouth worked, but nothing came out. Ellie reached out to put her hand on his chest. Their eyes met. Tears formed in his as she put a finger to his lips. "That was fun last night. But we can't, not again. If we do, it has to be serious, and right now? I want a career in the SES. I want to explore deep space. I think you want the same thing." She pulled his face to hers for a long and passionate kiss. Cain disappeared into the moment until someone cleared their throat.

Lieutenant Simonds stood at the end of the hallway, watching them. "If you two are ready, we can go now," he said without rolling his eyes. He turned, shaking his head at the youth of the day, enjoying their field trip a little more than the rest of the group.

He walked straight through the door and into the corridor, turning right for the short walk to the hatch that accessed Deck 10.

The others followed, Cain a little sheepishly, but Leaper helped him by talking with him over the mindlink, keeping his thought voice from carrying to the rest of them. It was the little things that made a big difference. Stinky had been the leader that DI Katlind wanted him to be. The team put their personal concerns aside and stepped forward as one.

The lieutenant had already reported to Space School that Black Leaper's team should be assigned together. He wouldn't bother with an update to his report about Cain and Ellie. Recruits were young and if they were really close, who was he to get in their way. He envied them because he knew, this team would be going to space and he'd be stuck on the Traveler. He admitted to himself that he would have run from the Android, too. He didn't have what it took to deal with a real emergency. The assignments group must have seen that, and he tipped his hat to them. Leave the excitement to those who lived for it. He had his eye on an ensign in engineering and she had her eye on him, he thought. *It wouldn't be bad to settle down on the Traveler*, he thought to himself. *It wouldn't be bad at all.*

With a flourish, he opened the hatch and let the winds waft the unique and harsh smell of the Livestock Level over the recruits. Some of the recruits choked, others, like Black Leaper and Cain, breathed in with reverence, becoming quickly accustomed. Leaper led the others as he followed the catwalk to the stairs and down to the grassland that fed the remaining livestock. Without the Wolfoids, the pig population had grown extensively, requiring a significant culling by the Androids to restore balance. With the reintroduction of humans to the RV Traveler, Deck 10 was back in full use. Human shepherds and Aurochs shared the responsibility to maintain the herds that fed the crew, at least those who ate meat.

Lieutenant Simonds walked down the stairs to greet their waiting escorts. A massive Aurochs bull stood casually next to two hover cars. His horns curved from the side of his head, outward and then back forward, menacing anyone who would look the bull in the eye as long as that person didn't know that the Aurochs were peaceful and friendly. The horns were a holdover from past days when they needed such hardware on their heads to hold predators at bay.

"Good morning, my friends!" the lieutenant called as he approached. Cain didn't catch the names of their escorts. He would have forgotten them anyway. They'd already been introduced to a seemingly endless parade of people. Of all the people he'd met since arriving on the spaceship, he wouldn't forget Daksha. The Tortoid had made an impact on him and he couldn't wait to talk with him more. Daksha left him with many questions and the desire to find the answers. He clearly saw why his great-great-grandfather considered Master Aadi to be his mentor.

They put one team into each hover car, and departed on a rapid circumnavigation of Deck 10. The Aurochs pounded across the plain as he ran free, keeping pace with the cars. Aurochs were legendary for their speed, a reputation that was well-earned. The wind whipped past the open windows as they zipped along. It was a tight squeeze since the Wolfoid took up a great deal of space. Tandry, Ellie, and Mixial squeezed into the front while the boys were stuffed into the back. Between Stinky and Cain, Briz stood with his front legs braced against the front seat. With that much fur in the back, Cain started to sweat. He hung his head out the window on one side and the Wolfoid had his muzzle out the other, ears flapping in the breeze.

The grassland flew by as they passed herds of some kind of hornless cow, pigs, and chickens that had been added recently. Aurochs could be seen around the plains, grazing and keeping the animals together. They saw a couple Wolfoids running through the grasses, too. Maybe they came from the planet for a visit or they were crewmembers on a ship temporarily at the space station. The Traveler was open to everyone. Cain was sure there'd be someone fishing on Deck 5, although he'd been told the conditions were harsh, like fishing during a hurricane, but some found that exciting.

He liked an adrenaline rush as much as the next person, but in his mind, vacations were meant for relaxation. Maybe deep space exploration wasn't as exciting as he thought it would be. He'd heard that it was minutes of sheer terror followed by months of extreme boredom. He'd have to talk with more spacers and see what they had to say.

They passed herd after herd, along with bots, Androids, and Aurochs. The overall feeling was serene. It was like traveling across the Plains of Propiscius. Leaper watched the sky, knowing that it was artificial, but the light seemed pure, like that on a bright, sunny day. They asked the driver about the source of the light. He explained about the bioluminescence system that made up the lowest panels of the ceiling. The ceiling was the next cylinder of concentric cylinders that made up the five spinning decks of each core section. One hundred meters of structure created the ring stability, in-between were decks where people lived and worked, and the system that provided light to the main levels.

The hover cars circumnavigated the entire deck, then turned toward the ramp spiraling upward. The rollup door opened as they approached and they sped up the wide ramp. The Aurochs stayed on the Livestock Level, tipping his horns to them as they drove away and the door closed behind them.

They stopped most of the way up the ramp as a wall panel slid aside, revealing an entry into the between decks. Most people took the radial elevators beyond the core's fore and aft bulkheads to get to the decks between levels. Besides engineering, this was where the majority of the work aboard Space Station Traveler happened. With numerous labs, berthing, dining halls, manufacturing facilities, and more, one would never have to leave the area between levels in order to live a fulfilling life.

Cain looked at the others. They shook their heads. Live your entire life indoors? Live in space on a spaceship, but never go anywhere?

No way. They all agreed on that. "Deep space," Briz 'shouted' out of the blue. His vocalization device raised the volume, but nothing like what he really meant. It was up to the others to pick up the torch and carry it.

"Deep space!" the rest of the team yelled, thrusting their fists into the air.

Lieutenant Simonds watched with mild amusement, not knowing what caused the sudden celebration, but he approved. If someone else wanted to go, then that made it easy for people like him to stay. He'd go if they made him, but he didn't want it. He expected the Traveler to be his home for the rest of his life. Maybe he'd even work his way up to captain. Captain Simonds. He liked the ring of that.

The two teams checked out one of the labs that specifically dealt with the air on the Livestock Level. The recruits had first-hand knowledge of the smell, and this was the area that managed the toxicity, keeping it within a range that wasn't harmful to people. That meant filtering and air handling. Next stop, the machinery room, then ventilation.

With SI Hendricks' death, the powers that be decided to send the recruits on three separate tours of the ship. The teams wouldn't wait on each other. Cain figured it was to expose fewer students to hazards by keeping the others away from him. He remained certain that the Android had targeted him and that it wouldn't be the last attack. He asked the lieutenant if he could have a blaster, but Simonds only laughed. Cain wanted to remind him that their last escort died a hideous death that a blaster may have been able to prevent, but bit his tongue and kept the comment to himself.

The entire team was wary. Tandry asked Mixial to stay out in front of them, make sure the way was clear, but the 'cat reminded her that she couldn't read the Androids. They were a blank to her. If that was where the threat would come from, then Mixial would be no help.

Cain knew that from his great-great-grandparents. The indomitable Golden Warrior was little help on board the Traveler except for his prescience, something that few 'cats had. Mixial did not, but as with G-War, if the threat wasn't to her human, then she may not sense it. Mixial remained aware and settled for alerting the team to the presence of the old style Androids.

It would have to do. Cain hated being afraid to turn a corner, wondering what was there. He couldn't live his life in fear, and they wouldn't give him a blaster. Mixial agreed to share her vision with him, show him what was around the corner. In a fight, the greatest advantage one could have was more time. Cain appreciated the team's concern and contribution to his health and well-being. What mattered most was that they believed him. Black Leaper probably had something to do with that, because he had fought with the Android and seen that it didn't care about him, only what it took to get to Cain. The Wolfoid was convinced the Android was after his friend.

Why wouldn't the others believe him? Because they'd never experienced hatred and evil before. His great-grandparents told stories of the Bat-Ravens, the horror those creatures projected directly into their minds that they'd never forgotten. The stories of the Android attack on the Wolfoids, on Braden and Micah. Those tales dominated his thoughts ever since he saw the look in the Android's mechanical eyes. That was the only Android he'd ever seen up close and he'd never forget that look.

Malevolence.

As they toured the facilities and learned how the systems worked for power, air, and fluid control, Cain noted that there weren't any Androids working, when there should have been.

Maybe someone had taken his claim seriously. And that freed him to learn what he needed about the spaceship's systems. The ship was life and he couldn't afford to be the distraction. He'd never been the weak link on a team before and didn't want to start. Cain stayed next to Briz. A running dialogue between the two held the entire team's interest. Leaper was both pleased and proud.

Fluid and air flow were similar in regards to the forces applied. The pipelines running through the decks between the levels had a slight slant that followed the direction of spin. Otherwise, the fluids would have to maintain additional pressure to drive them perpendicular to the centrifugal force. The little downhill twist significantly reduced the amount of standing pressure within the system, which increased the longevity between replacement. Most pipes were glass-lined, eliminating any chemical interaction with the pipes themselves. In most cases, the piping was four millennia old. The valves were replaced at regular intervals, but the pipes themselves were original.

Four thousand years. It was mind-boggling. The ancients had the technology to build the ship. In the last one hundred and thirty-seven years, Cygnus had relearned much of what the ancients destroyed during their civil war, but even with the recovered knowledge, the people of Vii could not have built the RV Traveler. They didn't have the infrastructure or equipment or legions of intelligent shipbuilders. They had yet to catch up on thousands of years of advancements.

But they moved forward in a different area. The survivors from Cygnus VI had made advancements of their own that enabled deep space travel without taking thousands of years to make the trips.

The ISE jumped Cygnus past its ancestors, literally and figuratively, and created the need for the Space Exploration Service. The first explorers had paved the way, experimented, created procedures to handle the unknowns of the interstellar universe, established Space School, and instilled the desire in children to touch the stars. Leaper, Cain, Tandry, Ellie, and Briz represented a new generation.

The schools were maturing on Vii, but many were still not connected technologically. Cain and his peers were from those schools that enjoyed the advantage of power and interconnectivity. Until Cain's school burned down, that is.

That thought brought Cain back to the moment where the instructors had selected two valves for replacement. The recruits were to do the work under the watchful eye of an Android that was responsible for the system. Cain was happy to see a newer generation Android show up. He relaxed and could focus on the task at hand, which was breaking one valve free without losing containment within the piping system.

Stinky and Cain followed their checklist from top to bottom as they worked through the isolation of the valve, its removal, and finally installation of the replacement. They hit it with a hand torch at the end to ensure the gaskets filled the spaces. They attached the air hose and did an air check on their valve and the attached piping, confirming a closed system where the fluids would remain contained. Once the Android checked their work and declared it sound, it opened the isolation valves and returned the system to service. It went from one to the next, through the different groups.

Briz had the pleasure of working with the Android on his system. The Rabbit fumbled when it came to detail work, but when he and the Android talked restricted flow, turbulence, and pressure micro-variations, even the Android had to stop and think. The Android did the hands-on work with the valve while he and Briz ran through numerous calculations, assessing the value of system optimization.

In the end, they determined that the system was capable of more, but that it had been over-engineered in the first place, delivering within the desired pressure and volume ranges while retaining excess capacity. Being filled with fluid at all times was probably the single greatest improvement recommendation without changing any of the associated hardware. Air created unwanted turbulence. The system was designed well, but was too big for the needs. It was over-engineered and lost its efficiencies. They could have used pipe of a smaller diameter. On a ship of that size, reducing the pipe sizes to exactly what was needed would have saved gross tons in weight. Just a little over thirty kilometers long, with probably hundreds of thousands of kilometers in piping that was too big. The reduced weight would have made a big difference.

The Android and Briz chatted like old friends, even though the Android's voice was mechanically plain, without inflection. Briz spoke with an animation that showed a zest for all things technical.

"Whatever ship I'm on, I want him there, too!" Cain whispered to Stinky. The Wolfoid nodded vigorously. Briz stopped his conversation and looked directly at Cain, nose twitching and ears dipping as he appreciated the compliment. "Of course you heard me," Cain whispered, shaking his head. Rabbits had incredible hearing, plus their eyes were on the sides of the head, so they could see directly behind them with their peripheral vision. It was difficult to sneak up on a Rabbit, but not impossible, as Cain and Stinky had demonstrated on numerous occasions, enjoying their ongoing game of Scare the Rabbit.

The teams were sent through the twisting and cramped spaces between decks in search of systems issues. Their goal was to recommend solutions to the problems to the Android instructor.

To Cain, it seemed like a treasure hunt, so he was happy as could be. The Android wanted the recruits to explore individually, but Lieutenant Simonds overruled it, saying that with the recent aberrant behavior in the presence of the recruits--he avoided the word "Android--he wanted the exploration done in their recruit teams.

Stinky led the way into the maze of piping, cables, and machinery. Cain brought up the rear as a precaution since Stinky didn't want to take any chances, just in case the Androids really were out to get Braden and Micah's descendent.

Briz was second and constantly held up the team as he was easily distracted, going off on a tangent to look at some inane piece of equipment and study it before returning to the group. Finally, the Wolfoid gave up and told Briz to follow his nose. The rest would come along for the ride, but he challenged Briz to share his understanding of the systems with the rest of the team over their mindlink. With Mixial's help in keeping the mindlink active, the team was treated to a running commentary of mathematical calculations, physics formulas, and mechanical engineering standards.

They weren't close enough for Cain to make faces at Stinky, but he listened as well as he could, until the Rabbit squealed in fear. Then Cain was focused like a laser as he ran forward.

Cain passed Ellie and Tandry, who ran forward to help a friend, but not as quickly as Cain's headlong rush. forward but cautiously. How quickly they learned that if one of them was in trouble, they were all in trouble. The three of them ran ahead, half crouching to avoid the piping overhead. Stinky was already with Briz, pulling him back from something that the others couldn't see. The Hillcat hissed.

The blood from a deep cut across Briz's foreleg stained his silky white fur. Cain had been raised to always keep numbweed with him, and being on the spaceship was no exception. Although he didn't carry much, he had enough to pack into the Rabbit's wound.

"You get too close to the real work?" Cain asked casually, thinking Briz got himself into some bad piping. He expected the Rabbit to answer, but only saw fear in his eyes. Cain looked around rapidly, thinking the Androids had made a surprise attack. Black Leaper pointed ahead. One of the mutant vines had penetrated into the section and was wrapped around a heavy coupling through which the ship's power flowed. Light reflected from its metal leaves as they moved of their own accord, back and forth in front of the equipment.

"Let's report it. It's not safe in here!" Tandry offered with wide eyes.

"If we go, we fail," Stinky replied simply. "Our mission was to find issues and return with recommendations. I'd like to think we found a big issue. I know the vines are throughout the ship, but have they dug through power couplings before?"

They looked to Briz for an answer, figuring it was something he would know. He still wasn't talking, so Cain shook him, knowing that the pain from the wound would have lessened with the numbweed. "Come on, Briz. We need you on this one. What can we do to stop that thing from getting into the power?"

The Rabbit's eyes seemed hollow as he started to talk, his vocalization device translating his speech as monotone, devoid of emotion. "The vines are metal, but they're also organic. They use their blood to move dissolved metals into the leaves, solidifying them, growing them."

"A bio-mechanical construct? We'd always assumed they were alien, didn't we?" the Wolfoid asked. Cain shrugged. That was what he thought.

"The Android in engineering told me that they'd made progress using electrical discharge, but were still experimenting at how they could reverse the growth, not just stop it," Briz answered. He stood up and looked at his arm.

"We're here with you, Briz. Just tell us what we need to do," Stinky told the Rabbit.

"We need a handheld computer. And then we need a communication device." The team looked at each other. As the team leader, Stinky had been given one. He held it up for the others to see.

"Mixial and I will go and get a handheld from the Android. What do I tell it?" Tandry offered. She was shorter and could run without being hunched over like the others.

"That we need it to help us make the best recommendation for problem resolution. It'll accept that answer," Briz advised. Tandry nodded once and was off. Mixial ran past to get in front of her, leading the way out of the maze.

The others settled in to wait, not taking their eyes from the vine and its deadly leaves.

Man Against Machine

When Tandry returned with the handheld computer, she gave the thumbs up. The Android had surrendered it without question. As soon as he had both pieces of equipment, Briz got to work, turning the communication device into a poor-man's scanner to look for radio-frequency emissions. He hoped that they were technological and not biological. If its intelligence came from the organic side, then the communication device would be useless in detecting it, otherwise his jury-rigged contraption would be able to detect the emissions.

The Rabbit started furiously coding, using snippets of code from within the handheld itself to fill the routine processes. Once the handheld was synced with their device, he perused the entire radio-frequency spectrum. He picked up a great deal of emissions and spent a long time sorting through them.

Finally, he shook his head. "I'm not finding anything from the vine."

"We're kind of far away..." Cain started to say. Briz stopped what he was doing.

"Yes. Take the device as close as you can. I've isolated the signals not associated with the vine, so if there is anything, it should be obvious." The rest of the team looked at each other. No one volunteered.

"Fine!" Cain surrendered, but as he reached for the device, Ellie grabbed his arm.

"I'll do it." Before he could protest, she scooped up the communication device and started crawling toward the power coupling and its vine protector. She crawled on an indirect route, keeping piping and other equipment between the vine and herself. When she could hide no longer, she reached out tentatively and pushed the device incrementally closer, checking with Briz to see if he had anything.

She cursed herself for always being last to volunteer for positions that would help the team. Cain was always first with his hand in the air, followed closely by Leaper. Tandry took the tasks that she was most comfortable with, technological work like what Briz was good at. And that left Ellie, on the outside looking in.

No more, she said to herself as she half-stood and moved toward the vines. Cain yelled something, but she didn't hear him. She inched forward, holding the communication device before her. Briz said something, but his vocalization device didn't project strongly enough for her to make out what it was. She stopped, turned, and saw Cain waving.

'What? I can't hear you?' she said over the mindlink

'Back away, slowly. Briz said he found what he was looking for. I'm proud of you,' Cain said. Ellie looked frustrated. She wondered if he knew he was projecting to all of them.

She was brought back to the moment as the communication device was violently ripped from her hand. The vine had slapped it away with an offshoot vine in the overhead. She jumped back and looked at her hand. The razor sharp leaf had only hit the device. To her surprise, her flesh was intact. The device was on the deck, beneath the vine, but out of the reach of its flailing leaves. Ellie crabbed backward until she could rejoin the team. She punched Cain when she was within arm's reach.

"What?"

"I'm proud of you?" she said accusingly.

"We all are. I wouldn't have gotten that close!" Tandry came to Cain's rescue. Ellie shook her head and looked to Briz to take the conversation somewhere, anywhere else.

"It's mechanical, passing instructions via the V Band of EHF, some fifty-three gigahertz. Let me dial it in and see what we can do." Briz's small Rabbit hands flew across the handheld keyboard, coding, splicing, and rewriting. He activated the communication device in broadcast mode and the vine went crazy. The leaves started hacking at the power coupling. Briz adjusted the settings and the vine calmed, then the leaves went limp.

"Throw something over there," Briz ordered. Ellie pulled a granola bar from her packet, eased closer, and underhanded it toward the vine. It hit, bounced off a leaf, and dropped to the floor. Briz chittered in excitement, hopping up and down. The others cheered.

One leaf started vibrating, then another, then the whole vine was shaking and the leaves were slapping back and forth, attacking the power coupling with renewed vigor.

Briz immersed himself once again in the handheld as the others pulled him back, farther away from the danger of a ruptured pipe, but probably not far enough if the power flow was unleashed into the space.

"Let it go, Briz! We have to get out of here!" Stinky 'shouted' over his vocalization device. Briz pulled away from the hands that sought to guide him away from the vine infestation. He squatted on his haunches and continued to code, eyes focused intently on the small screen.

The others looked at each other, unsure of what to do next. Black Leaper took a deep breath, ready to bark the order for them all to leave, when Briz brightened.

"I've got it now." He activated his program, made a small adjustment on a slide-bar, then watched as the leaves instantly stopped hacking at nearby surfaces and drooped, almost to the deck. The vine lost all strength. Briz pulled free and walked closer, carefully adjusting settings on his device.

The clang of metal hitting metal shocked them back to a different reality, as they hadn't seen what caused the noise. Then another and another. The leaves fell from the vines, crashing against pipes and equipment on their way to the deck.. Briz bounced up and down, his pink nose twitching.

The team spread out as they approached the vine. It was noticeably shriveled, the deck littered with its razor sharp, metal leaves.

"Did you kill it?" Cain asked. Mixial sniffed the leaves, carefully stepped past them, and squatted to pee on the base of the vine. No one tried to stop her.

"I think so," the Rabbit stammered. "We need to find another one and test it to see if the comm protocols of the vines are universal or local," he added excitedly.

Cain carefully moved the leaves with the toe of his boot until he found the communication device. It was scratched but functioning well, as demonstrated by the death of the vine. Cain almost keyed it to talk with the Android, then looked to Stinky, the team leader. He handed it to the Wolfoid with a smile, but Stinky held up his hands and pointed to Briz. The Rabbit traded the handheld computer for the comm device and keyed it, talking quickly with the Android and requesting that he join them.

After many pats on the back, the Android arrived. Its artificial skin covered a face devoid of expression. It pointed with its hand for the recruits to lead the way. Cain went first. When he reflected on his choice, he felt like he was putting the others at an unreasonable risk since they were between the Android and him. Stinky told him not to worry about it, because they had Briz on their side.

Cain laughed as he made his way through the maze of piping to the dead vine and deck littered with metal leaves. The Android reviewed Briz's program on the handheld computer, then took the communication device and looked at it, too. Its Android eyes fixed on a random point and it froze as it communicated with someone or something else. The recruits watched as the process continued. The Android turned its head, told them all to standby, then resumed its former position.

The recruit team from Class Beta 37 shifted uncomfortably as the wait seemed interminable. Mixial was sound asleep under a piece of machinery that generated enough heat to make her comfortable.

When the Android looked up at them, Cain could have sworn the thing looked pleased.

"By using the ship-wide communication system and the main computer to run your program, the vine infestation has been eradicated. Dr. Johns has sent his compliments to you, Briz, and said that there is a medal waiting for you. He would like to meet with you as soon as you return to the New Command Center," the Android finished and walked away.

And that was how the RV Traveler was cleansed of the vines that human scientists had created then lost control of. Once the alien theory was discounted, other options presented themselves, or so Briz told them. The rest of his team still considered him a genius and too valuable to send to space with the others.

A New Partnership

Briz was having none of it and insisted that he was staying with the team. Master Daksha also had his ideas regarding Black Leaper and his team, but didn't share them with the others. They only suspected.

The Tortoid had nostrils and didn't process smells like other creatures, so when they tried to explain why the teammates called the Wolfoid "Stinky," it was completely lost on him. He adamantly refused to join the recruits in using nicknames that he considered the denigration of all humanity.

Daksha also talked extensively with Mixial. Tandry expected it was related to the eventual takeover of Vii by the 'cats, as they were always plotting something. Mixial's duplicity in the great obstacle course debacle had still gone unaddressed. After the fire, the recruits from Leaper's team avoided talking about it, but Tandry didn't forget.

Maybe the 'cats wouldn't take over the planet, but Tandry expected that they thought they already had. Most people of any influence were bonded with 'cats. Mixial wondered why Cain hadn't. He was gifted and most importantly, he descended from those who always had 'cats in their lives. She asked, but he shrugged off her question.

A Tortoid, a Rabbit, and a Wolfoid. Sounded like the start of the companions as gathered by Braden and Micah. Throw in an Android attack and it looked like history was repeating itself. Judging by the emotions that Ellie and Cain were projecting, it also looked like the couple was set. All Cain needed was a 'cat to keep him on the straight and narrow.

"Come here, you two!" Tandry belted out of nowhere, looking pointedly at Cain and Ellie. They were in billeting. The shipboard training was complete and the next day, they'd be returning to Vii. Confused, Cain and Ellie joined her.

"So?" Tandry asked, which only served to further confuse her two other recruits. They shook their heads. "You've been sneaking into his room every night. You keep us all awake, then you spend the day fighting as if you're not in love. Are you two the only ones who don't see it?" Cain stood perfectly still, scanning the area with only his eyes to see if anyone else was listening.

They were, they all were.

"So?" Tandry repeated her question.

"I don't know what you want," Cain ventured. Ellie remained silent, also hesitant to move.

"Go for a walk, on the Livestock Level, and talk about what you want out of life, like adults, instead of the feint-parry-thrust game you've been playing." Without question, the young couple departed, more to get out of the spotlight of their classmates than to follow Tandry's order. Their recruit badges gave them access to the main decks, so in they went, making sure the hatch closed behind them.

They were alone. For the first time, they were alone and in the open. Cain leaned toward her and she responded, kissing him fully, in the artificial light of day. She held out her hand and he took it. They walked down the steps and into the grasses, holding hands as lovers did. They walked and they talked. They had much in common. They had shared goals. They felt like they were also in competition. There were limited positions on SES ships. They didn't know of any married couples serving together.

And none of that mattered. After walking for only a short time, Cain dropped to one knee and proposed, simply, without poetry, without thought, trusting his feelings.

Lost in the moment, Ellie agreed.

Mixial let the rest of the team in berthing know before Cain even stood up. The 'cat wasn't pleased with her human's meddling, but accepted it as 'cats had done for centuries, knowing that at some point, the Hillcat would have to clean up the messes made by her person. In the interim, she'd resume her conversation with Master Daksha, who she always found fascinating and unperturbed by human emotion.

If only the humans could see how dysfunctional they were and tried to be more like the 'cats. Mixial sighed heavily, understanding that without thumbs, the 'cats would always be at a disadvantage. Who else could open things for them? *If only the fabricator would serve fresh meat*, Mixial lamented to herself, *then I wouldn't have to get dirty hunting. Or servants. Yes. I like the idea of servants,* the 'cat mused.

When Cain and Ellie returned to the berthing, Stinky's and the other four teams had maxed the fabricator in producing snacks and treats for an ad hoc celebration. They even had wine, to which Lieutenant Simonds turned a blind eye, while sipping from his own glass. Doctor Kanter made an untimely visit with her entourage. She accepted that her work with the teams was done and joined the celebration. Cain and Ellie were uncomfortable, but accepted the well wishes and then retreated to Ellie's room, where they celebrated privately.

The Return Home

Black Leaper's team took their recliners in the matter transfer chamber, five for the recruits and one for the 'cat. Daksha had joined them and took the seventh spot. The second team took the other five recliners and with a full house, Holly gave them the usual instructions, directing them to stay still until they were safely back on Planet Vii. Cain resisted the temptation to hold Ellie's hand.

Aletha came into his mind suddenly, and he fought against it. He could see her shaking her head at him, hands on hips, disappointed. He pinched his eyes closed and prayed that the transfer process would start and he'd be spared her judgment.

And his own.

Ellie wondered what Cain was thinking about as she watched him clamp his eyes shut and clench his jaw. She didn't think he was afraid of the transfer process. She'd ask when they hit the planet.

Behind Cain, the walls shimmered and darkness descended on the bodies carefully still in their recliners. The computer dance began and the next thing the travelers knew, they were nauseous and waking in the matter transfer chamber beneath New Sanctuary.

No one moved for a long time. Although they'd become close, no one wanted to be first to puke. Finally, Stinky slid his front legs off the chair, slowly sliding until they were on the floor. First one back paw, then the other, and he found himself standing. He looked from one pale face to the next, grinning. He took a few tentative steps, then strode boldly toward the wall as it slide aside. Stinky turned and cocked his head.

"Well, what are you all waiting for? Did we learn to be lazy on the ship?" Stinky taunted the rest. Cain was next off his chair, followed by Ellie, then Tandry, who coughed twice and heaved. Mixial showed sympathy for her human by hacking up a hairball. Cain looked closely at Daksha.

"I think Daksha's dead!" Cain said, fighting his nausea as he hurried to the Tortoid. The smell of puke didn't help.

Daksha was on the recliner, legs tucked up against his shell, unblinking, looking more like a statue than a living creature. As Cain touched his neck, the Tortoid blinked, nodded once, and started floating. After that, the rest climbed down and on unsteady legs, walked from the room.

Doctor Johns was waiting for them, and heartily welcomed Briz, pumping his furry white hand until they thought the Rabbit's arm was going to come off. The elder human beckoned Leaper's team to follow him. The Tortoid joined the parade that headed into the bowels of New Sanctuary's underground.

The team arrived, feeling much better after the vigorous walk, and were handed glasses of water to further improve their post-transfer health. "Maybe you should have water set up outside the chamber?" Tandry said off-handedly to no one in particular.

Dr. Johns looked sideways at her then started clapping. "That's why we need you!" he shouted so the others in the New Command Center could hear. "Someone who can see what we cannot, since we are too close. We need you. All of you." The old scientist beamed and the others working at their stations stood, watching the group of young recruits expectantly.

Cain and Ellie held hands while the others shifted. Briz was front and center, failing miserably at trying to hide. Mixial bumped against the old doctor's leg, rubbing against it unashamedly before heading to the elevator. She stood there, then looked back as no one moved. An angry yowl elicited a response from the nearest technician, who ran over to activate the elevator. The 'cat didn't give him a second look as she strolled in, tail held high, showing plenty of 'cat butt to everyone in the Command Center. Tandry hung her head, at a loss for words.

Dr. Johns snickered. "Where were we? Oh, yes, of course," he started. "Recruit Brisbois, please step forward." The Rabbit reluctantly stepped next to the tall human clone.

"I'm afraid I'm not very good at this, so I'll defer to Holly and let him do the honors." The hologram instantly materialized, beaming a friendly smile at all present. He then shrunk his image to match the Rabbit's size.

"Attention to orders!" the hologram called out, his voice reverberating through the speakers of the New Command Center. "To all who shall see these presents, greetings. Recruit Brisbois, the Council of Elders has awarded you the Space Star First Class for your work in determining how to remove the threat of the vines aboard the Space Station Traveler. With your team from Recruit Training Class Beta 37, you refused to run, remaining exposed to the dangers of the vines and their deadly metallic leaves. You rallied your team around your vision that the threat could be neutralized and with unwavering dedication, you personally created the means by which the entire space station was cleared of this persistent menace. One hundred and thirty-six years have passed since the vines were first encountered and finally, we are free. The Council of Elders thanks you, Recruit Brisbois, for all you have done."

Dr. Johns produced a small, five-pointed, platinum star and pinned it to the Rabbit's harness strap. The clapping and cheering commenced, but the doctor wasn't finished. He pointed to Cain and Ellie, calling them forward. He put a hand on Briz's small shoulder as he tried to escape, making him stay.

"Recruit Cain and Recruit Ellie, you are awarded the Space Star Second Class for your willingness to sacrifice yourselves as you engaged the vines at close range. Your selflessness made the technical solution possible. And Recruit Tandry and Recruit Black Leaper, your leadership and support helped your entire team to realize success, a success not only for you, but all of humanity, all the people of Vii. You are awarded the Space Star Third Class. And a final award, and one that probably matters the most to you and your team, your training as part of class 37-B is at an end and your training as crewmembers aboard the Deep Space Exploration Vessel, Cygnus-12, will begin, effective immediately, by order of Admiral Jesper, Commander, Space Exploration Service."

As Dr. Johns pinned the Space Stars on the other four recruits, Briz hopped excitedly, happy that he hadn't been put into Research and Development.

Leaper started the handshakes and hugs. The others followed suit, and then those on duty in the New Command Center formed a line to greet the new ensigns, the title that came with graduation from Space School. Last through was Daksha, who asked that they form a circle around him. He spoke to them over the mindlink, always preferring that over the vocalization device, which he maintained did not adequately translate the Tortoid's thoughts into speech.

'Congratulations to all of you!' He nodded and blinked rapidly. *'Cygnus-12 is currently in refit at the De'atesh shipyard. What you'll be getting is an entirely new ship, with the largest capacity and exploration capability of any in the fleet. I am quite pleased to have you on board,'* he said with a twinkle in his Tortoid eye.

"Have us on board, you said. You're coming?" Cain asked.

'I'm the Commander of Cygnus-12. I just happened to be on board the Traveler reviewing some of the new equipment I'll be getting when I heard about a recruit with an exceptionally brilliant mind. You can all thank Briz for that. Dr. Johns suggested I meet with him as you wanted a shipborne assignment, didn't you?' he asked the Rabbit, who bobbed his head excitedly.

'And then I saw the rest of you in action. My goal is not just to go to space, but to go with people who will make a difference and then make sure that we come home. And there we are. You have ten days of leave awarded to you and that will start as soon as we enjoy a picnic in your honor, in the sun. I am afraid that once on the ship, we won't get much sun so I advise you to get your fill now.' Daksha nodded to let them know he was done and started swimming toward the elevator, which had been upgraded from the old days and could now hold their entire team with plenty room to spare.

Once the few seconds of transit ended, the doors opened to bright sunshine, temporarily blinding them as they fumbled their way through the small lobby and into the outdoors. The air was markedly different from the clean, recycled, and dry air of the New Command Center. They drank it in, unsure of what to do next as they still couldn't see clearly.

'Hey, you two. Come here,' a rough and rude voice ordered Cain and Ellie. They blinked and shielded their eyes to see who was speaking, while looking at each other to make sure that the voice was talking to them.

'Really? Is this what I'm going to be saddled with? Really?' a second, feminine voice added, heavily filled with disdain.

Two Hillcats waited impatiently in the shade of a larger palm tree. They crouched, paws tucked underneath them, as they watched the two humans approach.

'I'll take that one,' the large black male said, tipping his chin toward Ellie.

'Fine,' the other spit out, not sounding fine at all. She was a radiant white, not quite as large as the male, but her crystalline green eyes seemed

to dominate the area.

"Are you, you know, bonding with us?" Cain asked out loud.

'Look, master of the obvious speaks,' the female 'cat said in her thought voice.

"I'm sorry. I didn't mean to offend you, but I thought the bonding would be a little more pleasant," Cain said, trying to soften the tone of his new best friend. Ellie nodded, wearing a look as if she'd just eaten a cactus.

'It didn't mean to offend us! Ha,' the male 'cat replied, chuckling to himself. *'If nothing else, it'll be a good laugh, like watching a kitten fall-into-the-lake kind of funny.'*

'Do you have names? We'd like to get to know you better, if we could,' Ellie said soothingly over the mindlink.

'I like that one. Do you want to trade?' the female 'cat asked.

'Too late. You're stuck with the dumb one,' he replied with a snicker.

'Fine!'

Cain thought he should have been offended. Nearly every one of his ancestors had bonded with a Hillcat and they all described the experience as magical, combined with the abrasive nature that Hillcats shared with their bonded humans. Cain shook his head and took a deep breath. All the disdain with none of the magic. He probably did something in a previous life to deserve it, or it was the ghost of Prince Axial De'atesh himself come back to haunt the descendent of his life-bonded human, Braden.

"Do you asses have names?" Cain taunted, trying to take control of the conversation.

'Yes,' the white 'cat answered, yawning and closing her magnificent eyes.

Ellie giggled. Cain had had enough. He turned and walked away. Ellie, still holding his hand, followed. She shrugged at the big male 'cat.

'Lutheann and he's Carnesto. Now do go before our heads explode from the inanity of it all,' Lutheann answered, looking like she was sound asleep.

Cain looked unhappy, and Ellie knew why. He had always idealized the bonding with a 'cat. She could feel Cain's emotions surge with the high of their new assignment, followed by the low of being called an idiot by a creature that would always be in his mind, followed by the waves of affection for Ellie. She wanted to calm him, help him forward. Having shared his mind, she knew that he was both selfish and selfless, accepting some things as a natural state, while fighting vigorously against others.

He felt it natural to partner with another person. He'd chosen Ellie and she felt honored, although she suspected that she was a second choice. She would never ask him as she didn't want to know and wanted to believe that she had him all to herself. "Let's get married, today!" she blurted out. He stopped and turned, smiling.

The discontent he felt over the bonding with Lutheann immediately evaporated. The rest of their day turned into a blur. Daksha officiated the wedding, which were informal affairs on Vii. It held little value outside the commitment that two people made to each other. For the SES, they recognized marriage and would put the couples together if possible, whether on the same ship or in support positions on the space station or in the shipyard.

And the couple was already together. A spaceship could be gone for years and it was lonely in space. At least for Cain and Ellie, it became a little less lonely on that day as they showed off their Space Star awards and celebrated a wedding. Briz was happy to have the attention off him, if only for a little while.

He just wanted to get back to his room and check some calculations based on what he'd seen on the Traveler, and he needed to study more on the interdimensional space engine. There was so much potential, but he needed more technical information as well as theory, maybe even the original notes from the research center on Cygnus VI. He started walking off, thinking he'd talk with Holly, when Tandry corralled him and stopped him. She was his minder for that evening to make sure he didn't do exactly what he had just tried to do.

Mixial crouched with Lutheann and Carnesto, plotting the demise of the entire human race, Tandry suspected, or at least that of the three humans they called their own.

Cain stood by while Ellie called her parents, who were a little put out that they didn't have the chance to attend their only daughter's wedding.

Cain's parents were even less cordial, implying that they got married because they had to. Ellie prevented Cain from hanging up on them. His wife smiled at him and in that moment, everything was okay. That was what he wanted from her and what he needed.

He breathed deeply of the air at the oasis lake, the same air that his ancestors had breathed in over a hundred years prior. He understood why they loved this place as their secret getaway. It was crowded now, with a city growing on its outskirts. New Sanctuary, with its oasis, had become the center of the known world, a place everyone visited and many stayed. The schools were the most technologically advanced and the lifestyle was comparable to that which the ancients themselves enjoyed.

Cain liked it, but at the same time, longed for the open range, green fields, and trees. Ellie liked the city and all of its comforts. Similar to a spaceship, but on a grand scale.

"Let's hike to Livestel, maybe see some of the rainforest?" Cain suggested. "I don't feel like visiting family, taking a long trip that won't be fun."

She understood. "Will we ever visit Greentree?" she prodded, knowing the answer already.

"There's nothing for me there," he answered flatly, instantly thinking of Aletha, thinking he should call her, but then knowing that he could not. He thought she'd be crushed, but he was secretly afraid that she would not be. Tears threatened to fall. He blinked rapidly and looked away. Ellie knew something was wrong, that she'd opened a deep wound. She figured it was the girlfriend he'd lamented those months ago during their initial training. She didn't want to know how strong his feelings were for her. Ellie reconciled herself with the fact that they weren't going for a visit. There was no risk of running into the other woman if they weren't in Greentree.

And this was her wedding day! She punched Cain in the arm, hard. He winced, his angry face instantly appeared and glared at her. "That's enough of that, mister! This is our day, so stop moping and let's have some fun," she said with a big grin. They ran to the woods, leaving the others behind, then slowing to a walk and talking about the day and their future. It was the kind of talk that married people had. It took a while for them to notice that 'cats were following them—a large black male and an all-white female with green eyes that seemed to glow.

'Is this our life now?' Ellie asked over the mindlink.

'Yes,' came the simple reply from Carnesto.

"Are you two partners?" Cain asked aloud, as much to annoy the 'cats as to speak where he was more comfortable.

'No, and you are stupid for even thinking that. This foul creature likes domestics,' Lutheann responded in disgust.

'You say that like it's a bad thing,' Carnesto added joyfully. *'Now that we're going to space...'*

'We're nothing of the sort, you cretin.' Cain was happy that the other 'cat was on the receiving end of Lutheann's venom and not him. *'Your time is coming, human,'* she added. Cain didn't know if he should sympathize with Carnesto or be happy that it wasn't his time yet. He shrugged to himself, while Ellie chuckled.

"So, yes, this is our life now," Cain sympathized. "Let's visit Livestel. I think Stinky is heading home tomorrow. We can travel with him, then hike along the rainforest for a couple days. Nothing too taxing, just a chance to have some time to ourselves. Be alone, if you know what I mean."

"Relatively alone, if you get my drift," Ellie clarified, nodding in the direction of the two 'cats.

A Return to Space School

The five members of the team returned to New Sanctuary at the appointed time, ten days after they had been turned loose. They all had stories of their escapades, but the least vocal were Cain and Ellie, as they'd enjoyed each other's company like newlyweds do, which doesn't make for great stories to share. They were happy and the others accepted that.

Briz never left New Sanctuary. He spent every minute of all ten days belly deep in everything he could find on the ISE, and when he wasn't studying the technical materials, he was talking with the engineers. He was probably the most energized out of all the new ensigns. Tandry was exhausted from her ten days of nonstop partying at her home in Westerly.

Ellie wanted to take a shuttle to Jefferson City, but Cain wasn't in a good mood and that probably wouldn't have been the best way to meet his new in-laws. She invited them to New Sanctuary for a short visit during the training. They said that they'd see, still not happy with the whole situation.

Master Daksha stayed close with Briz during their time off and once the ensigns returned, he remained with the team for the first week before he needed to return to his ship. After two more weeks, they'd join him on the Cygnus-12. They had a great deal to learn before they could start learning how the ship really worked. There was theory, then there was the mundane, day-to-day tasks, critical for operations.

And checklists, endless checklists.

The team returned to Space School, happy for the diversion after the first week. DI Katlind was waiting for them, having already deposited her new crop of recruits at the classroom for the day. Black Leaper was first to greet her, but his joy was short-lived. The rest of the team stopped in their tracks upon seeing her dark scowl.

In a voice barely audible, she said the dreaded words, "Obstacle course." Cain had the audacity to laugh, pointing to their new uniforms. The short Discipline Instruction strode to him and jabbed a finger in his chest. "No discipline in your nasty bodies already? Take my eyes off you for five minutes and you revert to wild beasts. OBSTACLE COURSE!" The spittle flying from her face convinced them that this was no joke. They raced from the indoor platform, up the stairs, and turned toward the obstacle course. As they ran at breakneck speed, they started to laugh. The more things changed, the more they remained the same.

"What are you miscreants looking at?" the DI snarled at the three Hillcats looking at her, curious expressions on their 'cat faces.

I think I like this one,' Lutheann said over the mindlink, eliciting a snort of derision from Katlind.

Hurry along, human, your charges are waiting for your gentle hand to guide them through the obstacles of life,' Carnesto offered.

"And you mangy beasts could use some discipline. You better be out there by the time I get there!" she threatened, then turned and ran from the station. The 'cats looked at each other.

'She can't be serious?' Carnesto asked the others.

'You saw her mind. Of course she's serious. She burned down the observation tower to make a point. I don't think throwing us in the mud pond would be beyond her,' Mixial told them.

'I'd like to see her try,' Carnesto said in his most macho thought voice.

'So would I,' Lutheann added. *'I would like to see her throw you in the pit. So, she burned it down on purpose? The rest of the story is always more interesting.'* The white 'cat bolted away, followed closely by the smaller Mixial.

Hillcats were far faster than any human. It didn't take them long to overtake the DI. They passed her quickly, then continued until they caught up with Stinky and his team. When they passed, the Wolfoid dropped to all fours and bolted ahead. The 'cats had been running for a while so they weren't ready to race. Only Carnesto felt it necessary to win the race and he surged forward, taking the lead and reaching the obstacle courses a few bounds in front of Leaper. The other two 'cats arrived and then the ensigns. When DI Katlind arrived, the rest had caught their breath and were standing comfortably.

"Go!" the DI shouted without preamble. The team ran toward the first obstacle where Cain gave Ellie a hand up to reach the top of the wall. She scrambled up, then held a hand out for Tandry. Cain squatted two paces out from the wall. First Briz, then Stinky used him as a springboard, vaulting easily to the top of the wall. Before he could stand up, the three 'cats, in rapid succession, did the same thing, leaping high and catching the wall with their sharp claws, pulling themselves onto the platform before running down the ramp on the other side.

Cain used the wall to kick high enough to catch the hands of his teammates, who pulled him up and they were off. They figured the 'cats would run around the mud pit. No.

As Tandry jumped to catch the rope, Mixial, timed perfectly, landed high on her human's back, figuring that she'd catch a ride across. Tandry grunted with the impact and flew forward, the rope hitting her in the face. She flailed for it, missing and falling into the muddy water. Mixial splashed down, then struggled mightily to climb atop her human as the only dry refuge. Tandry was angry and dove under the water, swimming toward the edge. Lutheann and Carnesto looked at each other, then casually started walking around the mud pit.

DI Katlind had to look away so the ensigns wouldn't see her laughing. The others ran and hit the rope like professionals, swinging across to safely land on the other side. Cain and Briz hurried down the slope to help pull Tandry from the mud, leaving the swimming 'cat behind as they ran for the balance beam.

Tandry smiled as she dripped. Sometimes the best revenge was unplanned.

Space School Graduates

The team returned to their old rooms after the obstacle course. Mixial couldn't get the mud from her fur, so she showered with Tandry, scratching her frequently to let her know the full extent of her discomfort. After a toweling and a hot air blow dry, Mixial felt better, declared them even, and returned to the company of her fellow 'cats, who looked at her in mild amusement. A 'cat found the best humor in others' misfortune.

DI Katlind was waiting for the team as they casually strolled back to the common area, immediately uncomfortable with their approach to the day.

"No discipline. This team has no discipline. I'm a complete failure. Am I going to have to go on board that metal monster in order to keep you snot-nosed kids in line?" she asked rhetorically. The ensigns shook their heads as the 'cats watched. The DI avoided looking at the Hillcats, knowing that they were in her head and aware of how she really felt.

"Space stars for all of you? I have to say that I've been on board the Traveler a couple times, and those vines gave me the willies." She dropped the tough-guy act. "I'm proud of you, Briz, all of you." She sat down and motioned the others to drag chairs into a semicircle around her.

Briz recounted the tale for her and she nodded as he went. She clapped when he finished.

"I've petitioned to join the crew of Cygnus-12, but I probably won't be accepted," she told them. Despite their protests, she shook her head. "No. Spaceships are highly technical. You have to understand things, be skilled in ways that a knuckle-dragger like me could never. Sure, I've listened to all the lectures, but only to the twelfth week, before it gets to the important stuff. No, I'm afraid I don't have enough to offer."

"I'll tutor you. You'll be fine. And Pickles, the Lizard Man from Patesh's team, he can fill in what I don't cover. Do you need me to put in a good word for you?" Briz offered sincerely.

"When I need a recruit to vouch for me, then maybe they shouldn't pick me!" She watched as the ensigns were taken aback, disappointed. "I'm sorry, that's not what I meant," she quickly corrected herself.

"Spaceships are unique places where everyone does three or four jobs, every one task as important as the next. I don't know, we'll see. And yes, Ensign Brisbois, if you would be so kind as to put in a good word for me, I would appreciate it. Because I can't imagine what a sorry state that ship will be in if you don't have some adult supervision! And would you look at this?" She pointed to Cain and Ellie. "A married couple. In my barracks! Well, it wouldn't be the first time fun's been had in here," she said with her eyebrows raised and an odd smile.

DI Katlind reviewed their schedule and most importantly, what they were supposed to learn in their last few days at Space School. The team was graduating a full six weeks early and some of that knowledge was deemed critical. They'd accelerate through those classes and then graduate, formally, in a small ceremony in the Dean's office. Then they'd be whisked away to New Sanctuary, where they'd spend another week training with the ground support people, before transferring to the Traveler and catching a shuttle to their ship.

That was the plan, and the DI made sure they met each of their goals while she also managed the new recruits in class Gamma 37, the third class of the year. She ran them to the dining hall early, before the other class, and turned them loose to get to their classroom. Once in class, they were embroiled in a crash course on ship dynamics, construction theory, and the basics of living in space, enough information that they wouldn't blow anything up in the first few weeks before they were settled in and properly afraid of everything that could kill them in the depths of space.

No one would get there in time.

Save the ship, then save the people. The ship was life. The teammates thought they had the proper respect for the ship.

The 'cats had the proper disdain for a life aboard ship where there would be no grass under their paws, no wildlife to hunt, and no fresh meat. They shared their angst with their humans in odd ways, subliminally, openly, and constantly.

Cain and Ellie started to fight. Tandry stepped in and helped them understand what they were feeling. The emotions of their 'cats had seeped into their consciousness and their individuality had started to blur. The acerbic nature of their bonded 'cats did not blend well with the partnering of Cain and Ellie.

Tandry punched them both in their arms, explained what it was, and told them to figure it out. Leaper and Briz nodded vigorously, only partially understanding the human psyche. The entire team knew they were better together than apart. Mixial had sharp words for Lutheann and Carnesto, too.

When Cain and Ellie retired for the evening, they stayed together, although the bunks gave little privacy. Their 'cats slept nearby and gave them peace of mind that no one would sneak up on them, a trait passed down over the generations. Humans who bonded with 'cats were safer, because the 'cats watched over them and warned them if danger approached. Cain and Ellie slept soundly, and that was what they embraced from each of the 'cats, their willingness to stand between their humans and harm. The 'cats' words were cynical, but their actions were never in doubt.

After seven mind-bending days, the instructors declared Black Leaper's team to be minimally capable, the only rating that mattered as that meant they were cleared to go to space. The graduation was held in the Dean's office, with the menagerie that made up the team, including three Hillcats.

A surprise came when Ellie's parents walked in. She reluctantly hugged them and introduced Cain. Her dad got into a power handshake contest, finally declaring a draw after an uncomfortable amount of time and an angry look from his wife. The conversation was stilted, since there was no time to talk. The ceremony was quick, formally pinning on a single gold bar rank marker that rested above their Space Stars, platinum for first class, gold for second class, and a striped silver for third class. Leaper's team was the most highly decorated team ever to graduate.

Cain's in-laws remained unimpressed and scowled the entire time. He closed his eyes, trying to calm himself. Then he got desperate. *'Is there anything I can do?'* Cain asked over his mindlink with the 'cat.

She answered with some choice words vividly describing how she could kill the offending member of the family. Cain smirked until Ellie gave him the same look her mother had given her father. *'Anything else?'*

'Humans…' she said impatiently. *'He has no choice but to like you, and he will. Stop trying so hard. Be yourself, the one who will protect his daughter, and you'll be fine.*

Now leave me alone, I think I hear a squirrel.' Lutheann walked to the door and waited. Cain was positive she could open the door herself, but he caved and opened it for her. As soon as he closed it behind her, Carnesto appeared. Cain opened it once more, then quietly closed it behind the large black 'cat. When he turned, Mixial was standing there. He took a deep breath and opened the door a third time. After closing it one final time, he returned to his seat, finding that everyone was watching him. Ellie's mother seemed quite pleased.

Ellie gave him a look that suggested she'd tell him later. He couldn't wait.

The ceremony continued for three more minutes before finishing.

"The 'cats couldn't wait for three minutes?" he asked Ellie, even though she wouldn't know what motivated a 'cat, as he or any other human didn't know. She shrugged and worked her way between her parents, hanging off an arm of each to guide them outside. The ensigns had thirty minutes before they had to report to the subway for their short trip to New Sanctuary. Cain followed his new family out.

The other ensigns joined them in an area between the Space School buildings that was reminiscent of the ancients with paved walks, roads, gleaming white buildings, and windows sparkling under the sun's magnificence.

"So, you two are married," Ellie's father, Paxton, began. Once again, Ellie's mother Mikaila intervened, stopping the middle-aged man in his tracks.

"We are so happy to finally meet you," she said with a big smile, pulling Cain in for a matronly hug. Mikaila was short and round with red cheeks that suggested she was more ready with a smile than her partner. Paxton watched from outside the tight circle formed by Cain, Ellie, and Mikaila. Cain's eyes met those of his father-in-law. Despite their wives' joy, Paxton was not happy about the situation at all. It must have taken a monumental effort for Mikaila to get him to come to the graduation, all that way for less than an hour.

'Make an effort, please,' Ellie encouraged Cain in her thought voice. He gave a curt nod, then disengaged himself from the women.

"So, what do you do, Paxton?" Cain asked, trying to sound sincere.

"What, Ellie doesn't talk about us?" her father snipped back.

"Fine," Cain answered, stepping aside and kissing Ellie gently on the cheek. "I'll meet you at the subway." Cain walked off, refusing to listen as Ellie begged him to come back. He wasn't trying to manipulate her or drive a wedge between her and her parents. He saw himself as the wedge and decided, all by himself, that the best way to deal with the friction was by avoiding it. He knew that he would never have any kind of relationship with Paxton and that hurt. He heard Mikaila berating the older man as Cain continued to walk away, trying to look like a proud ensign while feeling like a failure.

He'd always felt that Aletha's father treated him like his own son, with the nurturing support and wisdom that came from such a relationship. Cain found shade beneath a large tree. Leaning against it, his thoughts drifted back to Aletha, her beauty and love for him, the joy of hugging her, looking into her eyes.

"What have I done?" he lamented, cursing himself, punching the tree and shredding the skin on his hand. He gasped with the pain, then watched the blood well from the open wounds. He let it run down his fingers and drip onto the ground. Cain fell to his knees and stayed that way until his legs started to ache. The blood dried and caked over his hand.

When he stood, Ellie was behind him. She looked at his red eyes through puffy eyes of her own. With a force of will, Cain pushed Aletha into a corner of his mind and closed the door. Some of his warmth was trapped back there, too. There was only one person he knew he could be himself with, and she wasn't there. He had to try to be that person all the time. He took a deep breath.

"Aren't we a pair?" Ellie asked, sensing something was off but unable to see past the barrier that Cain had uncharacteristically erected in his mind. "They didn't tell me they were coming." She tried to apologize, taking his hand and finally noticing his injured knuckles. "What did you do?" she asked, alarmed.

"Isn't that the right question," he replied flatly. "It'll be fine. Let's get to the subway. I can wash it off there."

They walked in silence. Their big day, graduation from Space School, and they felt horrible.

'The squirrels were quite tasty,' Lutheann offered to lighten the mood. Carnesto agreed.

"Our life now," Cain and Ellie said together, both laughing, strained but laughing.

Last Preps to Join the Crew

After a week of follow-on instruction in the bowels of the New Command Center, only Briz was able to see straight. The others felt like their brains had melted, but there would be no more time off to recover. It was a race to get to the ship and be familiarized before it departed. When they finished the last conversations with the engineers, the team packed its meager belongings and reported to the matter transfer chamber.

"Look what the 'cat dragged in!" DI Katlind barked at the team as they approached. The ensigns rushed forward to slap hands with their Discipline Instructor.

"Thanks, Briz," she said in a normal tone. "I have to admit that your support made the difference." She nodded to Dr. Johns, who was walking with the team and the three 'cats.

"I am glad you approve of your new shipmate, and there's one more surprise." Dr. Johns pointed into the chamber where the Lizard Man Peekaless examined the equipment connected to one of the recliners. "Your first stop is the Traveler, but once you arrive, you'll turn around and transfer to the shipyard along the asteroid belt. Then you'll board the Cygnus-12. Once out of the construction dock, you'll test the new EM Drive within our solar system. After that, you'll fly beyond this system's gravity well, to interstellar space. The Cygnus-12 is the only ISE-capable ship that can also travel within the well!" the doctor shared excitedly, before continuing.

"Once outside our system and with sufficient dark matter is surrounding the ship, you'll bank it into the engine. And then, you'll be able to engage the ISE! It's so exciting. I really wish I were younger so I could join you. The newest engine will take you farther than we've ever gone before." Dr. Johns beamed at the group. Cain didn't think the old doctor looked like he wanted to go along. He seemed perfectly happy within the New Command Center, indoors, with all that technology and comfort at his fingertips.

His time had come and gone and he was happy to pass the responsibility to a younger generation. One of his former clones had led the team that discovered the interdimensional space engine. From that single event, the entirety of the new Cygnus space program was born. Dr. Johns continued to be cloned, but each time he returned with a shorter and shorter lifespan. Fresh from the cloning tank as an old man, he always joked that his genes were tired.

There was some truth to that.

The nine new crew members destined for Cygnus-12 took their seats within the matter transfer chamber. They were joined by two humans, one reporting to the Traveler for work and one visiting his parents who'd chosen to live there. It was a diverse group, with different duties, different goals, each living life as they needed to for themselves and their families.

Cain liked the world that his ancestors had created. Braden's first goal had been to find Old Tech to trade for untold riches, but his goal changed once he met the southerners. After that, he opened a trade route and established free trade throughout the south. On the journey, he discovered the Old Tech he'd been searching for, but realized the world wasn't ready for it, although they could benefit greatly from it. Together with Micah and their companions, they established the safety protocols to prevent another civil war like the one that nearly destroyed all of humanity. All these years later, the protocols were still in place and although there would always be differences of opinion and downright hostility, there were ways to resolve it without resorting to open warfare.

Even if the worst happened, combatants couldn't use Old Tech to wage war. There were too many checks and balances, not the least of which was Holly himself, the Artificial Intelligence who was instrumental in saving the ancients' knowledge.

Cain looked at Ellie as Holly ran through the instructions—don't move, stay relaxed, don't touch anyone else. The usual. Cain wondered how different things would have been had he not joined the Space Exploration Service. He suspected they would not be better. He felt that he was on a path to realize his full potential. He knew, deep in his heart, that he was destined for things beyond Vii. Aletha both held him back and drove him. He was angry with her, for just a moment, then settled into his usual sadness when thinking about her, so far away.

All this as his eyes were locked on his wife. She smiled at him.

'If I wasn't strapped into this chair, I'd come over there and scratch you stupid!' Lutheann told him over their mindlink.

Cain glared at the shimmering white 'cat, not knowing whether to be angry or confused. He settled on confused as the room faded to black.

They woke up three days later in the matter transfer chamber on the RV Traveler. The wall slid aside, revealing the exit where Hermes and Lieutenant Simonds stood patiently.

They almost made it without someone saying goodbye to their breakfast, but when Lutheann and Carnesto both started gagging and coughing, Briz lost it, followed closely by Tandry. Cain was fine, until he stepped into whatever foulness had been the 'cats' breakfast. He tried to turn away as his mouth watered and his light breakfast threatened to make an appearance. He couldn't hold back the tide and heaved mightily, arching the chunky orange mess into Leaper's pelt. The Wolfoid jumped and shook, spraying puke everywhere.

Ellie, Katlind, and one of the new crew members were the only ones to escape unscathed. The lieutenant had to walk away, whether to laugh at the slapstick comedy or to avoid joining the heave-fest, Cain didn't know and didn't care as he finally made his way from the chamber, spattered with spew and his boots covered in slippery goo. Stinky looked less than amused.

Once they were in the open air of engineering, Lieutenant Simonds held a hand over his nose as he talked with them. "I think we need to get you cleaned up and then we're in a hurry. This transfer took three days. There was a meteor storm that got in the way of the data stream. So, yes, you are a day and a half behind schedule. Get cleaned up while we process the chamber for your next transfer. There's no time to put you on a shuttle. Make sure you drink plenty of electrolytes. I'm not sure you should eat anything. The transfer process doesn't seem to be too kind to this group." The lieutenant was serious with his jest, so he escorted them to a crew lounge, where they could shower, order new uniforms from the fabricator, and get the required drinks.

Lieutenant Simonds raised an eyebrow at Cain and Ellie as they chose to shower together, taking longer than the others. But he didn't say anything. He had yet to ask out the ensign who was the target of his affections, so he envied those who found love so easily.

If he only knew.

The reason he wanted the others to hurry was so he could show them how the clean-up from the vine infestation was progressing. He walked them past the elevator and continued up the sloping deck of engineering as it rotated within the ship to create an artificial gravity. The lieutenant suddenly stopped and smiled at them.

"Do you notice anything?" They looked. There were no vines and no evidence of where they had penetrated the bulkhead, trailed down the wall and through the catwalk, and then into the floor. He pointed behind them. They'd walked past the area where the vines had made their home for hundreds of years. The damage had already been repaired and engineering was whole once again.

"And it's all your fault, Ensign Brisbois!" The lieutenant pointed to the Space Star First Class on the Rabbit's harness. "Not many people have one of those. Wear it with pride."

"I am," Briz answered, nose twitching, ears perked and held high. The other members of Leaper's team slapped Briz on the back, beaming their pride, too.

'Hungry,' Carnesto told Ellie. She shrugged and turned away. She felt a gentle tapping on the back of her leg. Carnesto sat there, a forlorn look on his 'cat face, his black fur gleaming under the artificial lights of engineering.

"How much longer will we be here? Does he have time to go to the Livestock level and hunt?" Ellie asked the lieutenant. Lutheann and Mixial both angled in close, anxious for the right answer.

"He most assuredly does not. Someone took too long in the shower!" the lieutenant blurted out. Ellie turned bright red and Cain looked at the floor, refusing to meet anyone's eyes, especially those of an unhappy 'cat.

"The transfer chamber should be clean by now, so we need to go," the lieutenant stated dismissively, ushering the Cygnus-12 crew members forward.

"Sorry, Luthey, maybe next time," Cain tried to console the 'cat.

'What next time?' she asked sarcastically. *'We're going onto a deep space exploration ship in mere moments, then we fly through a bunch of empty space, until we get to this special empty space, where we can cross a vast distance to more empty space. Then we dither around out there looking for who knows what when you've got a hungry*

'cat right here, and the means to address that necessity only a kilometer away. I think humans suck.'

Ellie stared at him, but he refused to blink. Her eyes started to water, but before she blinked, she told him, 'Better get used to it, otherwise it could be a real long journey.'

'It's already been a long journey. Ahhh, I think I'm dying from starvation!' Carnesto winked as he rolled onto his back, feigning distress. Lutheann pounced on him and raked his chest with half-open claws. The team worked their way around the 'cats, heading for the chamber.

"They always like that?" the DI asked.

"Yes, they are, DI," Cain answered, walking hand-in-hand with Ellie, feeling at ease on board the ship, despite the slight disorientation from the spinning deck.

"My friends call me Lindy and since you haven't noticed, I'm an ensign, just like you," she said, pointing to the gold bar on her collar.

"Lindy it is." Cain offered his hand and they shook. "Welcome aboard. We're about to get our butts kicked in a whole different way." Cain turned to the Lizard Man. "What do you think, Pickles?"

"About what?" he asked, his vocalization device interpreting the question as matter of fact.

"Going to space! This is the big one, Pickles. You have to be excited," Cain said with a grin.

"I am giddy and overjoyed, all at the same time." The device translated the words emotionlessly.

Briz bounced along happily while Leaper kept leaning a little to one side trying to compensate for the unnatural effect on his balance.

"Hey! Everyone hold up," Lieutenant Simonds interjected, as his unfocused eyes suggested he was communicating using his neural implant. "I almost forgot. Everyone on a deep space exploration ship has to have the neural implant and since you rushed through your training, you don't have them. We need to get those installed before you leave," the lieutenant told them. Then he pointed to the 'cats.

"And you three, here's a visitor badge that'll give you access to the Livestock Level. Don't lose it and don't eat anything you're not supposed to." Faster than the eye could follow, Carnesto had the badge in his mouth and the three 'cats were running for the nearest elevator. Ellie shared the directions over the mindlink and surprisingly, he thanked her.

The lieutenant ushered them down the corridor that the 'cats disappeared into, took the elevator to an area between the main decks of the core, then to a small lab. Five of the team went first and received their neural implants, a device the size of a grain of rice that was attached to their optic nerve behind their eye and then interfaced with their brain. They would see a small screen appear in front of one eye, where they could readily interact with Holly or the artificial intelligence on board their ship.

The system had remained unchanged from the time of the ancients, as they had no better technology. Many swore that Holly used what he gathered from people's minds to keep them under control. Others simply appreciated ready access to the knowledge of the known universe. That wasn't to be taken lightly and people were only given neural implants for a reason. Access could also be denied for other reasons. Having an implant didn't mean you'd always have access to everything.

The SES was different. Spaceships were so complex that access to information was critical to sustained operations. At any point in time, any crew member might need information that was out of their specialty. There might not be time to find the right person. Neural implants improved the survivability of the ship and that improved the survivability of the crew.

Save the ship - get your neural implant, now! Cain joked to himself as if advertising a new pocketknife.

The Wolfoid, Rabbit, and Lizard Man went first as implants for their species were still new. Implant technology had been made for humans, but upgraded in the past century to include all intelligent species. Holly was still refining the processes to tune the implant to the others, so their acclimation would take the longest. First in, last out.

The humans were run through as if it were an assembly line. They spent a total of ten minutes each getting it done, three at a time. The entire process for all was completed in thirty minutes. Cain and Ellie had the misfortune of experiencing the 'cats making a kill right as they were waking up from the implantation, so their disorientation was magnified. They were given an extra two minutes to figure things out.

Lindy had no sympathy. Despite her assurance to the contrary, she would always be their Discipline Instructor, unwavering in her commitment to keep them from being distracted and losing focus on their primary mission. She seemed immune to the effects of the neural implant on personal balance. The others were shaky as they stood, while she jumped from the bed in the med lab, indifferent to the effects from her new technology.

"I bet Holly's having a field day with what's coming through that link," Cain quipped to Ellie as he tried to fight off the growing headache taking over his mind. He and Ellie leaned on each other as they staggered from the room. When the team was accounted for and declared free to leave, far different than being declared fit for duty, they slowly made their way back toward the matter transfer chamber. Lieutenant Simonds led the way, asking that those with 'cats request their furry counterparts join them in short order. Tandry contacted Mixial over the mindlink, receiving the 'cat's gratified purr in response as she was whiskers deep into the small pig that Lutheann had killed. Tandry hoped that it was wild and not one from somebody's domestic herd.

She lied to the lieutenant that the 'cats were already on their way, knowing that the Hillcats would show in their own good time regardless of any external pressure. Cain shook his head, slowly, as the headache persisted, despite drinking water and taking the pills that he was given after the process.

The return trip to engineering seemed to take half the time and before they knew it, they found themselves outside the matter transfer chamber, where they unsurprisingly found no 'cats waiting.

Lieutenant Simonds raised his eyebrows at Tandry, who grinned and shrugged, holding her hands up in surrender.

"While we wait for an indeterminate amount of time," the lieutenant said pointedly, "practice with your neural implants. Pull up information on your new ship. Try moving around while you have a window open. I'll ask Hermes to lock out the terminals in this section so you can't do any damage."

They did that, amazed at how easy it was to access the files, bring up pictures, schematics, watch videos, and find information. Briz squatted where he was with a euphoric look on his Rabbit face. His nose didn't twitch and his eyes remained unfocused as he stared at a spot in the distance, only seeing what was projected into the window before his eye. His big ears flicked, turning as if trying to catch sounds behind him in a world that only he was a part of. The others wondered how they could keep him from remaining embroiled in the technological world that had just been opened to him.

Leaper opened his window, then closed it. Then opened it, then closed it. "I don't like it. I need to be able to see and it doesn't process smells at all. How can you assess the situation if you can't smell anything? Bah! It's all fog!" The Wolfoid waved a dismissive paw.

The humans seemed to take it in stride, understanding it as a tool to help them with the complexities of keeping a deep space exploration ship functioning. Like Stinky, they felt the window in front of one eye to be disorienting. They played around for a little bit, looking at the file structure and how to find information, but were too anxious to see their spaceship to delve deeply into the world of the AI.

Ensign Peekaless had a unique experience. The others assumed he would become the self-proclaimed historian of their travels. He perused information that only he could see, nodding and talking with himself aloud, not realizing that his vocalization device was playing his thoughts. "Interesting. Right there. Yes. I'll add you to my journal. And what is that? Come here, you. Oh, look at that! Interesting. No, that's not right. If I could delete your silliness, I would. I shall lock you out of my window. Be gone, evil misinformation! Be gone, I tell you. And look at that! Interesting…"

"Pickles. Pickles!" Cain tried to get the Lizard Man's attention, but decided to leave him be, just until the 'cats arrived. They all looked at the catwalk expectantly.

Lieutenant Simonds was growing impatient, tapping his foot, arms crossed, and glaring at Tandry, who was frantically negotiating the 'cats' return over the mindlink.

When the three of them finally appeared and waddled along the appropriately named catwalk, the team started clapping. Carnesto stopped so he could wave a paw at them as a mocking one-finger salute. He laid down where he was until Ellie threw a small connector at him. She missed but when she reloaded, he acquiesced and caught up with the others to catch the elevator down.

'What? It takes time to eat four years' worth of food and we should be sleeping now, not on the longest death march of our lives!' Lutheann told the group over the mindlink.

'We're not going to be gone for four years! That was the old missions. A year, tops,' Cain answered in his thought voice.

They waited impatiently as the three Hillcats sauntered to them. They were in no hurry to climb aboard the recliner as the last thing they wanted was to lose their hard-earned meal. They strolled into the chamber and took the chairs closest to the exit, hoping to escape before the pukefest began.

The next step in the journey was about to begin. They were to be transferred through clear space to the growing shipyard outside the asteroid belt where most of the raw materials needed for a ship's construction could be found. The Cygnus-12, their ship, waited for them to arrive.

Four humans—Cain, Ellie, Tandry, and Lindy. One Wolfoid—Black Leaper. One Rabbit—Briz. One Lizard Man—Pickles. And three Hillcats—Lutheann, Carnesto, and Mixial. Ten intelligent creatures representing a broad section of humanity were heading into space.

They were the people of Vii.

Cygnus-12

Having a clear line of sight without atmospheric anomalies to deal with greatly expedited the matter transfer process. Holly was able to deliver the crew members in four hours. The travelers had no idea how long it had taken as only moments passed in their consciousness. No one moved for a long time, then as if in slow motion, they moved, first one leg, then the other, sitting up carefully, stepping to the floor, and with glacial quickness, they walked out the door.

Cain braced himself for the sound of puke splashing on the deck, but it didn't come. The longer they could fight off the queasiness, the more likely they could avoid it entirely.

Master Daksha was waiting for them with the ship's captain, Captain Rand. The greetings were quick and tame. Captain Rand was a rather tall human, skeletally thin. Lindy wondered how he made it through Space School as he appeared to lack almost all musculature. He saw her critical eye looking him over.

"Deep space can do a number on you if you spend too much time in zero-gravity, zero-g that is." He stopped to look at them all and they crowded around him to better hear as the corridors of the shipyard were busy and loud. "On our last trip out, we lost the spin of the core and our food processor went out. We survived one whole year like that, but it does a number on one's body."

The new crew members hadn't heard that. As a matter of fact, they'd heard about successes, but no one had thought to ask about failures. What happened when missions failed?

"You should have seen me six months ago. I've filled out a bit since then. I have a ways to go still." He smiled before continuing. "And yes, the mission was a resounding success. We mapped two new star systems, one of which had a planet in the habitable zone that looked to be fifty percent water. Very promising indeed. A second mission is going there when the ship is ready." He pointed out the clear impact window to a spaceship, massive compared to those in the adjacent docks. The habitat section of the shipyard was spinning to maintain the appearance of gravity, while the ships were best constructed in zero-g, where the parts and pieces could be more easily moved. The window they looked through was at their feet as they were pressed against the inside of the outer hull. It was a simple design, austere in its trappings. The facility served one purpose, as a place for workers to rest between shifts and were more comfortable doing detail work with instrumentation. Everything else happened in spacesuits, outside in zero-g.

The Cygnus-12 was in a shipyard dock, looking small compared to the new ship it was next to, but they shared a similar design. The Cygnus-12 had the standard doughnut-shaped main module, the core where the crew lived and worked and where all the ship functions took place. But the Cygnus-12 also had a spindle extending aft from the center core of the main module.

This spindle set the Cygnus-12 apart from the other deep space exploration ships which appeared to be doughnut-shaped only. They had no astrodynamics and if caught in solar winds or worse, a planet's atmosphere, then the ship would most likely be destroyed. The original exploration ships stayed outside of solar systems in the interstellar void where dark matter was prevalent and the possibility of external forces impacting the ship were almost nonexistent.

"What's the tail for on our ship?" Briz asked.

The captain shook his head. "I'll show you."

After that, they only made small talk as they worked their way through the shipyard's habitat toward the shuttle bay. Their first stop was in astro-physiology where they were all fitted for space suits. The shop had suits for all members of humanity, whether human, Wolfoid, Rabbit, Tortoid, Hillcat, or Lizard Man. They even had a suit for an Aurochs, although it was beyond comprehension that an Aurochs would be floating around in space.

Getting the Hillcats into spacesuits required multiple humans, resulted in much yowling, numerous scratches, and finally, hateful glares through their small helmets.

"What the hell, Lutheann? You picked us to bond with! We were going to space, which meant that you knew you were going to space. So shut up and take it like an adult!" Cain yelled. That earned him a scratch, but the 'cat's claws didn't penetrate the suit, so no blood. Cain pushed her away, and that was all it took. The Hillcat snarled and pounced, smacking her helmet against Cain's face as he she kept trying to get her fangs through the faceplate and into his neck. He rolled her from him, and she came back at him with a powerful leap.

Cain turned slightly and helped her sail past. Her suited claws slid over his uniform. He readied himself for another attack, but she circled warily, looking for a way to hurt her human.

He didn't wait. Cain rushed at the 'cat, catching her suit-covered tail as she attempted to dodge. He dragged her with him until he could get a good grip on her body. Then he attempted to throw her against the bulkhead. She was able to wrap her legs around his arm and started climbing toward his face. He jumped toward the bulkhead, attempting to squash the 'cat between his body and the steel plates, but she pushed off at the last second as he slammed into the unforgiving metal. She wrapped all four legs around his neck and started banging her helmet on the top of his head.

He pinned her against him and turned around, finally managing to beat her against the bulkhead until she let go. She dropped to the deck, stunned. He staggered forward, blood running freely down his head where the helmet had cut into his soft flesh. When he saw Lutheann lying in a heap, he carefully picked her up and cradled her in his arms.

"I'm not sure I've ever seen anything like that in my whole life," Captain Rand told Master Daksha. The Tortoid craned his neck sideways to look at the gangly human, and the ship's commander blinked slowly as he thought.

"I think we're in for an interesting trip. I had planned for a one-year survey, but I think that might be too long. How many body bags are we bringing along?" the Tortoid asked.

"One for each of the crew, Master Daksha, as per Standard Operating Procedures," the captain replied.

Ellie looked at them both. "Who puts the last crew member into her body bag?"

"Now that is one question we don't want to learn the answer to!" And the captain laughed heartily, watching to make sure that both Cain and the 'cat were okay.

'What were you trying to do, Lutheann?' Cain asked, gently stroking the limp 'cat's spacesuit.

'I wanted to make sure you'd stand up for yourself, as well as fight me and fight for me. Do you understand?' Clarity returned to her eyes as she continued to allow Cain to hold her. *'I also want you to know that I'm not happy about going aboard a spaceship. I had no choice in the matter and neither did he.'* She nodded toward Carnesto.

'What do you mean?' Cain asked in his thought voice.

'We were volunteered by the 'cat council. The bloodline of Prince Axial De'atesh's humans must be protected to the full extent that the Hillcat Nation can provide. It is what we must do.'

'Why wait until now?' Cain was curious how he had been the only one of his family without a 'cat and it took the imminence of space travel for the 'cats to take action.

'You were always watched, but your departure for Space School caught us all unaware. Then your engagement with the Android made it a necessity for someone to join you. Then you graduate early. So you're stuck with me and she's stuck with him. We were the only 'cats with the misfortune of being within shouting distance of New Sanctuary when the call came in. I hate wearing this thing, if your thick brain didn't already figure that out,' she said matter-of-factly.

'I appreciate your candor, pretty lady. We'll have you out of that thing as soon as we get aboard Cygnus. This little scuffle only delayed that. So let me get suited up. It seems that everyone else is ready and waiting on me.' Cain stood, only to be ordered to sit back down while a medical technician arrived and doctored the cut on his head. He was happy to see her use numbweed, as those on Vii had for centuries. Modern medicine didn't have an alternative. Cain was gratified that he didn't need stitches. The numbweed worked to stop the bleeding and soon, he was suited up and ready for the transport to take them to the Cygnus-12.

The shuttle was flown by a Wolfoid from the shipyard, who expertly maneuvered the craft away from the habitat, following the station's rotation and then flying clear. The trip across the spatial void took no time at all. Daksha and Rand watched the new crew members as they looked out the shuttle's windows. They knew the ship. It was the crew that would require nearly all of their attention. They saw they were connected to the spindle, the tail that was unique to the Cygnus-12.

The construction docks didn't move, so the landing was a painless affair. The airlocks grappled and all movement stopped. The hatch cycled and opened into a short, round passageway. The new and old crew floated free within the shuttle, nearly all of them, their first experience in zero-g. They pulled themselves along using the handholds within the tube.

The new ensigns had used their neural implants to look at the design drawings of their spaceship and expected to land at the center of the doughnut-shaped main core where the hangar deck was located. The spindle section was all new. The construction of it had started a full year before the Cygnus-12 returned from their previous mission to deep space. The main support anchors were reinforced within the hub of the rotating section, and that was where the spindle attached. The ISE required a significant upgrade to develop an interdimensional vortex large enough to include the new tail.

The new ensigns still didn't know what the spindle was for.

Captain Rand led the way into his ship, the lights responding by turning on as he entered the airlock space. The far hatch was still sealed in case of an emergency decompression. Until the outside hatch to space was closed and breathable atmosphere confirmed, they'd keep wearing their suits.

The ship was life. Redundancies were key concepts learned through hard lessons.

They watched the clear tube retract around the closed and cycled hatch of their spaceship. The shuttle hesitated for only a moment as thrusters cleared it from the immediate vicinity, then the main engines drove it away, back to the shipyard's habitat module.

Cain, Ellie, and Tandry removed the suits from their 'cats first, to show them that their discomfort hadn't gone unnoticed. Then the rest followed the disrobing process.

"Welcome aboard the Cygnus, your home for the foreseeable future. I am happy to be here. This is a great ship. Saved our lives. And with this section, we don't have to dispatch a shuttle for an extended mission in the heliosphere of a solar system. We're taking the Cygnus! This spindle is made up of the new EM Drive, a conical engine that bounces ion particles from a solid end plate, recovering them through a cone to recycle them. It builds forward momentum rather quickly, we've heard. I really want to see it in action. "We" means you, Briz. You're going to have to get up to speed on that as soon as you can. I've asked Jolly, our AI, to assist you in any way he can."

The ensigns clung to their handholds as they floated in the non-spinning ship. Everything was new, so they had no idea what to ask. Master Daksha bobbed his head in amusement.

"First things first, Captain. Let's show them to their quarters. Settle in for a few minutes, then let the tour begin. It's early, but it's already been a long day for our young charges. The real work starts tomorrow as we prepare the ship to leave space dock," Master Daksha offered.

"Well then, the ship's commander has spoken, and that's it. Tomorrow, our journey begins. Let's get you settled in first. Everything after that will be learning about the ship. Always remember, the ship is life. Save the ship, save the people."

"The ship is life!" the ensigns shouted in unison.

Getting Underway

"How many are in the crew?" Cain asked, curious because they'd seen few other crew members during their tour.

"The ship is heavily automated. I fear that nearly all of the crew is designated for maintenance duties, with secondary tasks within engineering, on the command deck, sensors, internal systems like life support, power generation, and elsewhere as needed throughout the ship. We only have thirty-seven total crew. We used to have thirty, but the EM Drive added too much new equipment. More people were needed to cover more territory. You'll work about eighteen hours and have six hours off. We don't run multiple shifts. We have overlapping work schedules and areas of responsibility, but when you are responsible for something, you own it. Any questions with what I've told you so far?" Captain Rand asked them.

They nodded as they digested the information. There would be little to no down time, ever. Cain had never contemplated what it meant to serve aboard a spaceship. He thought back to why he joined. The captain who'd run into a burning building to save lives, losing his in the process. He wanted to be that man, fearless, selfless.

He'd have to earn that title, which he'd known, but he hadn't thought what it meant beyond doing well in training. It would take an endless number of eighteen-hour days, but he'd get there. He'd be the one they could count on.

Having married crew members on board had been contemplated, but had not yet happened aboard the Cygnus-12. Cain and Ellie were the first ones. They were given a small recreation room that had been reconfigured. It was larger than the commander's quarters or even the captain's quarters. They felt guilty, but it wasn't that much larger and there were two of them occupying the space.

The ship could probably handle a crew five times the size of the one they had, but without the ability to resupply, they couldn't feed or service that many people. The crew was at an absolute minimum. It wouldn't take the loss of many people before the ship became non-operational. The captain said there was a backup plan, but he wouldn't share the details with them. They'd have to trust him, and more importantly, they'd have to survive and make sure the captain didn't have to implement the backup plan.

The ship is life. Save the ship! There was a reason that saying was the war cry of the Space Exploration Service.

The stark realization of why hit them as they followed the captain through the ship, talking with their new crewmates. The Cygnus-12 was huge, mostly for storage of supplies, every nook and cranny was filled to bursting with food stocks and spare parts, raw materials and manufactured goods. People were scarce, but nothing else seemed to be.

The fact that they were getting underway without knowing their assigned post and responsibilities scared the hell out of them. Only Briz seemed comfortable. They didn't know how he found the time, but he'd reviewed the schematics for the spindle section and the EM Drive. He'd studied the ISE, rather extensively, appreciative that the supplemental power needed to expand the interdimensional vortex was provided by auxiliary power generation in the spindle.

At least when they got underway, the ship would start spinning through space. Only the very center of the donut and the center of the spindle would be zero-g. Everyone else would allow them to keep their feet solidly on the deck. The equipment elevators, fluid piping, and other support systems ran through that zero-g space, to get the most work done with the least strain on mechanical systems.

The crew took responsibility for equipment and systems within and passing through their assigned areas, by deck, by section, by purpose.

Engineering had three main sections: interdimensional space engine, EM Drive, and power generation. The engines didn't require a human presence. They were heavily shielded to minimize particle bleed and had no serviceable parts within the engines themselves. Power feeds, cooling pumps, and other external components were strategically located to make it easier for one or two crew members to service efficiently. The cooling systems and energy transfer were the most labor intensive, requiring constant monitoring and adjustment. Over the decades, the SES had discovered that the engines ran with great efficiency, but when monitoring systems of any type were introduced, the dynamic changed. The observer effect stated that the act of observation will change the phenomenon being observed. Removing or diverting particles through measurement devices, by necessity, changed the flow of those particles and upset the delicate balance of the systems observed.

The SES determined that the change in the observed phenomenon was an acceptable variation for the value of being able to track the changes of the primary system. Without the measurements, the ISE could create a runaway loop, collapsing the vortex in on itself and destroying the ship. The vortex had to be controlled at point of origin and point of exodus. Movement without movement by using the vibrations and space within the dark matter itself.

Briz loved it. None of the others understood the internal workings of the ISE. Very few did and those types generally didn't volunteer for space duty. Briz was a rare creature indeed. When Master Daksha heard of him and his desire to stay with his team, the Tortoid went to the RV Traveler and personally intervened to ensure that Briz and anyone the Rabbit wanted was assigned to the Cygnus-12. The initial reason the others were assigned was solely due to the Rabbit.

When Daksha saw the team in action, he knew that he had his crew. The 'cats came as a surprise, but they'd figure that out as they went. He'd ordered additional real meat brought aboard and frozen in the cryo pods that lined every ship's external hull. He had enough meat for four years for the 'cats, three if they included it on rare occasions in the diet of the rest of the crew. If they were only gone for a year, then they could have a regular and substantial diet, something the captain looked forward to.

Logistics. Mission strategy. That's what made Master Daksha's position different than the ship's captain, who was responsible for ship operations. As the Mission Commander, Master Daksha was responsible for the scientific aspects of the mission, determining where they would go after the initial guidance from the SES, and how they would explore once they arrived. There were too many variables to make those decisions from a thousand light years away. One managed the ship, the other managed the mission.

The captain was instrumental in many decisions, but it took all of them to make deep space exploration a success.

Briz was assigned to engineering as Chief Engineer. At one time, he would have held the rank of commander, an old earth naval term. With the

SES, it didn't matter. The position was earned because of his knowledge and how he could best contribute to the ship. Cain, on the other hand, was assigned to the black and gray water systems. These were critical for the people on board, but immaterial to the ship's ability to fly through space. The black and gray water systems handled the sewage, sending as much as possible to recycling, and what couldn't be recycled was packaged for ejection.

Ellie cautioned the others in joking about Cain's assignment. He didn't take it well, except that he believed in the mission. He signed up to go exactly where he was going, to a different solar system, exploring.

On a different ship, Cain might not have seen what he wanted to see, but the Cygnus-12 didn't need to launch a shuttle filled with the explorers traveling slowly within a solar system. Cain was on the one ship that could do it all. It would penetrate the heliosphere and fly itself into the gravity well. He'd get to see it all firsthand!

On the monitors, of course, because where he worked, there were no portholes with a direct view of space. Cain committed to learning the systems in his control and making sure that they worked at peak efficiency. The crew deserved that. At the end of the work shift, he'd return to his quarters with Ellie and everything would be okay. He reasoned that if he couldn't do a good job at a bad job, they'd never give him a good job.

Ellie was assigned to engineering. She'd serve in the section within the core, the doughnut like ring. She'd serve within a Vii-normal environment where Cain would be working in half that. He'd have to adjust to feeling twice as heavy when he returned to his quarters after the shift. To help his daily adjustment, he only worked half his shift in the spindle section of the spaceship. The other systems were located within the core.

Tandry was assigned to stores and sensors. The two had nothing to do with each other, but sensors were mostly hands-off. Ship stores needed constant attention. There was a certain amount of fresh food offered daily to supplement what was provided by the fabricators.

Hydroponics and fresh growth took up an entire ring of the core module. Not only did that provide fresh vegetables and greens, it recycled carbon dioxide. It served as the ship's garden deck where all the people took time walking through each day to improve their oxygen saturation and general health. There was nothing like a stroll through a well-maintained garden to maintain one's spirits. Two Rabbits were assigned to the Cygnus-

12 with the primary responsibility of the garden ring. Their quarters were within the garden and some of the crew members suggested that they'd never left the garden level since reporting aboard. No one wanted to ask.

Pickles was assigned to the command deck as a sensor operator. His entire job was to collect data, catalogue it, and work with Jolly to analyze it. Anyone could look at the data, but only a couple people had that as a primary job. The others were envious until they realized what it entailed. Sitting in a chair and watching streams of data, looking for highlights or anomalies. And that was it.

At least the others were not just able to move about, but would be active throughout their work shifts. Cain needed that. The others did, too.

Lindy was assigned to recycling and fresh water systems, with a heavy reliance on maintenance. She and Cain would have to collaborate on much of their work. She needed help, claiming her fluid dynamics calculations were a little rusty. Briz had told her once that he'd tutor her, and he did not forget his promise. He committed two hours in separate one-hour sessions daily to work with her. One team, one mission. The ship was life.

Her main work station was in the low gravity of the central core, down a corridor from the hangar bay.

Leaper got the choicest assignment of all. He was aide de camp to Master Daksha. He would take care of whatever the commander needed, as well as assist the captain as directed. The drawback was that he wasn't exactly sure what he was going to be doing from one minute to the next. The commander and the captain both committed to keeping Leaper hopping. They said there was no chance of him gaining weight during their trip and that he had the steepest learning curve, as he was supposed to know everything about everything.

The 'cats decided that they liked the garden deck and were determined to live there. They could talk with their humans anywhere within the ship via their mindlink, so they didn't need to be in the same work space. So with some human help, they worked their way to the garden deck where they floated around, waiting for artificial gravity to return.

Lutheann was far happier than Cain expected. Their throw-down in the shipyard had cemented their bond and made them true partners in life. Cain found himself conversing with her more than he talked with his wife. He didn't know what that meant, but understood that it was probably not optimal.

He shrugged it off and focused on his work.

"All hands to work stations! All hands to work stations!" came the call over the ship-wide broadcast as well as over each crew member's neural implant. A strident flashing made Cain open his window, where he was treated to the announcement, with further instruction regarding where exactly he was supposed to be positioned based on what systems had failed in the past during initial movement from space dock.

"Oh great, I'm in here with the sewage pumps because this is the system most likely to fail!" he shouted to the space filled with machinery, but devoid of other life. He hadn't wondered about the chemical decontamination shower within his primary workspace, since most sections on the ship had them, but his seemed to be well-used. Suddenly, that concerned him. He queried Jolly regarding how many times the sewage system had failed.

'Only twice, Ensign Cain, but both were quickly resolved,' Jolly said happily. The AI's name was aptly chosen since he always seemed to enjoy his interactions with the crew.

"Why is the shower so well-used, then?" he asked.

'I probably shouldn't say anything, but a leakage is not considered a system failure. These things happen more often than we'd like to admit. The previous ensign assigned to these systems used the shower daily. Sometimes on multiple occasions,' Jolly said conspiratorially.

"Why did the other ensign leave the ship?"

'I just love all the humans who I have the pleasure of working with. Ensign Calmers wasn't calm at all. When the ship sections lost their ability to spin and the food processor failed, the ensign became quite upset. She was restrained frequently to prevent her from hurting herself. It was a traumatic experience. That's all I know, I'm afraid.'

"So, my predecessor became a basketcase. Not surprising. I'm afraid, too, Jolly. Just a little. I promise not to wig out on you, though. Lutheann will make sure that I stay on the straight and narrow. Now, I need your help. Please show me the primary systems and points of potential failure..." Cain and Jolly were so engaged that he didn't even feel the ship smoothly disengage from the dock and using thrusters only, move beyond the structure within which it had sat for more than six months.

Ellie and Briz pulled themselves around the engineering spaces, checking equipment, monitors, and more equipment. Briz was hard-pressed in zero-g. He seemed to flounder when trying to move. When he used his powerful back legs to launch himself, it was always too strong and he ended up crashing into whatever was in his way. The luster of engineering quickly wore off. Briz was miserable. All he wanted to do was watch the engines work, tune them to maximum efficiency, then see how much more he could get out of them.

Ellie found working in zero-g to be exhilarating. She swam like an old pro.

Tandry found that her job of moving stores around would be easy in zero-g, but she wouldn't be moving anything until after the artificial gravity was in place. Even with mechanical assistance, she saw that the stores job would involve plenty of manual labor. She decided that she'd worry about that when the time came. In the interim, she'd learn all she could about sensors.

Her work location was in one of the many sensor suites located in the outermost ring and against the exterior bulkhead. She was responsible for one third of the sensor suites, while two legacy crew members took the other two. Sensors required a great deal of power and as such, generated heat. Tandry's work conditions were challenging when the sensors operated at full power, as they were during the exodus from congested space. The radars and passive collectors drew energy in increasingly massive gulps. Despite the cold of space, Tandry soon dripped with sweat.

"Prepare for artificial gravity! I say again, prepare for artificial gravity!" the announcement blared into each space as well as flashing before each crew member's eye. The people pulled themselves into position, using their neural implant to inform Jolly that they were ready.

Once Jolly reported that the crew were one hundred percent compliant with the preparatory order, Captain Rand activated the ship's rotational system.

"Artificial Gravity engaged!" Jolly's voice warned them one final time as the ship started to spin, slowly at first to ease people into position. Feet and paws touched down and the crew's apparent weight increased until they felt loaded down under the burden of supporting their own bodies. It had been less than a full day that the new ensigns had been working in zero-g, so their adjustment time was minimal, but the legacy crew gasped, breathing heavily as they adjusted, even though Jolly set the rotation to one-half Vii-standard gravity for a few hours before slowly working up to a more normal artificial gravity, at least for those in the outer ring.

The 'cats enjoyed the return to normalcy. They were the most limited in zero-g and as usual, if they were miserable, they let everyone else know about it. They also resisted wearing their collars with the bracelets, an encoded band to give them access throughout the ship. They slipped out of the collars, leaving them where they dropped. On the garden deck, at least they could run and feel dirt under their paws.

The Rabbits requested access to their laser pistols to deal with a new vermin infestation, so Master Daksha committed to making a daily trip to the garden deck to help keep the peace. The humans Cain, Ellie, and Tandry also said they'd stop by at regular intervals to make sure that the Rabbits didn't go to war with the Hillcats.

With the return of even partial gravity, Briz worked like one possessed. He was fascinated with the operation of the EM Drive and disappointed that he had only a few hours to review the system before it was engaged. The engineer from the legacy crew hadn't dealt with the EM Drive before.

Ellie and Briz looked at each other. "We're taking a new engine for a test drive and we don't have an expert on board?"

"But we do, Ensign Brisbois and Ensign Ellie. All the knowledge regarding the EM Drive is contained within my consciousness. Anything that could possibly need done, I can explain to any member of the crew. Have no fear. We will figure this out together and the EM Drive will be the next great evolutionary leap for the people of Cygnus," Jolly spoke to them using the sound system within the core engineering space.

Ellie was still confused. "But we've launched into space without an expert on the engine. What if something happens to you?" Ellie questioned the sanity of the process.

"We won't leave our solar system until we are satisfied that everyone is comfortable with their roles on board the Cygnus-12. We rushed from space dock as we were well behind schedule, but that was considered an acceptable delay because the commander deemed Ensign Brisbois and I, quote, well worth the wait, unquote." Ellie started to laugh.

"So, Lindy isn't the only one who owes Briz?" Ellie strolled across the space to where the Rabbit sat, poring over the numbers streaming across his screens. She slapped him on the back, and he almost launched out of his seat. At least there was enough gravity to hold him down.

"Don't scare me like that!" Briz cautioned. Ellie leaned against him and rubbed her face against his neck and ears. He started giggling and tried to push her away. She scratched his ears briefly before walking back to her station. She liked having gravity.

"Great job, Briz! It's my honor to ride your coattails," Ellie yelled over her shoulder, sincerely appreciating having him on board.

"But I don't wear a coat," Briz countered. Ellie waved it off as she went back to work.

"And you need to teach me how this thing works, just in case we lose Jolly and you!" The Rabbit shuddered. He was still young enough that his mortality had never entered his mind. He looked up briefly, then shrugged the question away. He would learn the EM Drive first. After that, he'd teach the others.

Master Daksha floated on the bridge, not far behind Captain Rand. The Tortoid held a strap in his mouth so he could better manage the ship's spin without having to constantly swim. Whereas the rest of the crew was more comfortable with gravity, Daksha preferred the zero-g state. The Hawkoid who worked with the sensor suites also liked zero-g, but he and Daksha were heavily outnumbered.

Captain Rand was surrounded by monitors and touch screens. His job was to ensure a functioning spaceship, and he was fully immersed in the information and technical issues involved in its operation. He not only worked with the screens, he always had his window open with Jolly. His mind was constantly engaged with information. Like Briz, Captain Rand was a certified genius, but that was also his curse. He couldn't leave the ship when it was in space. He was as integral to its operation as Jolly, as every member of the crew. The captain gave them direction as necessary to keep the ship going. Other crew members on the command deck were engaged in their own tasks and generally never received orders directly from the captain.

Leaper was off on a task. The captain intended to have a banquet in the hangar bay on the hangar deck, after they secured the EM Drive following the first test. They'd traded their long range exploration ships for smaller shuttles since the Cygnus-12 could head directly into the gravity well, no longer confined to interstellar space. The entire crew had become explorers, not just those who were able to take an exploration ship into the solar system.

Lieutenant Chirit, the Hawkoid, liked the addition of the new spindle section and expected that he'd spend his off time there, enjoying flight. He'd previously spent time on the garden deck, but the overhead was low and if anyone was walking the pathway, then it made for a tight squeeze to fly past. *The spindle, maybe I can move my quarters there,* he thought as he checked and rechecked the stars to make sure the astronavigation program was registering correctly and that they remained on course.

The star charts were critical. The star locations had to be exactly defined for the correct calculations to feed into the ISE. Even the most minute errors would deliver the spaceship too far away from a target solar system, and it would take a month to build up sufficient dark matter within the ISE for another activation. Time was limited because supplies were limited. Getting the calculations right was the most important task that all the crew members contributed to prior to an ISE activation.

Chirit had time. They wouldn't be using the ISE for a while. The intent was to fly around the Cygnus system using the EM Drive. If there were any issues that couldn't be corrected, they'd return to space dock as a last resort. The supplies for their full mission had been loaded, and once that was done, they could leave and the mission clock started ticking.

The SES didn't like wasting supplies. If you were burning through your food supplies, the leadership wanted to see a ship exploring. A mission couldn't be replaced so if the Cygnus-12 only flew around the solar system and then couldn't leave, its mission would be scrubbed. It would be skipped and the exploration delayed. They were close to reaching out, making a difference for all of Vii, and no one wanted to wait.

So they went to space with half the crew being new and a quarter of those having been on board for less than a full day. No one was concerned, not Daksha, not Rand. Motivation and attitude on board any deep space exploration vessel were the most desirable attributes among the crew. Everyone was on the same journey, but on their own journey, too. Space was a big empty place, the ship being its own analogy, as the crew could spend days on board and not run across another intelligent being.

Sometimes the greatest exploration was done inside one's own mind. There would be plenty of time for internal reflection.

Jolly kept tabs on all the crew. It was the AI's job to make sure that depression didn't rear its ugly head to incapacitate anyone or take them from their desired path. He'd struggled on the last cruise after they lost spin and food fabrication. As the crew's rations were cut and then cut again, combined with struggling to operate in zero-g, many of them suffered. One of them even airlocked himself. It wasn't the first suicide of a deep space explorer, but it was the only one within the last decade. Captain Rand and Master Daksha took it hard, but they refused to quit, believing that the hard lessons wouldn't be learned if they didn't carry them forward. The new drive made it possible to keep the crew together and make more timely decisions.

When they lost spin on the last cruise, the exploration ship was deep into the well of the new solar system. They sent the recall notice, which took days to get to the ship and then it took months for the ship to change course, followed by more months as it rebuilt its speed to return to the Cygnus-12. That extra time made the trip nearly unbearable. Through force of will they survived. The information they gathered on that trip was far too valuable to be lost. They returned with it, heroes, but with one less crew member. The captain and Master Daksha considered the mission a success, but their roles in it as complete failures. That was their burden to carry throughout their life's journey.

Deep space. Where the ship was life. Save the ship, save yourselves, no matter the cost to your own soul.

Master Daksha cast his dark thoughts away and asked Jolly to relay his message to the crew. The AI confirmed that he was ready.

"Esteemed crew of the Deep Space Exploration Vessel Cygnus-12, greetings! We embark today on a journey of great importance, and that's why we decided not to wait. We'll learn about our new EM Drive over the next couple weeks, then we'll head to our launch point outside of our solar system. From there, we'll activate the interdimensional space engine for a jump of over one thousand light years. We're heading in the direction of Earth! Our goal is to find a planet capable of supporting life, if not already inhabited, that we can use as an interim stop, maybe even a resupply point.

"Wouldn't that be something, if we could find a planet that was already inhabited?! We'd be the first to find other life beyond Cygnus, outside of

Earth itself. If we are successful and the EM Drive operates as expected, we'll be able to jump another thousand light years closer, then return while we still have plenty of supplies remaining. That is our mission. We have the highest hopes for success. The SES has wished us well on our journey. The other four active deep space exploration vessels will continue their missions in search of habitable planets closer to Vii. We are a one-of-a-kind spaceship and it is ours to take on a journey of discovery. It is ours to find the way back to Earth." Master Daksha finished his speech and waited. He wouldn't know how the people received his words until he talked with them later. Or sooner, he decided as he excused himself from the command deck and decided to head for engineering. The captain stood and clapped, nodding to the Tortoid.

Captain Rand asked Jolly to share his thoughts with the crew, so Jolly tapped the captain into the ship-wide broadcast. "The first thing we need to do is show the SES that the EM Drive works and not just works like it is supposed to, but works in a way that makes the Cygnus-12 the best damn spaceship in the fleet! Prepare the EM Drive for five percent power. The initial acceleration will top out at five Gs. Find your acceleration chairs and belt in. Start the countdown, Jolly," the captain ordered.

Each area had an acceleration chair, a cushioned couch with seatbelts, leaning against the wall at a thirty degree angle. As the apparent gravity pulled them downward from the sideways spin of the core, the blood would be forced toward their heads and not away. The crew would remain conscious. After the initial acceleration, they'd continue without feeling the force on their bodies. Then they could return to their stations. The captain expected an initial acceleration for thirty minutes, then they'd shut down the EM Drive and coast as they checked the status of all systems, comparing deviations against expected norms. Everything was calculated within a narrow range. Maybe the deviations weren't bad and that was part of the testing. They had to determine whether abnormalities were bad or not, and then make sure that there was no damage to the engine or its support systems.

The Rabbits on the garden deck found their chairs, snickering to themselves as the 'cats had nowhere to go, but Hillcats were mostly indifferent to the acceleration unless it was extreme. They were the most adaptable to space and those who liked it least. The three 'cats crouched where they were, leaning against small trees to keep themselves from sliding toward the aft-facing bulkhead.

The countdown continued over the speakers in each space. Briz waited until the last second before racing to his acceleration couch, strapping himself in as the red light stopped flashing and bathed the space in an eerie crimson twilight. *I'll have to change that*, Briz said to himself.

The EM Drive came to life without a sound. It generated momentum by bouncing electrons off a special panel near the core section of the ship. The electrons returned down long tubes in the spindle toward the power generation, where they were gathered through a series of angular surfaces that prevented deceleration. The electrons were then re-accelerated forward.

The Cygnus-12 smoothly moved through space, picking up speed quickly. Briz watched the indicators on the panel. Heat build-up was at a minimum and the nuclear power plant at the base of the spindle continued to generate the force that both accelerated and recovered the electrons. Briz marveled at the soundless propulsion taking their spaceship away from the ship construction facility.

Jolly, what's the maximum acceleration the EM Drive can achieve?' Briz asked over his neural implant.

'The drive has a governor built in to prevent runaway acceleration, which is calculated at hundreds of g-forces. That would kill every living thing on board, but not before the ship is torn apart. The spindle would accelerate through the core section. I don't have to explain how bad that would be, especially since the ISE is tied into power generation within the spindle itself. If anyone survived the loss of the spindle, that person wouldn't survive the cold vacuum of space without power,' Jolly said without emotion, trying not to sound sensational.

'Thank you for that, Jolly. I'll add that to my list, to review and understand the constraints under which the engine must operate.' Briz stared at a spot on the bulkhead as he communicated with the AI. The Rabbit wondered how he'd ever gotten along without an AI like Jolly in his head.

'Would you like me to maintain that list for you? We can review it multiple times during the day and set a schedule for resolution. What is the maximum amount of time you are willing to leave a task undone, say, two days?'

Briz's face took on a beatific look. Ellie wondered what Jolly said to create such a euphoric state. She decided she could use a pick-me-up as well.

'How are you doing, Cain?' she asked her husband while also sharing an image of their intertwined naked bodies, sweating from their exertions.

'I'm surviving. Thanks for that image, it'll have to hold me over for a while. Thank goodness none of the sewage systems have exploded. I'm kind of vulnerable here on the floor. I'm not trying to kill the mood, especially as, all of a sudden, I can't wait for the shift to end and to see you back in our quarters.' He smiled inwardly, trying to share love and happiness. He never knew if his emotions carried through, but he'd keep trying. *'And you, surviving engineering with our resident genius?'*

'Yes. I think he's just become one with Jolly. He has this really stupid look on his face. He can't even hold his ears up, he's concentrating so hard. I can't hear anything. I didn't expect an engine to operate without a sound,' she told him. They continued talking about the nuances of the ship and shipboard life, as good friends would do, keeping the promise of an evening that Ellie envisioned alive and well in the fore of their minds. Lutheann and Carnesto scoffed, knowing that they'd have to endure the tryst. The 'cats started making noise, hoping to deter the young couple.

Cain and Ellie both knew what the 'cats were doing, so they vowed to make things even more spectacular, just to show their furry companions what the humans were capable of. Carnesto offered to show what he was capable of, which earned him a vicious swat from Lutheann. *This is going to be a really long trip,* she lamented.

Set Course for Interstellar Space

The first week on board the Cygnus-12 passed in a flash. The ensigns were run ragged. Not only did they have their normal duties in their workspaces, there was a damage control exercise every hour. Cain didn't remember ever being so tired. When he crawled into the rack, despite the best of intentions, both he and Ellie were asleep almost instantly. The rest of the crew was in the same condition, except for Briz. He was operating on two hours of sleep each night with a one-hour nap during the day. He said he couldn't afford anything more decadent.

Sleep as decadence. The others were learning to do with just under six hours of sleep a day, wondering if they'd ever get a chance to sleep in and recover before they spent every shift sleepwalking.

At the end of the week, Captain Rand called for another celebration. They gathered on the hangar deck in the middle of the afternoon, when they still had enough energy to stand upright.

"Thank you all for coming," the captain said once everyone was there. The fact that the legacy crew members were all in attendance confirmed to the new additions that they didn't really have a choice, although the information that the captain would share had to be worthwhile. Why would they ever consider skipping it? This was the right place to be, no matter what. They wanted to hear what the captain had to say.

"The tests on the EM Drive have been nothing short of spectacular! We have fallen just beyond the most optimistic estimates on performance. We are effectively getting double the g-force acceleration without double the stress on the ship's structure. The five gees you feel each time we step on the gas? Well, that was ten gees in effective acceleration. We've been traveling twice as fast as what we're feeling. If it weren't for the sensors, and thank you to all the sensor suite operators." He nodded to them, one by one. "Our internal instruments are registering what we feel, so that's something we'll have to resolve, calculate the real acceleration and not just the apparent number. But that's geeky stuff and beside the point. What it really means is that we can explore a system in half the time we estimated and in less than a twentieth the time if we were to use a shuttle. This is leaps and bounds ahead of all other missions. EM Drives are now being built to retrofit every other deep space exploration ship in the fleet, including all new construction. As we miniaturize the drive, we'll fit them onto new shuttles as well, drastically cutting transit times within the system." The group cheered. Briz smiled, happy with how far he'd come in his knowledge of the drive. He'd been talking with Jolly and had a couple ideas to increase the real speed to three or even four times apparent acceleration.

"Tomorrow, we're going to head for interstellar space at maximum tolerable acceleration. After we've banked our dark matter into the ISE, we'll make the final calculations for a single move of one thousand, two hundred, thirty-five light years. A single jump of one third the way to Earth. Commander Daksha will explain the rest of the mission." The captain smiled broadly as he waved at the small crowd that represented the entirety of his crew, including the two Rabbits who stood closest to the hatch as they prepared their escape back to the garden deck and the three Hillcats.

Master Daksha swam forward and floated high enough to be seen by all. "We expect to arrive just beyond a star system that records from the Traveler suggest contains a habitable planet. The Traveler passed that system at eighty-one percent the speed of light, so there was no way they could explore it, although their sensor readings are rather extensive. We've used those logs to analyze the entire route and systems most likely to contain the kind of planets we're looking for. This is a little farther than we wanted to jump as it is right on the edge of the safe zone. That being said, three jumps of this length and we will be within spitting distance of Earth. Then our magnificent new EM Drive can take us home. Would you like to be the first members of humanity to return home after nearly five thousand years?"

The crew cheered and shook hands. They hadn't known that this mission might take them all the way to Earth. They thought they'd explore two systems and return to Vii, typical of a deep space mission.

"We are setting out to make history. The Cygnus-12 and its crew, thirty-seven strong, forty counting the 'cats." He nodded his Tortoid head in the direction of the Hillcats standing to the side. Cain, Ellie, and Tandry hadn't realized that they'd joined them. Tandry immediately joined her 'cat so she could scratch her ears.

"One Tortoid, one Hawkoid, three 'cats, three Rabbits, two Wolfoids, two Lizard Men, and twenty-eight humans set out from Cygnus on a journey to an old place, that's new to us, to let our forebears know that we survived, and that we've thrived. Cygnus rises from the ashes of our past to assume its rightful place as a space-faring people." The Tortoid looked around the hangar deck, stacked with crates of supplies and two small shuttles. The EM Drive changed how they looked at the universe. They could travel wherever they wanted, together. They could arrive in interstellar space, accelerate through the system's gravity well, and exit the other side without have to undertake the difficult slingshot maneuver around the sun or a large planet, then slowing down for half the journey in order to be recovered by the interstellar spaceship. None of that had to happen anymore. They could explore new solar systems over the course of weeks, not years.

The Tortoid realized everyone was looking at him while he daydreamed, so he decided to share.

"This means that we can explore new solar systems in real time. Maybe we will cut our journeys down to a month, take a large crew and explore more. Maybe even visit a few planets. What do you think about stepping foot, paw, or claw onto another world?" People shouted their willingness to volunteer for such a mission. The crew smiled and looked to each other, nodding.

Attitude and motivation. Captain Rand slapped Master Daksha on the shell, grinning. They couldn't ask for more from the crew, who worked hard to run the EM Drive and the damage control systems through their paces. He felt they were ready. The crew could always learn more, but the problems that came would never be the same. They would always be something new and the crew would have to show resilience and ingenuity to fix the issue and continue the mission.

There was good and then there was good enough. Later, the crew would be good. Presently, they were good enough.

"Enjoy the rest of your afternoon and evening. Return to your shifts tomorrow as per your normal schedule. Jolly is keeping us in a static position away from space debris. Everyone, get to know each other, enjoy yourselves, and tomorrow, the real mission starts," Daksha ended on a high note. Stinky pulled the coverings from a couple games that had been secreted away within the hangar deck, boxes and bean bags, darts, and various games of chance. Half the crew started setting up the boxes with the holes for the bean bag toss, while the other half went into an adjoining space to bring out the feast that Leaper had stashed.

Cain pulled Ellie close for a long hug and full kiss, then he ran off to help Leaper as Ellie joined Tandry setting up a game of corn hole. The rest of the crew moved through the newcomers, introducing themselves and making the others feel welcome. They broke out by species, until the games began, then everyone melded together as sections took on other sections and the crew became a homogenous mass.

Once the food was gone, the crew drifted away to enjoy their time off. The sudden erratic behavior from the 'cats, Lutheann and Carnesto, suggested their humans were fully enjoying themselves. They walked out with the next people, heading back to the garden deck where they'd be better able to fight off the emotional tidal wave that washed over them.

Captain Rand checked in with Jolly to make sure nothing needed his attention. It didn't. He stayed behind to clean up, telling everyone else to go. Leaper couldn't do that. Neither could Pickles, or the last ones out. They made short work of the celebration's remnants, each shaking hands with the captain and slapping Master Daksha's shell before excusing themselves.

When the captain and the commander were alone, Rand spoke first. "I like this group, Master Daksha. Thanks for finding them and getting them on board. It makes me think that Space School is too long. They need some base knowledge, but if they are right for the job, then we need to get them here, train them here where they learn what it means to be a deep space explorer, become a real spacer," the captain stated. The Tortoid bobbed his head, blinking slowly.

"I think we were lucky. It's not just our genius Rabbit. The dynamic of this group is like nothing I've ever seen before," the Tortoid's vocalization device was flat, not carrying any emotion, but the captain understood the passion that Daksha felt.

"I think we're going to have a great mission, and maybe we'll find something useful, too," he laughed as he headed toward the command deck. He wanted to personally check a few things before turning in. His quarters were only a few paces from his work station, although he was more than willing to sleep in his chair at his command console. He lived for the ship. The ship was his life.

Activate the ISE

It took five days to clear the gravity well of the Cygnus sun and exit the solar system. The crew didn't feel the difference as they transited through the outer edge of the heliosphere, the final barrier into interstellar space. The ship's EM Drive moved the ship through the solar winds without buffeting or extraneous movements. Once beyond their solar system, the ship smoothly turned and activating the EM Drive, worked to decelerate by flying in the opposite direction. When they came to a complete stop, the process of banking the dark matter began. The system was already half-filled, and Jolly estimated it would take a week to reach maximum capacity. It took much longer to fill the first half than the second half as the dark matter helped pull more into itself. Starting from empty, banking the system could take upwards of a month.

During the time the dark matter banked, Jolly, Briz, and a couple legacy crew members triple-checked the calculations for the jump. Briz devised two new formulas to validate the process, creating an additional redundancy before the ISE activated. The remainder of the crew prepared the ship to penetrate the heliosphere and enter the gravity well of the target solar system. The ISE moved the spaceship without movement. One instant they'd be outside the Cygnus star system and the next instant, they'd be outside the star system designated IC1396.

Very few people understood how the ISE really worked and one of those was Ensign Brisbois. Captain Rand had a tenuous grasp on the physics of the engine, but Briz and Jolly were the only ones who knew exactly how it worked. They were both comfortable that it was ready to take them where they wanted to go. Briz continued to work with minimal sleep. Captain Rand checked with Jolly, who assured him that the Rabbit was perfectly healthy. Maybe Briz had spent his whole life in search of his personal nirvana. Once linked with Jolly, the Rabbit had become one with the ship.

If I'm nice to them both, maybe they'll let me drive the ship around, just a little bit every now and then, the captain thought to himself, chuckling. His neural implant started flashing. He opened it to see that emergency alarms were sounding on the garden deck. He hit the alarm and ran from his post. The command deck was in the outermost ring of the core and the garden deck was the next ring, of five total before the center of the core where the hangar deck was located.

Jolly, what do you have? the captain asked as he jogged the corridors to the stairwell on his way to the garden deck.

There appears to be laser fire. Three of the sprinklers have activated and have extinguished the fire. I have no other information at this time. Smoke and mist in the area is inhibiting the visual sensors. I'm unable to share a view of the deck with you,' Jolly apologized.

The captain didn't concern himself with that as he arrived at the hatch moments later. It had closed automatically when fire was detected and the garden deck was unique with water sprinklers. The argon fire suppression system elsewhere through the ship would have killed all the plants and reduced their ability to scrub carbon dioxide from the air. The garden deck made long term space voyages possible.

The captain manually opened the hatch after Jolly confirmed that the fires were out. He ran down the center walk, not seeing anything. The smoke was being pulled into an exhaust vent, quickly clearing the air. A Rabbit called Allard popped out of berry bushes to his side, took aim and fired his small laser pistol. The captain dove, laying out in midair as he reached for the Rabbit and got a handful of harness. Allard struggled to free himself, but Rand wouldn't let go, wrestling the pistol out of the small white hand and receiving a vicious Rabbit-kick to his mid-section before the fuzzy white crew member hopped away.

A 'cat snarled up ahead.

"Everybody STOP!" the captain yelled. "Jolly! Turn off those sprinklers!" Captain Rand stuffed the pistol into a cargo pocket of his one piece duty jumpsuit.

"Cain, Ellie, and Tandry, report to the garden deck! You have two minutes to get here!" Captain Rand told Jolly to pass to the three ensigns. Another laser beam reached out from between lettuce leaves and the captain pounced on Beauchene, ripping the laser pistol from his small hand. The Rabbit bounded away.

"WHY?" the captain yelled at the ceiling not far above his head. He tapped his foot impatiently, arms crossed, a scowl darkening his face.

When the ensigns appeared, he was short and direct. "Get your 'cats and confine yourselves to your quarters until further notice."

"They aren't 'our' 'cats. It doesn't work that way," Tandry started to say. Rand cut her off with a dismissive wave.

"Get them off this deck, now!" He emphasized his sincerity by pointing at the hatch. "NOW!" he yelled.

The three ran away from him, unsure of where they were going as they called to the 'cats over the mindlink.

'Yes, master?' Carnesto asked sarcastically in a bored thought voice.

'Way to go, you furry cretin. You've gotten us all confined to quarters. Have you seen our quarters? And now there will be four of us in there! What the crap were you thinking? Of yourself, no doubt! Now, go! Get to our quarters and wait for us there. We'll be along with your fellow miscreant shortly!' she ended on a high note, not shouting over the mindlink, but loud enough for everyone on the ship to hear her. A couple other crew members showed up for damage control duty, but the captain waved them away.

'She's kind of mad, huh?' Cain asked Lutheann, sitting calmly next to him and leaning slightly against his leg.

'Yes, I think retreat is the best course of action. I shall find my way to your quarters without her seeing me,' the 'cat stated. Before the all-white Hillcat took a single step, Ellie's glare locked her in place.

'Too late,' Cain told her, acting as if he were the one who was going to get yelled at.

"And you let him make trouble! We women have to stick together and you let me down." Ellie shook her head while wagging her finger in the direction of the 'cat. Mixial and Tandry disappeared without a word escaping either of them. Rand watched with approval. His own anger disappeared as Ellie vented her spleen at their errant companions.

'To our quarters, ho!' the 'cat called and trotted toward the steps. Ellie kicked at her, but she deftly dodged and continued on her way without pause.

Ellie looked around her, embarrassed at having to leave her post. Cain looked away, not wanting to incur her wrath.

"Well," he finally started to say, "I guess we'll make the most of it. We could jump into the path of a meteor. That would resolve the situation rather neatly, I would think." He looked at her with big eyes and a half-smile.

She shook her head and snorted. The captain watched, suspecting that the situation was close to being resolved. He had to find Allard, the Rabbit who kicked him, and the other one who'd run off. Rand gave the pair a great deal of latitude. The Rabbits had kept the crew alive with just enough food on their last cruise.

The captain checked in with Jolly. No damage that he could see besides a few singed plants, and the Rabbits were already meticulously trimming them. Rand approached, couldn't think of anything to say, so he settled for wishing them luck. They offhandedly thanked him for removing the infestation. He thought better of arguing with them, expecting the 'cats would be back. He'd have to hide their laser pistols and then figure out how they got them.

Jolly kept it to himself, knowing that he'd given the Rabbits access. Sometimes things needed to be spiced up and this cruise was going too well, which put the older spacers on edge. He appreciated the opportunity to help, although he'd never admit it. He already had faked video footage showing the Rabbits helping themselves to the storage locker.

All in a day's work. He was comfortable with the calculations and as the banking reached one hundred percent, they'd set course for a record jump. Jolly looked forward to that. He insisted the Rabbits stop their war with the 'cats and prepare to enter their new existence. They were going to become explorers.

When Cain, Ellie, and the two 'cats squeezed into their quarters, Ellie became even angrier. Lutheann and Carnesto looked surprisingly remorseful as Ellie delivered a supreme tongue-lashing. At the end, she asked what they had to say for themselves.

Carnesto coughed once, looked at Lutheann, then spoke. *They started it.* He laid down and curled his tail toward his cat face, closing his eyes as if preparing to sleep. Ellie reached a hand under his chin and gently lifted his head, looking deep into his eyes.

"What. Did. You. Say?" she asked, clearly articulating the words and sending shards of ice with each one. No one tried to answer her question. Carnesto was confused as to what to do. His instincts told him to fight. His mind told him that he wouldn't win.

'I said, we're sorry and it won't happen again?'

"That's what I thought you said. Now if we can convince anyone that you're sincere, we can get you out of here. I think we're spinning up the ISE and I should be at my work station. I hate leaving Briz alone. He's so engaged with the systems, he'd fall through an open hatch if no one was watching over him. He needs me there to keep him safe while he does his genius stuff."

Cain activated his neural implant. *'Jolly, how long do you think we'll be confined to our quarters?'*

'You've already been released, Master Cain. The captain *wanted to make a point. He's done that. Now it would be best if you reported to your work stations. We'll be activating the ISE shortly.'* Cain smiled at Ellie as he changed his focus from the window before his eye to his partner's face.

Then he looked at the two 'cats who hadn't moved since they sat down in the quarters. "You two are on probation!" he lied. "Promise us that you won't antagonize the Rabbits," he demanded.

'Yes,' came two voices over the mindlink. Cain wondered what that meant, but wouldn't dwell on it.

Ellie got up, opened the door, and pointed into the corridor. "Get out." The two 'cats were off like a shot. She wondered how they were going to get through the hatches, given their collars were nowhere to be seen, but she didn't care as long as the two furballs weren't trapped in her quarters.

Cain gave Ellie a peck on the cheek, a lingering hand caressing her butt, and headed toward sewage central, what he'd taken to calling his workstation. He went down the wide stairs toward the central part of the core. Ellie ran after him, taking the stairs down one flight from their billeting to where the primary engineering section was located.

Ellie arrived as Briz was furry hands deep into one of the coolant couplers. "Let me do that, Briz." He described briefly what he thought needed fixing. Her arms were longer and she could leverage better within the tight space. She unhooked the line coupler and put the new one into place. She double checked her work as she'd been taught on the Traveler, then she closed the access panel. Briz didn't react when she gave him the thumbs up.

Once the tools were returned to their case, Ellie assumed her workstation, running through a long checklist of systems to verify on top of everything that Jolly had already done.

When the EM drive was in operation, it created g-forces during acceleration and they had to strap themselves in. The ISE was different—there was no acceleration. There were no restrictions on how the crew prepared for the ISE activation besides that they be in their work spaces and ready to work when they arrived. After an ISE jump, every system on the ship would be checked, verified, and double-checked. The ISE caused stresses that Jolly and the other ship AIs could not yet predict. Something would break and the people had to react.

Traveling as far as they were--one thousand, two hundred, thirty-five light years--none of their sensors gave them the slightest clue as to what was at their target destination. They were counting on data from the original mission, roughly two millennia ago, which was recent data as far as interstellar charting went.

Checklists were completed in all sections. Jolly compiled the reports and updated the progress for Captain Rand. Pickles received the updates, verified status of the crew members as a redundancy, and reported the status to the captain.

"All statuses show green, Captain," Pickles said through his vocalization device. The tone reflected a simple conversation, academic in nature, without underlying excitement or anxiety. To the Lizard Man, it was raw data and a simple validation that it was within desired parameters.

"Prepare to activate the ISE. Start the countdown, Jolly," the captain said over the ship-wide broadcast. Jolly started his countdown from ten. When Jolly reached zero, the ISE created a bubble around the ship, which expanded to encompass the spindle section. The energy surge made hair stand on end. Those without hair felt a tingling sensation. And then the bubble collapsed as they arrived at their destination.

Alarm klaxons rang throughout the ship and red lights flashed. Something had gone wrong.

Engineering's On Fire

When the alarms indicated a fire in engineering, Cain was off like a shot, feet barely touching the deck as he raced down the corridor and up the stairs, taking them three at a time.

Flames shot through the open hatch. Cain yelled, "Engineering's on fire!" as the klaxons continued to scream, echoing down the corridor away from him. He sensed, more than heard, the anguished cry.

The hatch was open. The automated fire suppression system had failed.

He ripped open the damage control panel and pulled the tank out. He threw it hastily over his shoulder, reached behind him with a well-practiced maneuver to start the flow of air, and wrapped the dangling mask across his face. He draped the fire hood over his head as he ran. He didn't have time to put on the whole outfit. People he knew were dying.

He hit the flames of the doorway at a dead run. The intense heat scorched his bare forearms as he passed, and he yelled into his mask as he slid to a stop in the middle of the space, looking for survivors. A Rabbit lay under a terminal, an ugly scorch mark cut across his white fur, leaving blackened hair around burned pink flesh underneath. The Rabbit moved– Briz was alive.

Cain slid him out from under the melting terminal. The Rabbit was dense and blocky, half Cain's height but the same weight. Cain pulled an equipment cover off the back of a chair, wrapping it around the Rabbit's head and over as much of his body as he could, then hefted him up, trying to avoid the injury. Cain lumbered toward the hatch, ducked his head, held his breath, and jumped through the flames. He deposited the Rabbit in the passageway and raced back into engineering. Ellie was in there somewhere.

He should have been alarmed that the flames didn't seem to hurt as much this time. The next victim was a Wolfoid, horribly torn apart from the force of an exploded containment vessel. He saw something odd about the way the Wolfoid's body, bigger than a human's, was laying on the floor.

A pink-fleshed hand snaked out from underneath the heavy gray fur. Without remorse, Cain heaved the Wolfoid's shattered body to the side. Ellie was dazed, but seemed to be okay. The Wolfoid must have taken the full force of the rupture, protecting her. Cain's breath caught as he looked at her silken black hair, the ends curled and brittle from the heat that had passed over her.

He pulled her to him as blue lights started to flash within engineering, signaling the imminent flooding of argon gas into the compartment. He kneeled, rolling her from a sitting position to over his shoulder. He stood without much effort. She wasn't heavy and laid easily over his shoulder as he hurried for the hatch. The flames had died down somewhat, but he still ran through, hoping speed would keep them safe. Once through, he stopped, took off his hood and breathed deeply of the better air in the corridor. The hatch to engineering closed.

The klaxons stopped as someone helped Ellie from his shoulder, and he looked at the closed hatch. Anyone still in the space would be denied oxygen, just like the fire. The argon gas was supposed to be flushed in a matter of seconds, but it would be too late. He was surprised that he didn't know how many people worked in the space. Three? Four?

"Holy Rising Star, Cain! You shouldn't have gone in there. Why the hell would you do something like that?" the captain's words were harsh, but his eyes were grateful. As the older man looked at the two survivors in the corridor, he added, "but I'm glad you did, son. Looks like you saved two lives, irreplaceable lives."

The two Hillcats waiting for Cain and Ellie in the corridor couldn't have agreed more. Carnesto yowled in pain as Ellie came back to her senses. The burns on her lower body attacked her with waves of agony. He put a furry paw on her head to help her through the worst of it.

Cain stood and looked at the closed hatch of engineering, but that wasn't what he saw. He saw a door to a school while flames belched from windows, scorching the walls above. This time, he was unafraid. He'd gone into the chaos and rescued the survivors. He'd done what he set out to do, be the man that the captain was.

"Aletha!" he yelled at the closed hatch.

"I'm who you need me to be," he sobbed, reaching his hand toward the metal, not touching it, knowing that it was hot. "Has it only been six months, my love?"

When he turned, Ellie sat there. The expression on her face told the whole story. She was crushed, her physical pain dwarfed by her emotional anguish. Lutheann glared at her human.

The captain hovered over Briz as other crew members arrived. There was a small medical lab on board the ship and it was run completely by bots. They put Briz on a stretcher and headed that way. A second stretcher appeared and Cain chased away a crew member from one end. He'd carry his wife, even though the pain in her eyes implied that he might be better off elsewhere. He couldn't take his eyes from her, apologizing over and over in his mind. The 'cats followed as Cain and a fellow from ship's stores navigated the hallway to the med lab, which was located one deck up from engineering.

Cain's arms started to ache. He saw the skin was bubbled up and down his forearms. Some of the blisters had popped and leaked clear fluid that ran down his fingers, wetting the stretcher's grips. He flexed his fingers and gripped the stretcher more tightly. It wouldn't do to drop Ellie.

The main table in the med lab was taken up by Briz as the bots worked on him, trimming the burnt fur away from the wound and using a healing laser to build up the skin. They put Ellie into a chair off to the side, where a second bot applied a pain reliever to her injuries to hold her over until the healing laser could work its magic on her.

"You saved me. You saved my life," Ellie said flatly, raising a hand painfully to stop Cain from interrupting. "You saved me to impress your Aletha." Cain hung his head, gently massaging Ellie's hand, even though the act exacerbated the pain in his arms. She looked at him for a long time. He thought she was finally finished and started to speak, but she stopped him once again. He didn't know what he was going to say anyway.

"I know," she consoled him. "I've known all along, but I hoped."

"Can we forget what happened?" he asked.

"Let's not talk about that right now. Thanks, Cain, for coming after me. If you hadn't, we'd both be dead." She nodded toward Briz, still out cold as the bot worked on him.

"I noticed that you rescued Briz first." She smiled, trying to change the subject. Cain didn't bite.

"I wanted to save you all. Briz was closest to the hatch, that's all," Cain murmured, not looking up. "We lost the Wolfoid, not Stinky, the other one. I don't even know his name." Cain started sobbing, letting the pain in his arms drive his anguish.

He'd won everything that he'd joined the SES for, while losing it all at the same time.

And that's what it's like being a hero.

Report!

The captain returned to the bridge after checking engineering. A coolant pump and storage tank had blown, overwhelmed by the new levels of power generated to build the larger interdimensional vortex. Some panels were fried and systems had been overloaded, but the actual damage could be repaired. Two maintenance bots were already engaged in replacing destroyed computer terminals. They'd have to fabricate a new pump and tank, but the spaceship was equipped for that.

Crew members, on the other hand, were not so easy to come by, especially their resident genius. The captain wanted to be notified as soon as Briz was awake. He wanted to know he was okay. He wanted to know that Cain and Ellie were okay. He wanted to mourn the loss of Lieutenant Strider, the Wolfoid from the legacy crew. He wanted to believe that the sacrifice was worth it.

"Ensign Peekaless, where are we?"

"Calculations complete, Captain. We are almost on top of the heliosphere for system IC1396. It appears that we have arrived exactly on target. EM drive is nominal. Dark Matter banking has already begun. The system is currently at two percent. Jolly estimates three and a half weeks to maximum capacity as long as we remain in interstellar space," Pickles reported.

"That's one relief. Thanks, Ensign. I'll be in the med lab." The captain excused himself and walked away, hunched over and looking as if he'd aged a decade in the past twenty minutes.

Master Daksha looked at the people remaining in the Command Center. "Sensors! Full sweep of the star system before us. Planets, life, the usual. Let's learn what we're here to learn," the Tortoid intoned through his vocalization device. "For those who've been hurt, this trip is for them."

The sensor operators reported as they activated their systems in passive mode first, as per the standard operating procedures, the SOP. The passive systems provided an immediate view of the solar system so the operators could better aim their active systems. The radars didn't work across a broad spectrum, the energy would dissipate to the point that none of it would return to the ship. A narrow beam was the only viable option. The passive sensors were critical in telling the operators where to point the active systems.

Master Daksha swam to the portholes that lined the outside bulkhead side of the command deck. He looked through them as the ship continued to spin, seeing the speck in the distance that was IC1396's star. They'd be going that way in a while, but there was no rush. Even with his ten years of deep space exploration missions, he'd never accompanied a shuttle crew into the well, into a foreign star's heliosphere. Finally, he would be the explorer he always envisioned himself to be.

He hoped the survivors of the explosion would recover. He really liked the Rabbit, and the human wasn't too bad either. He felt the loss of Strider, a crew member who'd survived their last problem-plagued cruise, using the old Earth term for a sea voyage. They'd inscribe his name on the plaque that adorned the bulkhead on the command deck below the names of the others who'd lost their lives while serving aboard the Cygnus-12.

Maybe they should call you the Widowmaker, the captain thought sarcastically. Eleven crew lost in three cruises of the Cygnus-12's career, and this trip had just begun.

The motto of the SES was "the ship is life, save the ship." And they'd done that, repeatedly. Everyone on board volunteered for the SES because they believed that the risk was worth it. For all humanity, they went to space, to find what was out there and return with knowledge for the betterment of all. And if they could return with word that Earth was there, alive and well, then that would make every death that much more meaningful.

"No more sacrifices, if you please, Cygnus-12," Daksha told the ship. Pickles looked up from his workstation, only briefly, then returned to parsing the significant amount of information that flowed through the sensors and into the ship.

"Ensign Tandry has discovered something, Commander. She'd like to talk with you," Pickles passed to the Tortoid, who immediately switched screens on his neural implant.

'*Ensign Tandry, you have something?*' Daksha queried without pause.

'*Yes, Master Daksha. I believe I've found a man-made signal. I asked Jolly to search the database, find if the RV Traveler left a signal buoy in this system. He confirmed that the Traveler left buoys, but none within one hundred light years of here,*' she reported breathlessly.

'*What do you recommend, Ensign?*' the commander asked, knowing what he'd do.

'*I request permission to use the active sensor to paint the source, query the signal, and see if we can learn more,*' she offered.

'*Granted and carry on. When do you think you'll have something?*'

'*At least a week, Master Daksha. I have a LOB, a line of bearing, into the system. I estimate the signal is coming from deep within the well. If it's closer, then we'll have the information sooner,*' she reported.

'*Thank you, Ensign. Carry on. By the way, what is that hideous noise in your workspace?*' The commander could hear something that didn't sound right.

'*That's Mixial. The sensors make a sound that seems to grate on her soul. Is there any way she could go to the med lab, then maybe return to the garden deck?*'

'*Yes, she's free to travel the ship. No fighting with the Rabbits, please. Good work, Ensign.*' Daksha continued to look out the window, watching intently as the solar system spun into view. *Who's out there*, he thought to himself. *Have we found life?*

A Rapid Recovery

When Briz awoke, he shot straight up in bed, knocking the med bot aside. He blinked rapidly as he looked around. "The containment vessel!" he 'shouted' through his scorched vocalization device.

"It blew, Briz. Engineering was on fire. Strider was next to it when it went." Ellie couldn't continue. The laser continued to work on her legs. Briz was in a bed shoved up against the wall. Cain was getting treated on the main bed. The burns to his arms weren't horrible and would have healed of their own accord, but with the bot's assistance, his physical injuries would heal more quickly and with less scarring.

His arms were the least of Cain's problems, though.

The captain stood outside the small med lab's hatch, pleased that Briz was awake. He'd been there when Cain made his revelation regarding some girlfriend that he seemed to love more than his wife. Rand wasn't sure how to handle the situation, but he knew that he couldn't allow discord among the crew. They had to work together, especially since they were down one valuable crew member, with three more injured. The people would have to step up. They could mourn later. He'd say a few words, launch the Wolfoid's body into space, and carry on with the mission. Before the crew came aboard, they made their wishes known regarding their remains should they die while serving. Strider wanted to be buried in space, a place he always wanted to be. Most others wished to be returned to Vii, if possible, for a more routine burial.

Rand entered the small lab and worked his way around the equipment, nodding to the three ensigns. He stopped at the end of the Rabbit's bed as he could get no closer. There was a great bandage wrapped around Briz's chest. His white fur was dirty, some of it scorched with the ends curled from the intense heat that rolled over him. His whiskers were gone and the hair on his ears was singed. He looked a mess, but the spark had returned to his eyes. That was what the captain wanted to see the most.

"Cain!" Captain Rand said, more loudly than intended. Cain sat up, wincing as the med bot gripped him more tightly to keep the laser focused. "I just want to say thank you for jumping into the fire. I have to say--" He looked pointedly at Ellie, who intently returned his look. "I don't care about your motivations. All I know is that your actions saved two crew members who survived the rupture. Your selfless actions--and you could have easily died in there with them--made the difference today. We save the ship and then we save the crew. But sometimes you have to save the crew first as without them, how can we save the ship? We need one crew, working together. That's for the good of all, for the good of the ship. When the bots release you, I need you back at your posts, see what needs repaired, and let's make sure we have our priorities correct. I know you'll be in pain and should probably be in bed recovering, but that's not who we are when we're out here. We're heading into the well soon and while we transit the system, activities will be minimal and you can take it easy. On a different note, I thought you'd like to know that we've detected a signal that's not natural."

"Intelligent life?" Cain asked.

"Could be. Master Daksha wants to explore, get a closer look, as do we all. He's never been within the heliosphere of a foreign star, although he's been on more missions than the rest of us. He's eager. I am too, and since this is the best ship in the fleet, we need it operating like it can when we head into the well, since we have no idea what we'll encounter. In the interim, we're banking dark matter and fixing the damage in engineering. I'd like you at your posts to assist as soon as the bots let you go," he repeated to the three ensigns.

The captain excused himself and headed back to the command deck. Briz was first to speak.

"Can I go?" he asked the med bot.

"Yes," it replied simply. The bots were programmed with advanced intelligence, but they weren't intelligent. They only worked within defined medical parameters. The bot should have informed Briz as soon as he was able to leave, but then again, maybe the captain had loosened the limitations within the med lab programming. He was the captain and it was his ship. He had the authority to do whatever needed to be done.

Briz struggled to get down. Cain and Ellie watched helplessly, as they were both held in place by the med bots. The Rabbit slid off the bed sideways, using Cain's bed in the middle of the small room to catch himself before he fell over. Once he had his big feet on the deck, he took a few tentative steps, then continued with more confidence through the hatch and down the corridor. He stopped, came back, and leaned into the doorway.

"Thanks, Cain, for saving my life. I don't know how I can pay you back, but know that I'll try. It's the Rabbit way." He held up a bandaged front hand to stop Cain from saying anything. Briz wasn't good at social interactions, even with his friends. "See you soon, Ellie, and thank you for working with me in engineering. It's just us now." His big ears drooped as he turned and shuffled away.

Leaving Cain and Ellie alone.

"It's just us now," she stated, repeating Briz's last words. Cain didn't know if she meant it in more than one way.

"I'm sorry," was all he could manage. The bot continued working the laser back and forth over the burned skin on one arm. The gentle whirring of the bot's gears seemed loud in the silence.

A green light appeared on the equipment next to Ellie, and the small bot moved away from her. It started on Cain's other arm. Ellie took that as her pass to leave.

She stood, gasping at the pain as she exercised the new skin on her legs. "I better get another uniform," she said to herself as she looked at what remained of her current jumpsuit. She laughed awkwardly, but her eyes twinkled. She squeezed in beside the bot and leaned toward Cain. He tried to look away, but she held his cheek in her hand and pulled his head closer.

"No matter what else," she whispered, "it's just us out here. No matter any other thoughts in our minds, any other desires in our hearts, it's just us, and you risked your life for me. I won't ever forget..." She hesitated, then brushed her lips against his cheek, kissing his eyes first, then kissing him fully, as lovers do. "I won't ever forget that you carried Briz out first," she said as she kissed him once more with a grin, then limped from the med lab.

"I don't deserve her either. I don't deserve either of them," Cain said to himself as he remained alone with the bots, his arms held in their firm but gentle grasp as they conducted the initial skin repairs. He exhaled and inhaled deeply. He had no idea what to do.

'Lutheann, where are you?' he asked in his thought voice, hoping the 'cat might have sage advice for him.

'We are waiting for someone to open the hatch so we can return to the garden deck. Our untimely removal earlier prevented the recovery of those awful devices you would have us wear,' she said, friction riding her tone as she wanted to be angry, but didn't want to further incite the humans. Cain smiled to himself. The punishment continued and hopefully the lesson was learned.

'Stinky! Is there any way you can let those furry miscreants back onto the garden deck? I think they are waiting at the hatch at the steps on radial ninety,' Cain asked his friend.

'Sure. I have absolutely nothing better to do than to cater to the whims of those two criminals,' the Wolfoid replied sarcastically. They both laughed as Leaper requested permission to leave the command deck, committing to help Cain.

The 'cats were waiting impatiently when Stinky arrived. They didn't acknowledge his presence as he joined them. They were ready to go through. Hillcats and Wolfoids had a long history of close cooperation as well as an ongoing interspecies rivalry. Dogs and cats. Genetics mandated a certain level of friction between them.

'Well?' Carnesto asked.

'I know you hate it on board the ship, but couldn't you at least try not to make everyone miserable?' he pleaded with them.

'We're 'cats. Is that really what you expect from us?' Carnesto countered.

'It is what I expect, Hillcat or no. This is a big ship and at the same time, this is a really small ship. I don't think anyone's ever been airlocked, but I think you two could be first, for the good of all humanity.' Leaper opened the hatch. Lutheann and Carnesto looked at him defiantly, unsure of his sincerity.

"Four, three, two, one," he counted down aloud, pulling his bracelet away when he reached zero. The 'cats jumped through as the hatch started sliding shut. Leaper had already turned and was walking away, indifferent to whether the 'cats went through or not.

Cain listened to the entire exchange between the Wolfoid and the 'cats. He knew that it wasn't supposed to be like this, suspecting that he wasn't bonded as humans and 'cats had bonded over the centuries. *'I really need you not to be an ass, Lutheann,'* he told her, unsure of what else he wanted to say.

'You want to know what to do next?' she asked, sounding compassionate. 'Keep on keeping on. You have work to do. You fill an important position on this ship. You are respected by your teammates, by the whole crew for that matter. Stop sulking and walk with your head held high. Take a lesson from the Hillcats. Don't be bothered by the minutiae. And when they let you go from that horrid place, bring us some food!'

Cain looked at a spot on the bulkhead as he contemplated Lutheann's words.

'Please,' she added as an afterthought.

I guess that's a start, he told himself. When the bots finished, he looked at the fresh pink skin on his arms. No hair remained, and he wondered if it might grow back at some point. He flexed his arms, getting the feel of the tight, new skin. It didn't hurt, maybe because the med bots had injected him with something. His jumpsuit was dirty, but it wasn't burned like Ellie's or Briz's.

He'd still shower and change when he returned to his workspace. There was nothing like feeling clean when reporting to work in sewage central.

Into the Well

It took ten days before Briz was comfortable with the repairs to the engineering section. He and Jolly determined that a simple doubling of the wall thickness would provide the necessary strength to prevent a future rupture. But, to keep the internal dimensions identical, the reinforced tank wall took more space than available. So that meant modifications to neighboring systems and structures. That took the most time as they engineered the flow rates in lesser systems to prevent a cascade of failures during the next ISE activation.

The captain visited engineering often. His eyes kept getting drawn to the workstation where Lieutenant Strider had worked. Ellie removed the chair as if no one had ever worked there, but they all remembered. The Wolfoid's ceremony was a brief event, taking ten minutes as they sent his body into the void of interstellar space. The sound of the cycling airlock represented the end of the ceremony. The final step was engraving his name on the command deck plate below the other ten names.

Jolly, the captain, and the crew investigated the accident from the beginning of the ISE activation to the rupture and determined that it was nothing that they should have or even could have foreseen. The rupture occurred in a minor system that even Briz suggested should not have been exposed to excess pressure. Every other ancillary system associated with the ISE was checked to ensure that no other weaknesses were found, doing their best to avoid another accident.

During this process, Briz discovered what he suggested was a way to take the ship into a solar system, into the well, as an endpoint of an ISE jump. This had never been tried for being too risky. The captain liked the idea, but wasn't willing to validate Briz's theory at the risk of the entire crew. When they returned to Vii, Briz could share his findings with the Research and Development team, and then they could find a ship with minimal or no crew to demonstrate viability. In the well, other obstacles presented themselves, like asteroids or space junk trapped within the heliosphere. No one wanted to contemplate how catastrophic it would be to jump into the middle of an asteroid field.

Briz was disappointed, but he understood. The empty workstation was a reminder of what could happen when things went wrong in deep space.

With the help of a daily trip to the med lab, Briz, Cain, and Ellie's physical injuries healed fully. With Master Daksha's leadership and guidance, the crew was focused on the anomaly that suggested there was intelligent life somewhere within the IC1396 system. The tragedy and the hope of new life brought the crew closer together, as shared suffering had brought people together for millennia.

Even Cain and Ellie acted like young lovers. The 'cats made better marriage counselors than anyone could have guessed. It also gave them something to do that didn't involve antagonizing the Rabbits on the garden deck. An uneasy peace existed between the two species as they occupied the same large space. The 'cats also ran the center walkway at full speed for as long as they could, to keep their bodies in shape as the nothingness of space attempted to press in on them. With the help of their humans, they held it at bay. And that benefitted them all.

"All hands to work stations! All hands to work stations!" came the call over the ship-wide broadcast. "Prepare to engage the EM drive."

The crew had been expecting the call for days and were relieved when it finally came. Relieved and excited. They were taking the big ship into the well to explore. The thirty-six remaining members of the crew and three 'cats would be heading into the system.

"As we enter a new phase of our journey, I want you to remember that it took our ancestors fifteen hundred years to travel from here to Cygnus VII, to our home of Vii. Our scientists have made it possible for us to go places in a single lifetime, where it took generations before. We are here because humanity has survived, within all of us. Humanity will not be denied, whether you have fur, feathers, or skin. Together, we represent the best that science and evolution could offer. Now it's time for this new generation of explorer to open the universe to those back home who are counting on us. With the captain's permission..." Rand nodded to Master Daksha. "Into your acceleration couches. Prepare to activate the EM drive. Let's see what's in there, shall we?" the commander ended his speech and assumed his position.

"When they're all in place, Jolly, let 'er rip. Start with five gravities of apparent acceleration and step it up to seven once everyone's vitals are confirmed and stable."

"Yes, Captain," Jolly confirmed. "The crew is in place. Accelerating now toward the heliosphere on Ensign Tandry's bearing. Five gees apparent, ten actual." After ten minutes, Jolly updated their status. "All crew nominal. Accelerating to seven gees apparent, fourteen actual."

The angular acceleration of the spinning ship countered some of the g-force inflicted in the direction of travel, but the crew started to struggle. No matter where they were, the acceleration weighed on them. Jolly continued at a constant acceleration until the first crew member passed out, then he trimmed the drive back until it maintained constant thrust, keeping the speed steady. They'd continue intermittent acceleration to cut their travel time in system. They also had the added acceleration from the heavy pull of IC1396's Class F star.

If for some reason they wanted to stop, they'd have to decelerate at a lesser g-force over a longer period of time. They understood that they'd most likely overfly a desired target if they discovered it too late, and then slow to a stop, returning to it at a more reasonable speed. It would be optimal to collect data as they passed and keep going until they exited the solar system where they could finish banking the dark matter and continue their journey.

But what if? What if there was intelligent life that they could meet and talk with? The scenario played itself over and over in Master Daksha's mind, always leading him to a conclusion of peaceful discovery.

Captain Rand was more cynical and feared the unknown intelligent life. History taught him that people might not welcome strangers. He didn't want to get into a fight with aliens, even though they had no evidence to suggest there was any intelligent life in the universe besides humanity. They had two Rabbit laser pistols and four blasters on board. Initially, he'd balked at any of it, but the SES had used convoluted logic to justify their inclusion as part of a standard ship loadout. He was suddenly happy to have the weapons on board.

The captain was terrified by the idea that a foreign intelligence could use weapons against them. Their ship wasn't built for warfare. He hadn't considered such a thing until they picked up the signal. The weapons of the ancients nearly destroyed Vii. If other humans ventured from Earth, they could have similar weapons, and because of that, Rand knew that he wouldn't sleep soundly until they were clear of IC1396 space. *To explore or not to explore, the question that would best be answered by a high-speed pass through the system,* he thought to himself. *I'm an explorer who doesn't want to find anything! I best not share that with Master Daksha...*

"Reducing acceleration to a constant two-tenths of one gravity. Crew members may now exit their acceleration couches," Jolly stated over the ship-wide intercom.

The Cygnus-12 had accelerated through the heliosphere and was now using absolute minimum power, but continuing to accelerate at an angle across the gravity well, using the sun's pull to add to their ever increasing speed. One never wanted to accelerate straight down the well, just in case power was lost, the ship wouldn't be headed directly toward something unpleasant to crash into. It was best to travel at a forty-five degree angle as long as possible. Eventually, the gravity would affect the ship, but with a little push, the gravity could be used to help accelerate the ship past and away from the body itself, the slingshot maneuver, used from the earliest recorded days of space flight.

Unfortunately, the bearing toward the signal was only five degrees away from a direct line to the IC1396 star. Jolly settled for ten degrees and increased monitoring of the EM drive, maintaining a constant zero-point-two acceleration. The closer they got to the sun, the faster the ship would accelerate. By the time they reached the center of the solar system, Jolly estimated the ship would reach fifty percent of light speed as it flew past, heading toward the far side of the heliosphere.

"Sensors, what have we gotten from our active scans?"

"Nothing so far," Pickles reported. "The source must be far inside the well and possibly on the other side of a planet. The three sensor operators have tried a variety of methods, both active and passive, with little effect. As we decrease the distance, fidelity will improve."

Both the commander and the captain expected improved clarity the closer they were to the source. Using his neural implant, Master Daksha activated the ship-wide broadcast. "Ensign Tandry and Lieutenant Chirit, please report to the command deck."

Sensors, a secondary mess, a small billeting section, dark matter collection, and the command deck were in the same wheel on the outermost section of the ship. Sensors and the command deck had portholes where anyone could watch the space outside the ship. Sometimes it was better to watch using the external monitors which compensated for the spin of the ship. One could easily get dizzy stargazing.

As those summoned arrived, Daksha asked for a full rundown on the system. He'd read the repots, but wanted to hear what the sensor operators had to say. The Tortoid appreciated the personal touch and knew that the operators would feel something that wasn't reflected in the data. He wanted to look them in the eyes when they told him what they felt.

Tandry deferred to the more senior member of the crew, the Hawkoid lieutenant called Chirit. "Yes, Master Daksha, you want to know about the system?"

"Yes, tell me everything as if I hadn't seen any of the data. Start from the beginning, Chirit. We have plenty of time," the commander prompted. The Hawkoid went through the mundane details of solar winds, the thirteen planets in the system, and estimated total of forty-three moons. The fifth and sixth planets were in the green zone, not too close and not too far away from the sun so life could thrive. It was the fifth planet that they were accelerating toward. The sixth planet was on a vector more than thirty degrees from their current course. Both the green zone planets looked to have oxygen-nitrogen atmospheres and both possibly had water.

At the end of the briefing, Master Daksha sat quietly and looked at the solar system chart that Jolly generated from the provided sensor information. Tandry and Chirit, using their neural implants, joined him in looking at the three-dimensional view of the system. The captain watched them closely.

"Captain Rand, please prepare for a slingshot around the fourth planet so that we may get closer to the fifth planet." Seeing the captain's discomfort, the Tortoid added, "Just in case. At this time, we are looking at both IC1396-5 and IC1396-6. But be ready, just in case we need to stop and orbit one or the other."

Rand pursed his lips and started running through flight vectors with Jolly. They were already moving rapidly and the greater the course change, the harder it would be the closer they approached to the planet. After a few moments, the captain immediately ordered a course change for a forty-degree offset from their current bearing. He wanted to angle the ship thirty degrees away from the heart of the well, where the fourth planet was currently aligned with the sun. They were on course at ten degrees off-center, and a maneuver to slingshot was too risky as they could very well slingshot directly into the sun. With the thirty degrees, if they had to abort the maneuver, they would continue safely across the gravity well, and not down its heart.

Jolly increased acceleration to one gravity as the thrusters adjusted the ship's heading. The crew quickly became disoriented as they were treated to the pull from three different directions: the spin of the ship, the current heading, and the attempt at changing their course. "Commander, I recommend we temporarily halt the spin of the ship until we are safely on our new heading. A nauseous crew will do us no good." The decision was the captain's but they were inside the well of a new solar system where the commander was in charge of exploration.

It was unprecedented territory. The commander resolved it quickly. "Do whatever is best for the ship and her crew, Captain."

"Prepare for zero-g," he passed over the ship-wide broadcast. Jolly monitored and updated ship's status as each crew member reported in. Every work station needed to be secured, even though most were solidly set in place with terminals that could be operated from a variety of positions, and crew would still have cups of water, or more likely coffee, that didn't need to splash about. With their acceleration, they would have apparent gravity, but they'd be walking on what was formerly the aft bulkheads of the corridors and workspaces.

It was not a recommended maneuver with crew elsewhere than their acceleration couches, but Jolly estimated it would take nearly a full day of the EM drive accelerating to change the ship's heading.

"Sensors?" Master Daksha asked when Jolly reported the crew 100% compliant with preparations for zero-g. The ship slowed its spin and stopped. Master Daksha swam into a new position and continued floating. He was the least affected by changes in gravity. "Sensors?" he repeated.

Tandry replied. The Hawkoid was completely incapacitated. The two forces still pulling at him kept him grounded, and not in a good way. "We are getting a much clearer signal. I'm working with Jolly to parse the data.

I'm not sure what it is, but we'll let you know as soon as we have something."

Mixial had returned to the garden deck where she and the other two 'cats hunched in a corner as the plants drooped sideways. They commiserated among themselves, without sharing their discomfort with the humans. They'd had enough of being in trouble and suspected the AI would give the Rabbits their lasers again. They hadn't foreseen that maneuver and it changed their perception of the situation.

Tandry had her neural implant open, working with Jolly to find patterns within the signal. *Jolly, have you run the signal through known ancients' programs? Let's try to determine what it is not first, then we can try again to figure out what it is.'*

'Excellent idea, Ensign Tandry. Since this is the first time we've encountered anything like this, there are no protocols in place. I've added that routine to my approach in analyzing new signals,' Jolly said happily. He was silent for only a few moments. *'There we have it! It's an old earth video signal. Playing it now.'* Tandry watched as math formulas appeared along with the table of elements, a stellar chart, and a number of other scientific information. Then pictures appeared of Earth, human beings, animals, and more.

'What is this, Jolly?'

'The signal was originally used as part of Earth's SETI project, the Search for Extra-Terrestrial Intelligence. It has found us, but I'm not sure we were what it was looking for,' Jolly pondered.

When Tandry reported in and shared the video with Daksha, he was beside himself. He watched the video seven times before making a decision. "Ensigns Ellie and Cain, please report to the command deck," he ordered.

Cain worked his way out of sewage central, walking on the bulkhead as he managed to crawl into the stairway. Looking up, he determined to use the handrail as a ladder in order to climb the two decks. Ellie showed up with the same quandary. She stood on the side of the hatch frame and looked across the stairs to the railing. Below her was a fall of thirty feet if she missed the jump. She caught sight of Cain as he slowly worked his way upward. He stopped to catch his breath, shaking his head.

"The ship wasn't made for forward acceleration without spinning. This ship design only used the ISE or thrusters, and didn't create gee forces through acceleration. I think a whole redesign is in order, otherwise someone's going to get hurt," Cain proclaimed within the void of the stairway. He braced himself to give Ellie a target to jump to. The hatch to the stairway appeared as a hole in the floor. Ellie needed to jump across the space, as she was pulled at an angle.

She braced herself and leaped. She didn't need as much force as she used and she body-slammed into her husband, who almost lost his grip. He wrapped an arm around her waist and held her there. They dangled over the drop down where the stairs led to the next deck. They each had an arm wrapped around the railing support, their feet wedged. They faced each other, bodies pressed tightly together. Cain was instantly aroused.

"Nothing like a death-defying stroll to the command deck to make you appreciate life," he whispered, his voice catching.

"I still haven't forgiven you," she whispered back, their lips nearly touching. He couldn't hold back, he leaned in and kissed her, gyrating slightly against her hard body. He almost let go, catching himself as he started to slip from the railing. She held him closely, rubbing her cheek against his. He pulled back to take a deep breath.

"I think Master Daksha is waiting on us, but I kind of like the way things are, right here." Cain smiled. Ellie started climbing and Cain used his free hand to cradle her butt as she passed. She didn't even flinch, expecting it as always.

'Yea! Shake that groove thing, right in his face!' Carnesto prodded.

'What's wrong with you?' Ellie replied hotly.

'I'm being supportive of my human. Accept it or I will scratch my claws on the bulkhead while you sleep and make you listen to it.' She shook her head and continued upward. Cain didn't know why she hesitated, but assumed that it was to allow him more time to feel and enjoy her round bits.

Cain followed her until they were opposite the hatch they needed to pass through.

It was the reverse of what Ellie had gone through to climb the railing. Cain held on with both hands and leaned as far from the railing as he could reach. Ellie used him as a springboard, catching the hatchway and scrambling out. She leaned back through and held out an arm, just like the obstacle course at Space School. He looked at her hand, thinking of that first time when she pulled her hand away and let him fall.

Not now, though. He jumped and trusted her fully as she caught him, swinging him to her where he could grab the edge of the hatch with his other hand. They worked him through, stood, and walked on the bulkhead until they reached the hatch to the command deck, which now stood over their heads. They used the hand grips across the ceiling to pull themselves upward, finally crawling through the hatch and reporting in.

"Holy Nova! What happened to you two?" Master Daksha exclaimed.

"There's no way to get here from there without some gymnastics. I'm a little rusty, but Ellie was fine," Cain said, thinking they were in trouble, so he tried to protect his wife.

"Commander, these ships were never designed for forward acceleration like we're getting with the EM drive," Captain Rand said, leaving the implication hanging.

"Oh my! I do apologize. How did you climb the stairs, then? I don't think I want to know. You should have said something. Don't put your lives at risk for something like this!" the commander apologized. "But since you're here, I'd like you two to deliver our message to our fellow Earthers. And yes, we found some, right here on the fifth planet. I'm afraid that we would probably not make a good impression by using my face in our video. We might scare them away. You two look…. How do I say this without being offensive? You look human, wholesome, happy. If we have to put a good face on all that Vii stands for, you two are it."

Cain and Ellie were flattered, but didn't want anyone to think that they represented all of Vii. They were young and the real leaders of the expedition were older, wiser, and more intelligent. So what if they were other species? "I think we should include all the species, give them a taste of who we really are," Cain suggested.

"Eventually, Ensign. Eventually. Their message suggests that this society is one hundred percent human. Now, I've worked up a short script. Tell me what you think." Cain and Ellie read the message. It was generic, only vaguely discussing where they'd come from and implying that the crew was diverse without going into detail regarding the true nature of the intelligent species of Vii and how they'd been genetically engineered using DNA spliced from humans until they evolved on their own and became equal with their forebears.

It was a message saying that a spaceship was hurtling toward their planet, with multiple claims that the Cygnus-12 came in peace. "Don't want to frighten the natives!" the Tortoid kept saying.

Cain and Ellie took a position standing on the rear portholes, formerly the aft bulkhead and currently the deck, where a limited amount of equipment was shown, just enough to convince any listener that the newcomers were on a spaceship. The young couple smiled at the point of light next to the pinpoint camera contained in all the terminals and read their lines, convincingly and naturally, finishing with a request that the receivers reply once they heard the message, since it would take a while to slow the ship if a meeting were to be arranged.

The commander broadcast the message to everyone in the ship, giving them time to comment so the message could be improved. It was short and generic, so no one had any comments. It set the tone that the commander wanted in his first message—peaceful explorers, human just like you.

"Send the message, Jolly, maximum power to the emitter, repeat it for the next twelve hours as we continue down the well. And you two," Master Daksha said, nodding to Cain and Ellie with his Tortoid head, "just stay here until we restore the spin. We don't need any more acrobatics. I can't believe I didn't think of that when I asked you to come here..."

Fellow Humans – The Decision

During the eleventh hour after the ship started broadcasting its message, they received a reply.

"Fellow humans! We greet you from the planet Concordia, the fifth planet in the system known as IC1396, but to us, it is Solar Two. We landed here a millennium ago in escape pods as our colony ship came apart. Debris is scattered along a path fifty light years long, little bits here and there as the ship traveled on a ballistic trajectory through interstellar space. At least this planet appeared to us while life remained. The survivors launched with what they could fit in the shuttles and traveled for nine months, arriving here with no food, no water, and little power. The crash landings claimed more lives and with few people and little technology, we've built what we have today, enough to send a signal into space but not enough to go there ourselves. We're transmitting maps of our world and the coordinates of a landing site in a separate data stream that will follow this message," a middle-aged man stated, enunciating clearly through a heavy accent. Behind him was a plain wall.

Daksha blinked slowly as he contemplated the message. He watched it four more times, slowing it down occasionally to study the man's facial expressions.

"What do you think?" he asked. The captain was twisted into a knot thinking about conspiracies, but didn't want to express his concerns in front of the crew. As they found out from Cain and Ellie's earlier adventure from their workspaces, he was trapped on the command deck until they returned the ship's spin. The crew needed to move around as some should be off shift and others on, while the rest had duties to accomplish in multiple spaces on multiple decks.

"Prepare for artificial gravity to be restored," the captain called to all crew, giving people time to think before answering the commander's question. Jolly confirmed that the crew had checked in and were ready, some very vocal about being ready as the toilets weren't completely accessible in the ship's current mode of gravity generation.

The ship started to spin, slowly at first, then sped up, flying through space like an old time projectile.

Master Daksha had the infinite patience of a Tortoid, but he knew he needed the other's input as he was blind to alternative courses of action. He wanted desperately to make contact with the refugees from Earth, meet them, hear their story, and tell them of Vii's successes.

Cain and Ellie made to leave, hoping to return to their workstations. The commander swam in front of them. "Ideas?" he asked.

Ellie put her hand on Cain's arm. She wanted to say something, not seeking his approval but letting him know she wanted to speak first. "Isn't this why we're out here, Master Daksha, to find a way back to Earth? But now that we've found other humans, we have to meet with them. Maybe this is our whole journey. We spend time with them, restock our supplies, turn this into a hub from which we launch further toward Earth. Can you imagine? Earth is within our reach. Two more jumps, logistically. It was a problem, until now. The EM drive lets us explore and look what we've found! I came to space for exactly this. It would be disappointing to fly past without stopping to say hello."

Everyone on the command deck looked at her. She and Cain had been passing the time with Stinky during their sequestration due to the prohibition of using the stairs. Black Leaper was still reeling from the loss of the only other Wolfoid on the spaceship. They were trying to cheer him up, but Ellie's answer to Master Daksha's question broke him from his reverie.

"Yes!" he said through his vocalization device, probably more loudly than intended. "If we don't, then what was Strider's death for? I think we have to." He ended with a resounding yip and bark, his device translating those exclamations as a flat-sounding "oorah."

"How do we protect ourselves?" the captain asked. "What if it's a trick?"

"Then those who go down in the shuttle will have a hard time. Issue the blasters and set up a reporting protocol. If we lose contact, then we'll move to an alternate location and launch the second shuttle. If we lose that one, we leave. The ship is life, save the ship," Master Daksha intoned.

"But when we return, we'll bring reinforcements and lots of blasters. If they mess with us, we'll make them pay," the captain said, as if it had already happened. The others looked at him oddly.

"What if they just want to shake our hands?" Ellie asked innocently.

"Then we'll do that, those of us with hands of course!" the commander swam in a circle, showing his thick legs and blinking rapidly as he bobbed his head laughing. The crew's morale was high, too. There was nothing like the first discovery of life outside Cygnus to buoy the spirits of the deep space explorers.

Cain and Ellie excused themselves. No one else offered input to the commander as those who spoke mirrored his own thoughts. The captain's concerns were appropriate and would be addressed with procedures, a landing SOP for contact with other humans.

The SES had contemplated meeting aliens, but nothing more. The previous space missions weren't equipped to land on a planet. Cygnus-12 would get to write the book, because contact was imminent and they had everything they needed to get up close and personal with the Concordians.

"Captain, put us into the neutral point between Concordia and its moon. I will take the team to the planet in shuttle one. I would like a cross-section of Vii to show the flag, as it may be. Cain and Ellie, their 'cats, Leaper, Chirit, and Senior Lieutenant Pace. We'll need you, too, Jolly! Make sure your link through the shuttle is secure so we don't lose contact. We don't want to be left behind," the commander said as he started his planning. He swam close to Ensign Peekaless and started narrating the details of the Landing SOP, as he decided to call it.

"And you're coming, too, Pickles," he said affectionately, using the Lizard Man's nickname.

A New World and New Life

'Get your collars and meet us outside the garden deck, we're going to the planet!' Cain told Lutheann using his thought voice.

'I'm sorry, I'm not sure I heard you right. You're saying that we're leaving the ship now to go home?'

'No,' Cain patiently explained, knowing that all the 'cats were listening in. Mixial was crushed at not getting to leave, but her human was remaining on board. *'We're still over twelve hundred light years from home. This is a new planet, Concordia, where humans crash-landed a thousand years ago, around the same time that our ancestors landed on Vii. They sound like they could use some help, so we're going to let them know that they aren't alone. And we need you two miscreants to keep us safe, just in case anyone has misguided intentions.'*

'What if these miscreants don't feel like going?' Carnesto countered.

'Sure. Try that and see if you can return to the 'cat nation. I know how things work. 'Cats can't lie to 'cats. They'll know you abandoned us, but if that's how you want it, I'm sure we can arrange for the Rabbits to get their laser pistols back. Now, just meet us in the corridor!'

'Fine,' Lutheann said, but her thought voice sounded pleased. The 'cats really hated being trapped on board and any opportunity to get off was a good one, in their minds.

Ellie and Cain ran down the corridor like kids heading for recess. The 'cats met them as they continued down the stairwell to the hangar deck where they met the others. Master Daksha floated serenely, but he blinked rapidly, betraying his excitement. Senior Lieutenant Pace was a young man, though still much older than Cain or Ellie. He'd made three cruises with the commander and was a stalwart companion. His knowledge of computers helped better integrate some of the key systems with Jolly. People assumed that Jolly took over any and all computerized systems, but some of it needed to be tweaked and the rest of it needed significant input. Pace filled the void.

Leaper was there, wearing his harness and carrying a spear, not a lightning spear like the Wolfoids usually carried but a plain carbon fiber one that the industrial fabricator had produced. The system was restricted from producing weaponry, more SES logic. They could carry weapons, but they couldn't produce more.

Cain and Ellie carried blasters, as did Pace and Pickles. The Lizard Man wore his skin suit that kept his skin from drying out whenever he wasn't in a rainforest-type environment. He had a special shower in his quarters that misted water over him while he rested, which was the only time he was out of his skin suit. The Lizard Man was an imposing figure, standing a head taller than the humans, with a deep, heavily-muscled chest and fangs for ripping his food. The fact that Pickles was an academic, non-violent, and most comfortable behind a computer was beside the point.

Chirit was flying around the hangar deck, enjoying the space to spread his wings. He had no chance to do that while working sensors, but he wasn't there for his wings. His Hawkoid eyes missed nothing and his ears were nearly as keen. He was a gifted sensor operator and had been mentoring Tandry during the voyage to bring her up to speed.

Without further delay, they loaded into the shuttle, secured themselves, and waited for word from the captain as Jolly executed the intricate maneuvers necessary to find and stop at the neutral point, that small area of space where the gravitational forces between the planet and its moon were in balance. There were four neutral points around planets with a single moon. The spaceship was flying backwards, using the EM drive to slow their momentum and the thrusters to adjust alignment. The ship continued to spin despite some bouts of nausea within the crew. The alternative, as they discovered, was complete immobilization. The med bots whipped up a concoction and delivered it, by species, to limit the effects of the artificial gravity.

The shuttle was a modified rocket with stubby wings sitting on top of a pair of oxygen/hydrogen engines. The shuttle only had enough fuel for one flight. It was self-sufficient in that it could recharge its own tanks once on the planet. In space, it had to be manually recharged. It was a tight squeeze on the inside. Pace took the pilot's seat and Ellie moved into the co-pilot's. Daksha wedged in between them, getting a strap thrown over his shell to hold him in place during the violence of entering the planet's atmosphere.

The Wolfoid squatted across two of the four side-seats. Cain and Pickles sat in the other two, while Chirit laid across their laps, protecting his tail feathers and wings. One Hillcat wedged herself under Cain's legs while a second was in front, sharing Ellie's seat with her. It was universal--no one was comfortable.

The commander and six crew members were the first ever from Cygnus VII to make contact with aliens, even if the aliens were human. The Cygnus-12 was making history.

"It won't do to scratch the paint on our way, would it, Commander?" Pace asked of Daksha, hoping to lighten the mood.

The ship rolled along the rails supporting it until it came to the hatch. The hangar bay had been cleared and vented. They waited for the red light to start flashing, showing that they were preparing to open the hangar bay. When the light flashed, the hatch folded away and the shuttle's crew looked into open space. Pace touched the thruster and it jumped the shuttle through the door. He carefully maneuvered away from the Cygnus-12 and turned the nose toward the planet.

"I hope they have something fresh to eat. Nothing like a big banquet, eh, Commander?" Pace chuckled as he eased the ship at a shallow angle toward the planet. He checked his entry vector and adjusted the course to fly toward the coordinates provided. They'd circle the planet twice before descending below the perpetual cloud cover and into the lower atmosphere, touching down on their tail, exiting via the aft ladder and slide.

The entry was rough as the shuttle skipped and dove. The nose heated, bathing the windshield in a dark orange glow as they continued downward. Pace struggled to keep the nose up to prevent the ship from diving too harshly. They rocked back and forth. Lutheann was stepped on and let out an angry yowl. The inside of the shuttle got hot. The humans sweated profusely, while Daksha and Pickles seemed right at home. The 'cats started whining hideously. Chirit looked at Cain and shook his head.

"I'm not really enjoying this part," Cain told nobody in particular. Ellie laughed and tried to reposition herself as far from the heat and fur of the 'cat as she could get, which was about a quarter of an inch. She shook her head, sympathizing with Cain.

Suddenly, the buffeting stopped and the ship's flight smoothed. A couple bounces through the clouds and a broad landscape appeared before them. The crew craned their necks to get a look at life on another planet. They passed over rolling countryside, green in the valleys, white on the mountains, the blue of water in rivers and lakes, the gray sky overhead.

The ship continued on course toward the landing coordinates provided by the people of Concordia. Jolly had chosen an overland route, as opposed to a flight path that would have taken them over a great ocean. They passed a great city between two rivers, an advanced city of gleaming metal and glass.

Vii had nothing that compared with the magnificence they saw. If a group of humans arrived on Concordia with nothing but the clothes on their backs in shuttles that were failing, how could they build such extravagance? Maybe they never had a civil war that set progress so far behind.

Then how could they not have any space travel?

"I'm not sure our hosts were completely honest with us," Cain said what the others were thinking.

Jolly, are you seeing this city?'

Yes. That's not the only surprise. There are two small spacecraft headed toward the Cygnus-12 at this time. They appeared shortly after your shuttle penetrated the atmosphere.'

'Captain Rand? Whoever is on those shuttles cannot get aboard the Cygnus-12. Do what you have to do to save the ship, even if you have to leave. We can't get back right now. We'll land and recharge the engines, then we'll meet you at the alternate neutral point,' Daksha shared with all of them via the neural implant.

'I'm afraid they have us boxed in. We'll take care of things first and then we'll move the ship. Good luck, Commander,' the captain said, sadness in his voice.

"Good luck, Captain," the Tortoid said through his vocalization device, looking at the landscape beyond the shuttles windows, unblinking as he tried to think of a way forward that didn't involve fighting the people of Concordia.

"Things just got a whole lot more interesting," Pace said, caressing the blaster at his hip.

Prepare to Repel Boarders

"Jolly! We need something to hold them off. We have two shuttles approaching from opposite sides. We have four airlocks. If we disable them, what kind of damage can they do to the ship?"

"If they're wearing space suits, they can use a cutting torch to breach the hatches. If we vent to space, that helps them, not us," Jolly answered.

"But we have to be ready. Activate the intercom, please." The captain hesitated for a moment then spoke clearly, "As you all know, we have probably hostile forces inbound. Put on your suits and prepare for zero-g and no atmosphere. The weapons locker is open. Gentlemen, go get your laser pistols and prepare to use them. We have a fight coming and we can't afford to lose, otherwise we condemn Master Daksha and the others on the planet surface. If we are not in place when they leave the planet, they'll die in the cold of space.

"Let's not make our guests feel welcome. Any and all ideas to drive them off the ship are welcome, and we need those ideas sooner rather than later. Every section, do what you can. I could have never imagined saying this, but here it is. Prepare to repel boarders." The captain closed his eyes and pursed his lips, only for a moment. He got up and rushed from the command deck, leaving it empty as he headed for the locker where his spacesuit hung.

Briz was frantic in engineering. He had a number of ideas but only he remained in his section. The Wolfoid had been killed and Ellie was on her way to the planet. Briz knew how to make things explode, but his precious ship! He ran through the scenario in his head—shuttle docks, airlock opens, bad guys enter wearing space suits and carrying blasters, bad guys cycle the system, and bad guys enter the ship. Once on board, they'd have to be dealt with one at a time and the Rabbit was wholly unsuited for that.

When the shuttle docked, the Concordians would still be on board. He had the EM drive and the entirety of the ship's power at his disposal. He pulled up his terminal, checked available materials, and dispatched the external maintenance bot to weld a bracket aft of the port airlock and attach it to the ship's main power. He sent a quick note to the captain, suggesting they concentrate on the starboard airlock as he'd take care of the one on the port side.

His small Rabbit fingers flew over the keyboard as he programmed the bot to do his bidding and make his trap work as he intended. He hoped that they would both be ready before the shuttle arrived. He had no way to test it and wasn't in the best state of mind. Briz was angry, almost to the point of being incoherent. How could anyone do something like this when the Cygnus-12 came in peace? Fury seized him and he gritted his teeth, nose twitching rapidly and ears drooping as he concentrated on the task at hand.

Beauchene and Allard, the Rabbits from the garden deck, hopped to the locker and took out their laser pistols, checking the charges and heading for the stairs. They'd set up a warm welcome for anyone entering the ship using the starboard airlock. Their spacesuits were bulky and hindered their vision, but getting exposed to the vacuum of space wasn't their idea of a good time.

Rastor, the other Lizard Man on the crew, went to his quarters where he kept a copy of his family's spear, a unique weapon topped with a trident. He hefted it appreciatively, gripped it tightly and ran down the corridor after the Rabbits. He'd left his spacesuit in his quarters. If there was going to be a fight, he wanted to be free. He knew that he couldn't stand toe to toe with enemies carrying blasters, but he could hold a hatchway and prevent them from accessing the stairs.

Save the ship.

Former DI Katlind stood her post in maintenance, following what was going on. She put on her spacesuit as instructed, then grabbed a metal bar and wrapped tape around it to make a handle. The airlocks were on the same deck where she worked. With a test swing of her weapon, she felt as ready as she'd ever be. She bit her lip and with purpose, walked from the maintenance shack.

"Jolly! You have to help us defend the ship," the captain pleaded, talking into the microphone of his spacesuit.

"I am programmed to respect the life of all intelligent creatures. I fear that there's little I can do to help. I can block corridors and secure hatches, make their movement through the ship as trying as possible, but I can't do anything to kill them outright."

"Anything you can do to keep them off this ship or eject them once on board would be greatly appreciated. I expect they'll be wearing space suits, so if we send them into space, you won't be killing them," Captain Rand suggested.

"Semantics, Captain. If we've disabled their shuttle and they are tossed into space, what is their chance of survival?" the AI countered.

"It's better than if I get my hands on them. No one can take this ship. That reminds me. Disable the controls on our remaining shuttle. Reactivate on the voice command of any two crew members only."

"The shuttle is locked out and the instructions are updated and have been sent to all crew members. Commander Daksha and the landing team are still airborne. They've flown past the designated landing coordinates and are looking for an alternative, as far away from the city as they have fuel for. The crew have elevated pulse and blood pressure, but otherwise they are physically fine." Jolly didn't add "for now" as he could only speak for the present. He was at a loss as to what the future held. He was trying to run projections, but had no information regarding what the Concordians were willing to do or capable of doing. He'd have to reconcile his programming with sending suited figures into space if he was to be of any help to his crew.

'How can I stand by and watch them be killed? Maybe there was a misunderstanding.' Jolly continued to try to reason with himself over what the next few hours would bring. The actions he knew he had to take contradicted his programming. If he took no action, there were more contradictions. The dichotomy demanded more and more of his computing power.

Briz typed furiously as the maintenance bot completed its work. Two I-beams supporting a post, shaped with a spear point welded onto the exterior of the spindle. A brace in the shape of a T anchored it. Briz needed to finish the programming to shunt power through a cable attached at the spear point's base at the right time. He watched the external view as the shuttle made its final approach.

Beauchene and Allard stood in a hatch down the corridor from the airlock, their laser pistols aimed forward. Rastor stood behind them, spear ready to defend them should anyone get too close. Two humans from maintenance joined them, large wrenches in their hands as they dreaded having to use them.

"We didn't start this!" one of the men shouted. "It's up to us to finish it, and then we rescue our crewmates!" He finished with a hearty yell and breathed heavily, psyching himself up for the encounter. The Rabbits were anxious. When they fired at the 'cats, they purposely aimed well over their heads. They didn't want to hurt anyone, but if they lost the ship, they'd lose their garden, and the Rabbits just couldn't have that.

Run and Hide

Pace stopped the steep descent so he could fly the ship past the landing coordinates provided by the Concordians. The shuttle slowly descended as he took it out to sea, banking slowly to turn back inland, far to the planet's south, trying to put a mountain range between the shuttle and the shining city.

"I suspect we won't get as far away as we'd like," Master Daksha suggested, not disappointed but resigned with their situation.

"No, but we won't make it easy on them," Pace insisted as he touched the engines to increase altitude, hopping the ship over one of the foothills leading to the mountain range. Clearing the top, the shuttle started dropping again. He could risk no more power if he wanted to land. They raced past a small village on the side of the hill as they headed toward a large valley, he skimmed across it, using the thrusters to invert the ship and the main engines to slow their breakneck speed. The passengers were thrown against their restraints and the 'cats howled as the engines jerked the ship to a mid-air stop. With the nose pointed skyward, the last of their fuel was expended to set the shuttle on its tail. The engines powered down and the shuttle began the long process of pulling oxygen and hydrogen from the air to refuel the tanks.

"Honey, I'm home," Senior Lieutenant Pace said flatly as he powered the systems down and opened the back hatch, extending the ladder and slide. One by one, the crew unbuckled and used the handholds under the seats to let themselves down. Chirit hopped off Pickle's shoulder, diving through the hatch before unfolding his wings, getting enough air to level out just before he hit the ground. He flew in a circle around the shuttle, higher and higher, sharing his view over the mindlink with the other crew members.

Livestock had been in the field when they rocketed in for their landing. Most of the animals had run toward the far end of the valley, though a couple hadn't cleared the area in time and were dead, fried beneath the flames of the engines' last burn. The others opted for the slide instead of the ladder. Cain dropped Lutheann and despite his warnings, she extended her claws which sent her tumbling. She hit the ground as a rolling ball of fur, but was immediately up and racing toward the nearby trees.

Chirit flew toward the village on the side of the hill, opposite where they landed. Men. Coming toward them. In the valley. With weapons. Rifles? Blasters?

The others cleared the shuttle and took stock of what they had. Not much. They hadn't planned for survival in a hostile environment. They had survival food bars and water packs for a crew half the size of what occupied the shuttle.

"I've made a huge mistake," Master Daksha said out loud, probably not intending to. He hovered at the bottom of the slide where the others gathered, minus the Hillcats who had already run into the woods.

"It's what all of us wanted to do. They'll pay for their duplicity, make no mistake," Cain said. Pace nodded his approval. Cain started running in the direction the 'cats had gone.

'Jolly, button up the shuttle please,' Commander Daksha said over his neural link as the others pushed him in front of them as they ran.

Chirit kept an eye on the men as they entered the valley. They were a long ways off, but didn't hurry when they pointed toward the figures running away from the small spaceship. The group of Concordians continued hiking toward the landing site. They had a long ways to go and Chirit estimated that it would take them a good twenty to thirty minutes to reach the shuttle.

"We have that long to run or set up an ambush. What do you want to do, Master Daksha?" Pace asked.

"We can't shoot first. We just can't. We have to win without fighting, or at least by hurting them as little as possible. I'll leave the tactics to you, Pace. It's not in a Tortoid's nature to fight, although I am able to use the thunderclap that my father, Master Aadi, passed to all his children." The thunderclap was a Tortoid's sonic blast, generated from within its mind. When used against a single enemy, the results were devastating. When used against a group, it incapacitated them long enough for others to rush in and disarm them. Master Daksha prepared himself to use it in defense of his crewmates.

Pace pushed Master Daksha as the landing party ran into the forest, slowing their pace to avoid the trees and better navigate the rocky terrain and bushy undergrowth.

"Pace, hold up!" Cain called. He'd heard the stories passed down through his family about the battles that his ancestors fought. He had played Braden versus the Bat-Ravens while growing up. All the kids in his family did. He'd always fancied himself a warrior. As the others stopped, he looked at his blaster. Play time was over. Now it was time to step up.

"Look at this area," Cain started, pointing to the small hills on either side of the cut they were running down. "Let's continue this way, tear up the undergrowth a bit to leave a trail, then we circle back on both sides overlooking this area. When they follow us through here, we drop that big tree in front of them, then we can fire down on them if they don't want to talk. We talk first, but we're ready to back it up with our blasters." Pace nodded and gestured for Pickles and Stinky to follow him as he pushed the floating commander in front of him. Cain and Ellie would take the opposite hillside. They waited, then made sure to stumble through enough bushes to leave a trail. After that, they carefully picked their way up the hillside and backtracked to gain the best vantage point. Pickles was designated to cut through the tree trunk as he was less accurate with the blaster, by his own admission. They figured that he simply didn't want to shoot anyone.

They couldn't blame him. They didn't want to either. Cain needed to know that he wouldn't fold under the pressure of battle, that he'd do what he had to. Ellie was cold and calculating about it. She hefted the blaster to get the feel and practiced aiming. She dialed in a narrow beam and settled in to wait.

The Hillcats appeared behind them as if by magic. *Where do you need us?'* Lutheann asked.

"Let us know when they enter this area, then cut off their retreat?" Cain asked, although it wasn't a question. He wanted their approval of his plan. Without a word, Lutheann and Carnesto padded away, back toward the mouth of the cut.

Chirit continued circling high above the group of men, seven of them, all carrying hand-held blasters, three with rifles, three with bows, and one older than the rest carrying a walking stick. They had reached the shuttle and walked around it, looking for a way in. The ladder and slide had been retracted when Jolly buttoned it up for them. The men seemed confused by the sounds coming from the ship, the sound of the oxygen/hydrogen generator refilling the storage tanks. The trail of the crew was easy to follow and soon it was obvious that was what they meant to do. They lined up, the men with the bows in front, then the older man, and the three men with rifles behind. They kept their weapons at the ready as they entered the forest, walking far more carefully than how they'd crossed the valley.

Chirit kept his Hawkoid eyes on them as they moved. Cain was pleased that they were following as he hoped. If they hadn't, there was no other plan. Although the group was well-armed, maybe they weren't used to operations against hostile humans. That gave them all hope. Cain shared his thoughts with Daksha, who felt the same. People who weren't good at making war might not be an enemy.

The group of men continued past the 'cats, who perched silently in the trees and out of sight of the men, who never bothered to look up. Cain chalked that one away for future reference. People tended to think two-dimensionally.

Into the area between the two groups of ambushers, they walked. Ellie raised her pistol over the rise before her and took aim. On Cain's order, Pickles fired, cutting cleanly through the large tree's trunk, starting a few small fires around it and beyond it. The men stopped when the blaster's narrow beam crackled the water in the trunk, popping and sizzling. The tree toppled, not directly across the cut as intended, but angled, back toward the men, who started shooting haphazardly at the hillside.

One Down, One to Go

The first shuttle matched the spin of the ship and eased in toward the portside airlock. When it touched the extended ring where the two ships would create a seal, Briz said one word to his terminal. "Now."

The EM drive cycled, instantly adding one gravity of thrust. The shuttle canted aft, impaling itself on the extended rod between the two I-beams. When it penetrated the skin of the ship and hit metal, power surged along its length, sending as much electricity as Briz thought the Cygnus-12 could spare into the Concordian shuttle. The lights on the intruders' ship exterior exploded as blue lines of power arced over the shuttle, sparking various systems to destruction. The shuttle ripped itself free of the power rod and drifted aft, yet another dead object floating in space.

"Yes!" Briz told his terminal. "Secure the EM drive," he added. He hadn't informed the crew of the maneuver and hoped that people weren't injured with the spaceship's sudden jerk forward.

Jolly was noticeably absent, but for the electrification stunt, the Rabbit didn't need him. Briz expected the AI was busy with the other shuttle. He tried to raise Jolly, but couldn't. Briz had never run into that before as his neural link with Jolly resulted in instantaneous communication and collaboration. Briz imagined the intruders had somehow cut Jolly off from the rest of the ship. That thought terrified him. He dug into his circuits and programs looking for the problem and soon forgot that a second shuttle was bearing down on them.

The second shuttle matched the spin of the ship, just like the first, and eased toward the airlock. With the size of the spindle section, it was possible that the second shuttle hadn't seen the demise of the first, although the instantaneous loss of communication should have suggested that something was wrong.

The second shuttle didn't seem bothered. It eased in, clamped onto the ring, and created the seal. Men rushed into the airlock and cycled it. They weren't wearing spacesuits, surprisingly, which could help the crew of the

Cygnus-12. First one man, then a second leaned out the hatch, pointing hand blasters. The Rabbits fired together. One shot scorched the bulkhead beside the hatch and the other hit the man full in the chest. He howled in pain and fell backward. Blasters were pointed out the hatch and fired down the corridor without aiming. Most weren't close, but the sheer volume of fire made the Rabbits retreat. The two humans and the Lizard Man waited. Blaster fire became better aimed and much of it splashed the open hatchway where they stood.

A crewman ran at the intruders from the opposite side, happy with the distraction from the others. Ensign Katlind swung at the first Concordian she saw, caving in his skull. She hit him a second time, just to be sure. She'd never killed anyone before. The ensign leaned back to swing at the next intruder coming through the airlock, but his blaster struck first. She gaped at the hole in her chest, frozen, surprised that she wasn't thrown backward. The pipe fell from fingers that she could no longer feel. Her legs giving out, she slumped against the bulkhead, wondering if this was it. Lindy didn't wonder long as the intruder shot her a second time and walked away.

Jolly, secure this hatch and blow the airlock. They aren't wearing suits! Jolly, where are you?' Rastor pleaded with the AI to help them as the first boarder stuck his blaster through the hatch. A viciously swung wrench broke his forearm and sent the blaster to the deck. The man called Bendall followed through, hitting the Concordian in the chest. Two blasters appeared from behind the injured man and fired into Bendall's face. He screamed, but only for a second as he crumpled. The second man, Gaven, dropped his wrench and picked up the dropped blaster, depressing the trigger and sending a beam of fire through the hatch at the boarding party. He kept the trigger depressed as he hosed the corridor with fire. The beam sputtered and the blaster died in his hand, but it bought them time. The survivors had retreated to the airlock and were plinking at the hatchway, short bursts of tight beams, hoping to catch a wayward arm from one of the ship's defenders.

"I can't raise Jolly. We'll have to manually close this hatch," Rastor told Gaven, who had picked up his wrench and now couldn't tear his eyes away from his friend, one of the other legacy crew members of the Cygnus-12. Rastor threw himself into pulling the hatch closed, his skin suit absorbing some but not all of the random hits from the blasters. Gaven joined him, slowly at first, but then put his shoulder into it. The hatch finally closed and they spun the actuator. Gaven's last act was to wedge his wrench into it and slow their ingress. In the interim, he hoped they'd be able to get Jolly to flush the corridor beyond, removing the air and killing the intruders.

"Jolly? Jolly, can you hear me?" Rastor continued to plead with the AI.

"Something happened and Jolly's gone. It's only us. So how do we manually vent the corridor on the other side of that hatch?" Rastor asked the other crewman. A loud clang answered them as one of the Concordians hit the hatch with something big and heavy. It sounded like a wrench, the one that his fellow crewman must have dropped into the corridor when he was shot.

The garden deck Rabbits were nowhere to be seen. *Briz? Are you there, Briz?* Rastor called using his neural implant. *Briz?*

"Jolly isn't answering and neither is Briz. What happened to that first shuttle? If Briz didn't take care of it, we're going to be trapped," Rastor said, wincing from the pain of his wounds. His skin suit hung in shreds, melted in places, ripped in others.

Take No Prisoners

"HOLD!" Master Daksha yelled with all the volume his vocalization device could muster. A couple more shots, and the men stopped firing. "We could have killed you easily, but chose not to. That's not our way. Why do you follow us, carrying weapons?"

The older Concordian walked toward the hillside. Not seeing anyone, he shrugged and yelled at the general area. "You scared our livestock with your landing in our valley. Then you ran carrying your weapons. We can only conclude that you are criminals who've stolen a ship or you are the start of an invasion of our area. In either case, we must defend ourselves. We've paid our tithes! We only ask to be left alone!"

"I think there's something that you haven't considered," the commander offered. "We are travelers, from a long ways away, and the people from the big city have misled us and are trying to steal our ship. We are like you. We only want to be left alone in peace. Put your weapons down and we will show ourselves so you can see that we aren't what you think we are," Master Daksha finished.

The old man argued with some of his people, then they put down their rifles, bows, and blasters. Pace stepped forward first, a brave act, if they had other weapons secreted away. Then Pickles joined him and the men shuffled their feet, looking frightened as the Lizard Man approached. They'd clearly never seen one of his kind before. Master Daksha floated over the rise and swam through the air toward them. Pace had holstered his blaster, but Cain and Ellie kept theirs trained on the backs of the shocked and unsuspecting men. The 'cats had climbed down the tree and now sat very close to the men, who hadn't noticed their approach. Chirit swooped close by them, and back-winged to a landing on a branch over their heads. Leaper joined them too, walking upright and showing his full height, equal with the Lizard Man.

"I am Commander Daksha of the spaceship Cygnus-12. We came here in peace from the Cygnus star system, exactly twelve hundred, thirty-five light years away. We are looking for a route back to Earth, as we all came from there. You see my crew and my friends, a Lizard Man, a Wolfoid, a Hawkoid, Hillcats, and I'm a Tortoid. We all have human DNA because of what the ancients did to help us better adapt to our home planet of Cygnus VII." Daksha waited for them to internalize his message.

Senior Lieutenant Pace walked toward them with his hand out. The men were human and shaking hands was universal, he hoped. "I'm Pace, Senior Lieutenant," he said simply. The older man hesitated briefly, then took the offered hand, gripping it firmly as he looked Pace in the eye.

'Are you two sensing anything?' Cain asked the 'cats using the mindlink.

'No. They are only herdsman, ranchers, and farmers. They are as angry with the authorities as you are.'

Cain shared the 'cats' insights with Master Daksha.

"Can you help us?" the Tortoid asked as he swam close and looked at the group of men before him. "We only need to buy time for our ship to refuel itself. Then we can return to our spaceship and continue on our way."

This started an argument among the men. Cain and Ellie stood, being sure to make plenty of noise as they climbed down the shallow slope. They holstered their blasters, trusting the 'cats' instincts and insight. The men continued to argue, claiming that anyone found helping the strangers would be punished. None of them wanted that.

Pace finally held up a hand and asked for quiet.

"We don't want to put you at risk, so return to your homes and forget that you ever saw us. We came in peace, and we'll leave in peace. That's all we wanted. It's too bad that we have to be afraid. I think there is much we could share, learn from each other," Pace said, sadness tingeing his voice.

"I've met my first aliens!" the small device around Black Leaper's neck projected loudly. The Wolfoid held a paw over his muzzle as he realized he'd blurted his thoughts out loud. His crewmates looked shocked, but the older man started to laugh and the others joined him as they looked at the creature, covered in rough black fur, standing upright on two back legs, and carrying a spear. The whites of his eyes showed beneath furry ears, above his long muzzle. Cain snickered first at his team leader, then he and Ellie joined the others standing in front of the Concordians. After a slap on the

Wolfoid's back, Cain took the time to shake each of the men's hands. Ellie followed, and the looks that the men were giving his wife made him uncomfortable. She could handle herself, although he waited for her to join him and made a show of holding her hand as they started walking back toward their shuttle.

Then they stopped to let the others pass. Trust was earned and they weren't yet at that point with these Concordians. Cain and Ellie had blasters and suggested they'd bring up the rear, keeping the 'cats close to watch for any duplicity. Pace nodded as he and Master Daksha led the older man down the cut and through the woods. The other members of the crew mixed in with the men, who started to talk freely, once they learned that they could readily communicate with the crew members from Vii.

The conversations varied, but were all based on learning about Cygnus VII. What was it like? They countered by asking what was it like on Concordia and what were the tithes that the villagers had paid.

"Daksha, you can call me Albert, of the village Fairsky. We manage the cattle herds, providing both milk and beef for the people of Concord, the capital city that you saw to the north."

"Cattle? From Earth? I suspect your ancestors settled here with fully intact spaceships then," Daksha said as he thought about the words that the man in the video shared.

"Yes, of course. Our ancestors arrived only a few hundred years ago. A colonization ship stopped here, woke half the passengers from their cryogenic sleep, put them on the planet with all the resources needed to establish a colony, and then the ship moved on. They left us with a couple shuttles, but that was it. You say you have a spaceship in orbit and you've traveled some twelve hundred light years to get here?"

Pace nodded and Albert continued, "They want your ship. Not this one, but the one that's in orbit. It's probably bigger, isn't it?"

"Yes, it is much bigger, as interstellar spaceships need to be. The power required for travel is rather extensive. We assumed the Concordians wanted the ship when we saw the two shuttles break out of the atmosphere after we were too far committed on our approach to the planet. We have a pretty spunky crew, though. I think the people on those ships won't be getting a warm welcome," Master Daksha said hopefully.

Kill them, kill them all.

Rastor gave up trying to contact anyone. "It's just us," he told the other man. "We don't have time to weld this hatch shut. Use the blaster and see if there's enough power to fuse the steel." The blaster lay on the floor next to the body of their crewmate. He picked it up, took aim at the mechanism, and fired. A small beam reached out, licked the steel, then died.

"I hope that was enough," Gaven said tentatively, still reeling from the loss of his friend. "Next deck up. Beneath the plates, we'll find atmospheric controls there. We might be able to vent the section."

"What are we waiting for?" Rastor said and grabbed a handful of the man's spacesuit as he leapt for the stairs, taking them two at a time heading upward, panting heavily as he left a trail of green blood behind him.

The man finally found his voice. "We have to avenge Bendall!" he cried

Rastor didn't slow down. He pushed forward, through the hatch and into the next level. Engineering was located there, along with secondary power generation. They didn't have far to run down the corridor before reaching the panel that Gaven indicated. He popped the quick connects and it up. A bank of lines and valves greeted him, along with a series of power conduits.

"It's pretty simple, actually. All we have to do is stop the flow of air into the corridor by closing this valve here," he said to himself as he cycled the handle and watched the indicator turn red. "Then we close this circuit, which is the failsafe to keep us from doing what we're about to do." Gaven ripped two wires out of a panel and spliced them, rolling the ends together.

"Then, we cycle this valve and there we have it!" The last valve flashed red, indicating that the section had been opened to space. He heard the whistling sound. "Wait, we shouldn't hear anything."

He turned to find Rastor, lying on the deck in a pool of his own blood. Beyond him, two men pointed blasters. He raised one hand while he tried to cycle the valve shut with the other. They shot him for his efforts to seal the ship, blasting him away from the open panel. The two Concordians approached, found both Cygnus crewmen to be dead, then checked the panel. Seeing only two valves that showed red, they cycled one, then the other. The whistling stopped and their ears popped as the air pressure balanced.

"Thank God. It's universal–green is good, red is wrong. What do you think this thing is?" The man nudged Rastor with his toe.

"I couldn't tell you, but it's dead now. I'd like to take that spear as a trophy, but I won't be able to sneak it back on the shuttle." He looked around to make sure no one was watching him as he tucked it into a nook in the corridor. "Let's clean out the rest of these freaks and take this ship!" he said to his partner, who smiled back and nodded.

They never saw the laser beams coming. One was shot through the neck, the other through the side of his head. They dropped, bloodlessly as their wounds were instantly cauterized by the power of the Rabbit's small laser pistols. Allard hopped to the hatchway and aimed inside, watching for more intruders. Beauchene checked on their crewmates, ears drooping when he found that neither was alive. They both ran toward engineering. They needed Briz's help.

The Concordians, They Come

Master Daksha and Albert were first from the woods, looking appreciatively at the shuttle from Cygnus-12.

"We're not alone," Pace whispered, seeing two men on the other side of the ship, studying it intently. Beyond those two was a small craft, with a bladed rotor on top of a bubble containing four seats. The engine was behind the bubble and there was a boom tail with a small, vertically oriented blade.

Where were the other two? Pace looked around frantically, sending Cain and Stinky one way, Ellie and Pickles the other. Pace pulled his blaster and got in front of the commander. The two men spotted them, positioned themselves behind the landing gear of the shuttle, and pointed weapons at the group.

"Put down your weapons!" one of them yelled. Pace looked back and watched the Concordians in the group meekly put their weapons on the ground and get on their knees. Albert shrugged and did the same, leaving Pace standing by himself. Chirit flew from the woods with Lutheann carefully balanced across his back. The Hawkoid struggled to rise above the trees, circling back over the forest to gain altitude.

Daksha asked Pace to put his blaster down and surrender as the others had. Cain, Stinky, Ellie, and Pickles had disappeared back into the woods.

The two men moved forward. Two other men appeared from behind their craft where'd they'd been unloading equipment of some sort. They joined their fellows, brandishing their blasters as they looked at the group in front of them.

"Aliens and traitors," one man spat, waving his blaster at the men on their knees. "And what the hell is this thing?" he snarled at the Tortoid.

"I am Commander Daksha," he answered. "Of the Space Exploration Service. We come in peace."

"Then you come as idiots," he shot back, scowling, carefully aiming his blaster at the Tortoid's head.

Chirit circled far to the side of the valley and glided in behind the Concordian aerial vehicle. Lutheann jumped to the ground when she could and Chirit rapidly gained altitude, reveling in the freedom of flight, knowing that on this world, his abilities were more unique than anything he could do aboard the ship.

Lutheann slinked to the landing struts of the shuttle, then padded silently forward toward the backs of the men with weapons, as Cain had asked her to, to stop the man threatening the commander. Blasters were trained on the other hostile Concordians from the forest, while Carnesto crouched between the villagers, trying to look inconspicuous, but one of the Concordians was eyeing him, unsure of what he was looking at.

When Lutheann attacks, fire. Please do not miss. Master Daksha, please float lower to the ground. Lutheann. You're up,' Cain instructed over the mindlink. The Tortoid descended until his thick feet touched the ground. The Hillcat, without a sound, leapt and landed on the scowling man's back, one claw ripping into his arm, making him drop his blaster. He screamed like a little girl as claws dug into his flesh, shredding his back, while seeking his throat for a killing blow. Narrow blaster beams licked out from the tree line, taking the other three men unaware. As the hostiles fell, the blaster fire stopped.

Carnesto pounced on the nearest man who had fallen, but was uninjured. The 'cat kicked the man's blaster away, then snarled in his face, showing his fangs and holding one paw high, claws ready to slash. The man froze. Pace was on him in an instant, twisting the man's arm savagely behind his back.

The man Lutheann had attacked whined and pleaded for his life while blood readily flowed from his wounds. The four crew members ran from the trees to take up positions around the Concordians.

"Why did you make us do that?" Daksha 'yelled' at the dying man. "We came in peace. Why wouldn't you just talk with us?" The Tortoid hovered over the man and watched as his eyes fluttered, before he collapsed.

The commander swam through the air until he was close to the man that Senior Lieutenant Pace held. He hovered for a few seconds, then turned to Albert. "Take your men and go. Forget you ever saw us. It looks like these men hate everyone, no matter who you are. How did they ever get to be in charge?"

"That's a long story, my friend, and I hope it's okay that I call you that. You've shown more care for our well-being than our own people." He waved his arm at his men, who were more than happy to go. They gathered their weapons and set off at a run, trying to put as much distance as possible between themselves and the dead men. They knew that there would be hell to pay, and they didn't want to be on the receiving end of it. Albert had been around long enough to know that when hell came, it wouldn't matter what they claimed. The government's men were dead in their valley. No one would come out of this unscathed.

Master Daksha turned toward the man who was still struggling within Pace's grasp. Cain offered a helping hand by taking the man's other arm and bending it backward against the elbow. He held his head high as he grunted in pain. Carnesto put his claws against the man's throat.

"Hold," Master Daksha said. "Is this really who we are?" Cain and Pace were angry, but pulled back, securing the man's arms without forcing him to be in pain.

The 'cat had never drawn the blood of a human before and found it to be a guilty pleasure. Lutheann sat idly by, licking the blood from her paws, close enough to her kill to be energized by it, but not close enough to get any more on her fur. Carnesto retracted his claw and before the man's eyes, licked the human's blood from the tip of his razor-sharp claw.

"Tell us, why did you come after us?" Master Daksha asked, beginning the interrogation of their prisoner.

"Because you didn't land where you were supposed to. Everything would have been clean if you had," he answered.

"Yes, I suppose so, clean for you, anyway. I suspect we would have been taken prisoner and judging by your reaction to the variety of people who arrived here from Cygnus VII, we probably would have been treated like animals, not equal to humans." The Tortoid hovered close, looking at the man's eyes without blinking, which the other found unnerving. He wouldn't look at the Tortoid.

Lutheann? Carnesto? Can you give us any insight?' Cain asked over the mindlink. The Hillcats could see into any human mind and know what they thought. They generally avoided that, for their own sanity as they considered human minds too chaotic, human emotions too strong.

'Yes. He's afraid that he'll be punished for failure. He's afraid of us, how quickly we dispatched the others in his group, especially with my, we'll call it an intervention of his leader. They are not used to being challenged. He doesn't know what to do,' Lutheann answered.

"So, you aren't used to being challenged? We will let you go, as soon as we can leave ourselves, and we'll be done with your planet. We'll mark this system as off limits and no one will ever return here. That's what your leaders want, that's what they'll get." Daksha spoke calmly while the man became more agitated.

'The people in the village are doomed when he is free,' Lutheann added unnecessarily.

"If anyone should seek revenge, my good man, it should be us. We can't have you harming the good people of Fairsky. You know something? They're afraid, too. They thought we were from Concord, here to punish them for some perceived slight. Is that how you do it? Rule with an iron fist? Anything other than strict obedience is punished." Daksha backed away from the man.

"Tie him to a tree. Chirit, if you would be so kind as to see what there is to see, look beyond the valley and tell us what's out there, I would appreciate it. Pace, please check the ship. We need to leave as soon as possible, so how long will that be? Pickles, please find us some water. Cain, Ellie, and the 'cats, maybe you can hunt something for all of us to eat. Leaper, if you could stay with me, I would feel much safer." Master Daksha swam toward the ship and floated upward. He used his neural implant to directly activate the ship's hatch. Chirit winged away, catching an updraft at the edge of the valley and soaring quickly to great heights. Once the Concordian was tied up, the others disappeared on their individual tasks.

Leaper stayed at the bottom of the ladder, watching the man struggle against his bonds. Leaper had put his spear aside and cradled one of the blasters instead. The other recovered blasters went to the humans of the crew as they were fitted exclusively for their hands and not a Wolfoid's paw, which had fingers but wasn't quite a hand. He could shoot the blaster if need be, as a test shot into the open valley confirmed. He walked close to the man, hoping to intimidate him until he stopped fighting. They stood and looked at each other.

"We abolished your way of life on Vii some one hundred, thirty-five years ago. My ancestors and those of this crew established the Council of Elders with representatives from all species to lead the people of Vii. They created the pure-heart test that only the 'cats and the Tortoids can administer. No one who is self-serving or power-mad will ever attain a position of authority over others. It has served us well and will continue as far into the future as we can see. Our way has allowed us to achieve space flight, where we can travel to the stars. Your way won't get you any of that. I thought you should know. Now, stop fighting against your ropes. The only value you have to us is that we can rest easier knowing that we didn't kill an unarmed man. Should you free yourself, one of the Hillcats will run you down and rip your throat out. The choice is yours." Leaper only guessed that Lutheann or Carnesto would revel in hunting a human with misplaced morals.

Leaper returned to his place at the bottom of the shuttle's ladder, noting that the human had stopped struggling and was sitting still, looking around him as if the Hillcats were ready to pounce. The Wolfoid figured his side task of guarding the prisoner had just become a whole lot easier.

Inside the shuttle, Pace shook his head. "Three more days, Master Daksha, and that's with us leaving at seventy percent of a full load. That will get us into space, but we'll run out of fuel as soon as we leave orbit. The Cygnus will probably have to come get us, but right now, I can't reach Jolly and that concerns me."

"Me, too," Daksha replied. "Three days. Is there any way we can hide the shuttle? Can we use their flying machine to help ourselves in some way?" Pace didn't know. He continued to check the shuttle's systems. Their approach and landing had been normal and all systems remained operational. They left the shuttle and sealed it behind them.

Their inability to contact Jolly was disconcerting, to say the least.

Chirit showed them the valley and the slopes beyond, leading to a great ocean. He also showed them more of the Concordian flying machines heading their way. Ten more, to be exact. "That's forty more people, with blasters. We can't fight that many," Pace said.

"No, we can't," Master Daksha conceded. "Let's use the woods as cover and work our way toward the village. They have the manpower to even the odds, and they aren't too happy with the powers that be. But, we'd put them at risk. Maybe hiding in the woods is the best option," Master Daksha thought out loud.

"Save the ship," Pace said. "We have to save the ship."

"We have another shuttle on board that can come and get us. We have to save the Cygnus-12 to have any hope. This shuttle here is useless if we don't have a spaceship to go home to. Recall everyone and then we'll head into the woods. Maybe at some point we'll be able to talk with Jolly, or anyone from the ship, find out that they are okay."

"What about him?" Pace asked.

"Let him go. We killed the others and won't be able to hide that. At least he knows the truth of why. Even if he lies, it can't be worse than any story they'd come up with to fill the void of information. Maybe our 'cat friends can get into his mind and force him to tell the truth?" Daksha suggested.

"Maybe, Commander. But for now, we need to go if we want to put any distance between us and the incoming Concordians." Pace used his neural implant to recall the crew. Leaper untied the prisoner and shooed him away, into the valley. The man started slowly, but a short burst from the blaster sent the man running.

The others were too far away for a quick return. With Chirit's help, they selected a clearing deep in the woods where they could meet and decide what to do next. Pushing the Tortoid between them, Pace and Leaper headed into the forest, taking the same path they had before. They left the bodies of the dead in the valley, lying in the shadow of their shuttle. Their former prisoner was running like a madman toward Fairsky. The landing party plunged into the foreign woods, leaving all that they knew behind them.

Deck by Deck

Allard and Beauchene ran into engineering where their fellow Rabbit was working feverishly on the computer.

"Have you figured a way to lock out the intruders?" Allard asked.

"Intruders?" Briz asked, confused.

"They're in the ship, Briz! Two of them were on this deck, and they're killing the crew!" Beauchene yelled.

"Killing the crew!" Briz repeated. He stopped his attempts to find where Jolly had gone and started bringing up the monitors showing the passageways of the ship, starting with those that sensed movement. Seven different screens displayed a total of ten intruders. They were on every deck but Briz's. He cycled the cameras showing the engineering section and corridors beyond. He stopped when he saw the four bodies. "Our people."

"And two of theirs," Allard said darkly.

"So what do we do?" Beauchene asked of the engineer.

"How am I supposed to know?" Briz countered, feeling the weight of the ship's safety on his shoulders. They watched as two intruders approached the command deck where the captain waited beside the hatch, holding something that looked like a length of pipe. Tandry was away from the door, facing it. Mixial was nowhere to be seen.

'Captain, you have two men just outside your hatch. They look ready to enter,' Briz passed over the neural implant. The captain did not respond using the implant, but nodded and firmed up his grip on the pipe.

One intruder stood back while the other activated the manual open on the hatch. It slid aside soundlessly. Tandry screamed and then put her hands up, not taking her eyes from them. The men looked through the hatch, but didn't see anything as the captain was pressed flat against the bulkhead. The closest man moved tentatively forward, keeping his blaster trained on Tandry. When he stepped through the hatch, Mixial dropped on him from above, scratching and clawing his head and neck. The other man jumped forward, trying to get a clear shot. The captain swung the pipe as if he were attempting to fell a tree with a single swing. The man's face seemed to wrap around the pipe as the Rabbits watched, horrified at the abject violence. Captain Rand let the pipe go as he turned to wrestle the blaster from the other Concordian.

Mixial had done her job well. The blaster was already on the deck and the man bled profusely from the wounds on his head and neck. Both hands dangled from shredded wrists. The 'cat jumped away, turning when she hit the deck, ready to reengage with the intruder, but there was no need. He swayed and fell, slapping the deck and spraying blood. The captain picked up the two blasters, handing one to Tandry, who had acted as bait to draw them in. She looked as determined as everyone else fighting against the intruders to their ship.

'I see no others on your deck, Captain,' Briz switched to the mindlink as he stood up, preparing to leave engineering.

"Wait! We can't guide them to the other boarders if we leave. The captain and the other two can clear the ship if we just stay here and tell them where to go!"

"I can do that no matter where I am in the ship. I've made some adjustments to my implant's interface. You have laser pistols and we need to help. Look there! They have six of our people trapped on the mess deck and another ten in billeting one deck above us. If we don't do something…" Briz let that trail off as he brought up the picture of the dead crew in the corridor just outside.

Briz looked from Allard to Beauchene. "The ship is life, save the ship," he said, grim determination in his voice, his vocalization device conveying his thoughts as he intended. "Let's get those two who are in your house." He nodded to the other two Rabbits and they hopped toward the door, happy to have Briz with them. They stopped by their dead crewmates first. Briz choked from the smell as he dug the blasters out from under the intruders.

'Captain, we're headed to the garden deck. If you take the stairs down from where you are, wait before entering. The Concordians are near that hatch. We will come in from the other side and flush them toward you. We have two laser pistols and two blasters.

These intruders won't know what hit them,' Briz offered. The captain acknowledged.

Rand seethed with anger. His ship had been befouled by the inhabitants of Concordia. Members of his crew were dead. Parts of the ship were damaged. Blasters were fired inside his precious and sensitive ship! He would berate himself later on how he'd let it happen, but the first thing he needed to do was secure the ship. Mixial went first, leaving bloody paw prints on the deck as she headed for the stairway. The captain followed and Tandry watched behind them.

The Rabbits bounded up the steps in the stairwell on the opposite side of the ship from where the captain descended. Knowing that the intruders were on the other side of the deck, the Rabbits raced up the two flights and ran through the hatch. Allard and Beauchene went one way and Briz went the other. It took no time before all three groups were converging on the intruders who were digging through the plants and helping themselves to some of the fresh vegetables. Briz fired first from a position behind a small bush. He missed, because he was a terrible shot. The other two were growing more confident. Their shots grazed one of the men. He howled in pain as the two intruders fired back, not aiming, just firing and running away from the threat.

Rand and Tandry stood ready, blasters aimed at the closed hatch. Even though they were ready for it, when it opened, they were surprised, but the Concordians weren't looking their way. Rand and Tandry fired, their narrow beams burning deep into the chests of both men. The intruders were thrown backwards, landing in heaps where they flopped until death.

Tandry vomited, spraying the captain and the deck before the hatchway. The captain gagged a couple times, then walked through, not looking at the mess behind him. He bent and picked up the men's blasters. Tandry tried to apologize, but Rand shook his head. "It's a horrible day for all of us. I hope we never forget the lessons we're learning here. Briz, how many left and where are they?" he asked as the Rabbits converged on their captain.

"Six. They've breached the mess deck, but the crew in billeting is holding them off," Briz reported.

"Down this stairwell and we come in behind them. Will the others in the corridor see us?" the captain asked. Briz nodded. "Then we need another diversion." Rand pursed his lips in thought. The garden deck Rabbits fussed over some damaged plants, making repairs as they could, reinforcing the dirt around the roots, and trying to put some normalcy back into their lives.

"If we could flood the deck with smoke, I think that would be to our advantage."

Briz shook his head, his big ears flopping back and forth. "Since there's more of us than them, we stand a greater chance of shooting our own people. Maybe we do like we did here. We attack on two fronts. Rabbits from the billeting side and you from this side. You clear the mess deck and we'll take care of the men in the corridor."

"You'll be exposed," Rand countered.

"Rabbits can run fast, turn sharply. We will make ourselves hard targets." The captain looked at the scar running across Briz's chest. His new fur had barely begun to grow out. The small Rabbit looked a mess, but the sparkle in his eyes said that he was determined to wrest the ship from Concordian control. The captain shared the same determination. He held out his human hand and the engineer took it.

Briz called to the other two Rabbits as he ran past, heading for the stairs opposite where the humans stood.

Tandry watched them go. She was spent. Her commitment had shattered with the first man she'd killed. Mixial tried to soothe her. The 'cat's first human victim was an ugly mess, and it was right in front of Tandry. She'd watched, but it didn't become personal until she herself had pulled the trigger. The captain understood as her emotions pulled her to a dark place. Mixial rubbed against her, purring loudly.

"Tandry, I need you with me. I can't take them alone. We have to do this together." She sat on the first step of the stairway, hugging her knees to her chest and rocking. She shook her head vigorously as the captain tried to calm her.

'We're in place and ready to go. Just give the word,' Briz passed via the neural implant.

'Hold on, Briz. We have a slight issue here. Soon. I'll let you know. Stay hidden!' the captain ordered.

'We need to hurry, Captain. I think the Concordians have explosives and are preparing to blast the hatch to billeting,' Briz said, anxiety creeping into his voice.

"Tandry! We have to go, now." She continued to shake her head. He grabbed her by her shoulders and roughly pulled her upright. "Ensign!" he snapped, inches from her face.

"Save the ship!" he growled. "We have no time for this. Mixial?" Rand asked. The 'cat continued to rub against her human's legs. He shoved Tandry away from him. The captain wrapped his hands around the handles of the two blasters, testing their weight and checking the dial for the settings. Ancient technology, identical to what they had on Vii. Maybe Concordia had a civil war just like on Cygnus VII, halting continued development.

Or maybe they thought they had developed enough, until they saw the Cygnus-12. Greed. Envy. Fear. They were driven for some reason to lie, steal, and murder. The captain drove himself into a rage.

He snarled as he stepped around the ensign, heading down the steps to the next level, where the mess deck was located. When he reached the hatch, he found it closed. As soon as he opened it, they'd know he was there, unless they were looking the other way, which was Briz's plan. His hand hovered over the manual open switch.

'I'm in place, Briz. When you go, I'll count to three and then open the hatch,' he told them, then added, *'and good luck, my friends. Save the ship.'*

'Save the ship,' the Rabbits responded together. Without waiting, Briz activated the hatch and the three Rabbits bounded through then bolted down the corridor. They jerked one way then another as they ran, occasionally jumping off the walls to foil their enemy's aim. But the two men were working on the hatch, their blasters at their feet. The Rabbits caught them by surprise and they hesitated, taken aback by the mad rush of harmless looking, fuzzy white creatures. Until the laser pistols lit up. The shots were sporadic, but with the only targets being the two humans crouched before the hatch to billeting, they hit as much as they missed.

When Briz touched the trigger on his blaster, it sprayed a wide flame over the two men. They screamed and batted helplessly at the fire, then they ran down the corridor away from their attackers. They didn't make it far as the combination of blaster fire and lasers cut them down.

The captain was forcing himself to count slowly. Maybe too slowly, he thought as he heard the screams when the hatch slid open before him. He took two steps into the corridor as the flaming figures fell, burning and dying in the corridor leading away from him, away from the mess deck. The corridor curved upward to his right where billeting was just beyond what he could see.

He had no time to worry about the Rabbits or the other crew. His people on the mess deck had barricaded themselves and were throwing anything at hand to hold their attackers at bay. One man stuck his head into the corridor to see what the screaming was about. The captain fired both blasters, neither accurately, but by waving the tips around, the narrow beam found its target and threw the intruder into the hatch frame, where he collapsed.

"Hey!" a shout rose from within carrying the accent of the Concordians. "Mack!"

Blaster fire splashed through the hatch and into the corridor. The crew inside knew their captain was coming, because he'd let them know by way of their neural implants. They'd built a barricade from some of the furniture, ripping it free from its restraints. With his crew's limited projectiles, it was surprising that the Concordians hadn't simply flamed the place and sealed it off. Maybe they decided that they needed a certain number of the crew to teach them how to operate the spaceship, something the captain hoped none of them would do willingly.

But he'd never been tortured. It wasn't a part of their training. They were explorers, not soldiers.

The captain jumped to the hatch and leaned an arm around it, aiming his blaster inside. The intruder fired first, hitting the captain's arm and horribly burning it. The captain screamed and fell, dropping his second blaster and rolling into the corridor. The intruder fired at the barricade of the defenders and moved to the side of the hatch, expecting a second attacker, assuming they traveled in pairs as the Concordians did.

"I'm the captain," Rand gasped as he held his arm, writhing in agony. The two bodies not far from him smoked, clouding the corridor and warranting a flashing red light. Briz was barely visible beyond, working on the device that the intruders had been attaching. "I'm the captain," he said one last time, barely audible, before he passed out.

The Concordians Are Gaining on You

The ten flying machines circled Cygnus-12's shuttle before landing in a wide semi-circle around it and the other machine parked nearby. Men poured out of the machines and arrayed themselves, weapons pointed menacingly toward the woods.

Master Daksha and the others were nowhere near. Chirit circled far to the side and high above the woods as he watched the Concordians, looking for whether they'd follow and how.

Their former prisoner stopped once he saw the inbound flying machines. He turned and waved to his comrades as he started walking back toward the shuttle.

The crew members from the Cygnus-12 quickly reached the small opening that Chirit had directed them to, some breathing more heavily than others. The 'cats were in the trees, legs dangling, looking relaxed as they watched and reached into the woods with their other senses.

"Distance. The more distance we put between us, the better off we'll be. There's one minor drawback, though. I fear that we might have to make Concordia our home. We haven't heard from Jolly since before we landed, about the time that the shuttles would have attacked the ship. We have to think like help's not coming," Cain suggested.

The Tortoid bobbed his head slowly as he thought about their options. He was having no luck as he fixated on the possible loss of the ship, trapped on a distant planet with no way to tell the SES where they were or what happened. And it was all his fault. His thoughts were dark with guilt.

"The hills. We have to put distance between us. Those flying machines of theirs had to weave as they entered the valley. The easiest way would have been for them to fly over the hills, but they didn't. I think they might be limited in how high they can go. So we climb, away from them, out of their reach," Pace offered.

Cain was fresh out of ideas. His ancestors had never had to run from an army while on a strange planet, with no friends to help them and no sanctuary to hide within. For the first time, he felt real fear reaching for him, the type of fear that could cripple a person. He gripped Ellie's hand tightly, happy to have her by his side. He was committed to protecting her, to give him a reason to keep going when all he wanted was to be back on the ship.

"We survive," he said out loud, talking as much to himself as the others. "I want to believe that the ship is still there. I don't know why our neural implants aren't allowing us to talk with them, but we'd know if something happened to the ship. We survive so the other shuttle can come get us. Then we leave this forsaken hell hole."

"I'll second that," Pace said, looking at the faces of those around him.

'Half of them are entering the woods, following your tracks,' Chirit reported over the mindlink. *'The others are spreading out, some back to their machines and others to the shuttle.'*

'Thanks, Chirit. Are there any birds here? I haven't heard a sound since we landed, not birds, not animals besides the livestock in the valley. Make sure they don't see you,' Pace commented. The Hawkoid flew higher and looked toward the sea, where there should have been birds. Maybe that was why the Concordians never looked up. There was nothing there.

The 'cats confirmed that there was wildlife, small creatures like squirrels and larger game like deer. They had yet to see any, but they sensed it was there and with that, could hunt it and kill it. They wouldn't want for something to eat. The longer the Hillcats went without food, the more deadly they'd become to anything that moved.

Master Daksha apologized for having to be pushed, until they found a vine that they could use as a rope. They tied this around Pace's waist and the Tortoid held the other end firmly in his beak-like mouth. Leaper and Carnesto raced ahead of the group, running fast on all fours. They scouted a route that took them away from the valley, away from Fairsky and toward the highest peak of the mountain range beyond.

Chirit circled, watching the progress of the men, but as the tree cover became heavier, he had to get closer to see. Blaster beams reached through the leaves, tracing lines of ozone all around him. He swerved and dove away, then flew past at high speed, heading in a direction ninety degrees to the route taken by his crewmates. He continued climbing slowly as he hoped to lead the Concordians astray. More beams licked out through the leaves, but they weren't a threat to him as put greater and greater distance between him and the attackers. He suddenly dove and skimmed the treetops as he flew toward his friends. Now that the others knew, he wouldn't be able to fly at all where he could be seen. The Concordians would be on the lookout for the alien in the sky.

'Sorry, but they're on to me,' Chirit apologized to the others.

'It's okay, my friend. Why aren't there any birds here? Maybe we'll find that out someday, should the Concordians choose peace, although I hope we don't have to wait long. Our crewmates will come for us. Believe that. They will come, and then maybe we can talk with the Concordians like adults,' Master Daksha said firmly in his thought voice.

They continued to hike through the woods, trying not to upset the undergrowth and leave a trace of their passing. Cain and Pickles both had knowledge of woodcraft, but the undergrowth wasn't like anything they were used to on Vii. As Cain looked back, he saw that a child could follow their trail.

"Pickles, let's clean this up and then leave some false trails," Cain suggested. The Lizard Man nodded, happier aboard a spaceship than traipsing around the woods in his skin suit, but he backtracked with Cain, brushing the grasses upright and sweeping their tracks from bare ground.

Cain, Pickles, and Lutheann raced off together, leaving tracks and broken branches to mark their passing. With a combination of Lizard Man boot prints and his own human boots, they left a trail deep into the woods that angled away from the original path. Once they found a stream, they waded through it, drinking and filling their flasks, before continuing.

Cain hadn't realized how thirsty he was or how dry Pickles had become. The Lizard Man submerged himself completely to rehydrate his suit. He floated in the water, but Cain could only guess that Pickles was happy. No human could read a Lizard Man's expression.

"We'll need to go soon," Cain urged, seeing that Lutheann stayed on the edge of the stream. She had no intention of jumping in.

'You're coming back to this side, right?' she said nonchalantly in her thought voice.

"Yes. We'll head out this way, leave some tracks, double back, head upstream as far as we can go, then cut back toward the others. Do you sense anything?"

'You should hurry,' she told them. Pickles immediately got out of the water, knowing that he'd be able to get back into it shortly for their trip upstream.

They ran from the water, tearing out plants as they climbed a small bank and dove into the woods. They had covered a short distance when Lutheann spoke to them over the mindlink. *'Change of plans. Turn right and pick up the pace. The first Concordians are in the stream and running after you.'*

'We can't speed up without leaving a trail. How many are there?' Cain asked.

'Four. The others are farther back. Much farther, but they follow these men on your trail. I will join you shortly.'

'Means they aren't following the others. What do you think, Pickles, a little ambush to show them that following us isn't a healthy way to live?' Cain said confidently in his thought voice. He wondered briefly how Lutheann was going to cross the stream, then cast it from his mind. Some things he simply needed to accept.

'I am not a good shot, my friend. I fear that I will be no help to you,' Pickles replied.

'Can you do the Lizard Man trick where you blend into a tree, make yourself invisible?'

'Yes, but only if I'm not wearing my skin suit. All Lizard Men can do this. It's in our genetic makeup.'

'Then we can use that. We'll find a big tree. They'll run past. You shoot them from behind, just spray the blaster fire in their direction and I'll be at their flank to finish them off. Can you do that?' Cain had no other plan and he was breathing heavily. They were running faster, but leaving a trail that was easier to follow. They weren't going to get away by making a false trail, because this was their real trail. They'd led the men away from the others, but directly to themselves.

'I've never shot anyone before,' the Lizard Man sadly stated.

'I'm new to it myself,' Cain tried to counter, but he'd fought the Android on the Traveler and had demonstrated that he was cool under fire, almost reveling in battle.

'I will count on you to clean up whatever mess I make of this, and you, too, Lutheann.'

"All we can do is the best we can do, my friend," Cain panted out loud. "Up here. Use this tree and I'll be over there, behind those rocks. We leave tracks just far enough beyond that area to draw them through." They ran twenty paces beyond a large tree that looked like an oak from back home. Pickles undressed and stuffed his suit under a bush. He held his blaster behind him as he leaned up against the tree and blended in with its bark.

The Hillcat disappeared into the brush. She was all white and wasn't as easy to conceal as the all black Carnesto, so she made herself scarce and if needed, she'd appear. She knew to stay clear of the blaster fire. She was still fired up from her previous kill and was more than willing to do it again, so she waited, maybe closer than she should have, but she had confidence that her abilities far exceeded those of the Concordians.

Cain picked his way around the small hill, taking care not to disturb any of the undergrowth. He crawled the last few feet into position as he heard the heavy pounding of men approaching at a dead run. Pickles was talking to him over the mindlink, encouraging him to hurry.

The men ran past, quicker than Pickles expected. When he stepped from the tree, the Concordians were already fifteen paces past. He fired into the ground behind the men, then waved the blaster, sending a thin flame through two of them and into the trees above. The other two dove away from the attack. Cain took aim and three narrow-beam blasts later, had taken the third man down. The fourth man had found cover and was firing back. Pickles dodged behind the tree and stopped firing. The man concentrated his blasts at Cain's position.

A white streak appeared on the trail and Cain fired quickly in the man's direction to keep him from seeing. The man lifted his blaster to return fire when Lutheann jumped from a full sprint, landing on his chest and knocking him backward. Cain scrambled from his position and ran after her. Pickles peeked out from behind his tree.

The Hillcat ripped and shredded, then jumped away. The man turned, blaster still in hand. She jumped on his arm and tore the weapon from his hand, then dashed way, returning from a different direction moments later.

Cain stayed back as Lutheann worked the man over. When he fell, she had him, slashing his neck and ending his life.

'Thanks, Pickles. You did what you had to do, and you saved us,' Cain said over the mindlink, knowing that his crewmate was distraught. Cain pointed to the bush where the skin suit was hidden. 'We need to go. This time, we leave no trail. Back to the stream and then we follow it as far as we can, before angling back toward the others. No trail,' Cain cautioned.

While Pickles got dressed, Cain collected the gear from the men, flasks, rations, blasters, but no other technology that he could see. Maybe they had neural implants like the crew from Cygnus-12, but he wasn't sure. These men looked hard, like they lived lives outside working with their hands. They didn't seem the type who used high technology, or something like a fabricator to deliver their food and server bots to clean their rooms.

"They're behind us, technologically. They are where we were one hundred, thirty-some years ago. But they don't have a Free Trader Braden with a vision and a Hillcat to help them see a better future. Maybe we could be that for them?" Cain said as Pickles finished and joined him, looking at the bodies of the Concordians.

"Are you delusional?" Pickles asked in shock. "They have an army of people trying to kill us. The population is afraid of them and they look on me and the others as freaks! No. We won't be the ones to enlighten them. We need to survive just until we can get out of here."

"I'm sorry, Pickles. You are right, of course, but who doesn't want to be the next Braden, the one who brought peace and a new era to Vii?" Cain slapped the Lizard Man's back and nodded. They headed into the woods, moving much slower as they used branches to brush their tracks and leave no trace of their passing. Lutheann padded into the brush and disappeared from sight as she moved ahead, making sure their way was clear.

They're in the Engine Room!

The intruder looked through the hatch at the body of the ship's captain. He looked back at the barricade and sensed that he'd broken their will to fight.

With a heavy accent, he instructed the crew as to what would come next. "Come out and no one else gets hurt. We want the ship. You want to live. You teach us what we need to know, then we all win. You might even be able to remain and crew the ship for us," he said as he stood, letting the blaster hang from his hand at his side.

The crew stood from behind the barricade, heads bowed in shame as they surrendered.

The man turned and stepped into the corridor, looking down at the captain.

He never saw the blaster beam that tore into his chest. Tandry stood there, holding the trigger down, frozen as she fired. The man launched backwards into the hatch frame, locked into position by the continuous fire.

A long-haired calico Hillcat bumped her hard, shaking her focus. She let off the trigger and watched the man collapse in a heap. The crew rushed from the mess deck, one took the dead man's blaster and two others came to the captain's aid. They wrapped an undershirt around his arm as they lifted him between them. The med lab was down the corridor, past billeting. They carried him around the two burnt bodies, tried not to disturb Briz as he worked to disarm the explosive device, and then into the med lab. The bots immediately took over.

Briz joined the group after he removed the device and those inside opened the hatch. Twenty crew and one Hillcat stood outside the med lab as the bots worked on the captain.

"How many are left on board our ship, Briz?" Tandry asked coldly as she fingered the blaster she still carried. Once she crossed the line of killing her second human being, she hardened. She was no longer tormented by the look of the first man she killed. She didn't think she could do it a second time until she saw the Captain Rand and blamed herself for not being there to keep him from getting hurt. She wouldn't make that mistake again.

Briz accessed the systems and found the last two. "They're in the ISE, checking out the engine. I need to get back to engineering!" Briz ran off before he told anyone why.

Tandry and Mixial followed Briz. Allard and Beauchene headed toward the stairs to the garden deck. The others milled about uncertainly. Sensor operators, mechanics, logisticians, a pilot. All were trained and cross-trained by the SES to be the best spacers they could be. None of that included military operations. They looked at each other and shifted uncomfortably. The only ones who remained in the corridor were human.

The oldest crew member, a lieutenant commander who specialized in life support, held up his hand to get everyone's attention.

"I think we're all afraid. I, for one, can only guess at what to do next. We have intruders on board our ship. There's only two of them left thanks to the heroic efforts of our captain and our crewmates. We know some of our crew have been killed. Others are on the planet, fighting for their lives, running for their lives, or already dead. We don't know because Jolly is nowhere to be found. We are in trouble, but there's nothing we can do if we don't help ourselves, if we don't retake our ship. Then we can figure out how to get our people back from the planet. We have blasters and we have the numbers. Let's go to the ISE and root them out of there!" Some of the others cheered, but the group was sedate.

"I don't think we should use blasters near the ISE. Dark matter is funneled through there," a maintenance crew member said, her voice small as she knew she was dampening their spirit. They all felt like they needed to do something.

"Good point, Cass," he nodded at his crewmate. "How about this... We put people at every exit from the ISE and then shoot them when they come out. They'll have to leave sometime." The others agreed and all of them jogged toward the stairway down, past engineering and power generation to the inner most ring of the spinning core, where the ISE and the dark matter banking system occupied the entire deck.

The group split up to camp outside the four separate hatches, three to the ISE, which was a complex space with numerous nooks and crannies, and one to the dark matter banking control room, which was a small place with limited systems and nowhere to hide.

Garinst, the lieutenant commander, accessed his neural implant and tried to raise Briz, but couldn't get him, so he sent one of his group to engineering to check on the young Rabbit. The rest waited, watching and nervously fingering blasters. Garinst wasn't military, but he understood that the safety of the ship came first. He cautioned those with blasters to be ready, but not to fire into the ISE space and not to accidentally pull the trigger. He put two people to the side of each hatch to grab the intruders should they choose to leave the engine room. Maybe they wouldn't have to kill them and that would make them feel better. As it was, they couldn't account for too many of the crew. They assumed they were dead, as many as eleven of their crewmates.

He shook off that concern. Save the ship first. Then they could take care of everything else.

When the crewman entered engineering, he found Briz fully embroiled in his keyboard and monitors. He pecked furiously to input long strings of commands.

"What are you working on, Briz? We need your help!" the young man pleaded.

The Rabbit didn't respond as he kept poking away, The man waited, impatiently. He had finally decided to grab the Rabbit to get his attention when Briz hit the enter key one last time and jumped up, startling his crewmate.

"Damn, Briz!" The man jumped back out of the Rabbit's way.

"Oh! I didn't see you come in. Wait a minute. I have to check two things and then we can do this." Briz disappeared into his own mind as he linked with the systems through his neural implant. He found the crew stationed around the closed hatches but outside the ISE. The two intruders were inside. "Perfect."

Briz pressed enter, setting off alarms and making the red warning lights flash as the ISE was flooded with argon gas like the engine room was on fire. Briz bounced up and down on his big back feet as his eyes stayed unfocused. He accessed the ship-wide communication system and spoke clearly. "All intruders have been eliminated. The ship is ours," Briz said proudly.

Hide

Cain, Pickles, and Lutheann met up with the others without further incident. The 'cats couldn't sense another human near them as they struggled upward, climbing past the hills and into the mountains.

"They must have abandoned the chase," Cain suggested as they huddled among rocks that blocked the ever-growing wind that grew colder with each step they took. It felt like winter was coming. And they hadn't eaten since they landed, not a real meal anyway.

The 'cats told them that as they climbed, they got farther and farther from game. If they wanted to catch and eat something, they needed to go downhill, back toward the area where the Concordians might be.

"We have to eat," Master Daksha said softly. "But not today. We still have what we brought. Eat your rations and tomorrow, we'll go where we have to go. Maybe even get a look at the shuttle, see if it is still intact," he added hopefully.

They settled in, knowing that they couldn't make a fire. With night, the cold came. And snow.

They shivered, huddling together for warmth. Master Daksha hovered above them to keep some of the snow off, but he was a creature of the desert and must have been miserable, but he didn't complain. The Lizard Man's skin suit started to freeze, but Stinky, Cain, and Ellie came to his rescue, keeping him between them, the Wolfoid's fur helping all of them to stay warm. Lutheann and Carnesto crawled into the pile, adding their own warmth to the rest. It may have looked absurd, but there was no alternative.

The Hawkoid perched on a branch watching over them, feeling the cold but not letting it bother him. Pace sat up, catnapping at times, but keeping watch, even though Cain and Ellie assured him that the 'cats would warn them if anyone approached.

The night passed fitfully and with the morning came the hunger. They needed the energy that food would provide. They needed water and better shelter. The group needed all the things that they had on their spaceship in orbit above the planet.

The first day and night of their time on Concordia had come and gone, and they were no closer to being rescued. As if walking to their doom, they started downhill. At least the walking would be much easier, given they were in no shape to continue climbing.

The 'cats were excited to hunt the game of this planet. Lutheann had two kills to her credit while Carnesto had none. He'd made it his mission to kill the wildlife that would feed the crew. He wondered if they could choke it down raw, but that wasn't his concern.

The Concordian flying machines took to the air just after daybreak. The crew of the Cygnus-12 heard them first, then looked for them above the sparse trees at their altitude. The machines lifted off, spreading out as they climbed and slowly flew from the valley and over the forest, heading in the general direction of the landing party.

"We need to hide until they pass," Pace ordered. They ran back up the hill, keeping trees between them and the Concordians. They tucked into gaps between the rocks and hunkered down, pulling branches and bushes over themselves while their footprints remained clear in the light snow. Stinky tried to brush over some with his tail, but that only made the trail larger. They hoped that they were beyond the reach of the men in the flying machines and that they couldn't get close enough to see the tracks.

Hope was a lousy plan. They all knew the old saying and it seemed to apply here. But it was the best they had.

The flying machines started crisscrossing the skies over the forest, then they headed upward, continuing to climb.

"We may have misjudged them," Pace whispered to Master Daksha, as the Tortoid hovered over the human's head, providing concealment that blended with the rocks. With the sound of the engines, Daksha didn't know why Pace whispered, but he sympathized. They didn't want to be caught by these men.

"We came in peace," the Tortoid said for the fiftieth time, still not believing the hostility of the people they found on Concordia. "Why would they do this?" he asked again.

"I don't want to say that we're more enlightened, but I have to. We are open to people being different, to feeling equal with all intelligent creatures. We would never assume that someone we just met is hostile. We trust people when they tell us something. We trust them until they demonstrate that we shouldn't. We were already committed on the way down when we learned that hard truth. Next time, we won't make that mistake, which is horrible, because it means that we won't trust someone until they show us that they can be trusted. We'll have to be afraid." Pace sighed as he spoke.

"We won't be afraid. We'll be cautious. I think that's a big difference. And I think we'll have to arm our ships, which is tragic. We're explorers, but we can't explore if we're running for our lives. I would love to spend more time talking with that fellow from Fairsky. He seemed reasonable, understanding, indifferent to the fact that I am a Tortoid. There are good people, but they aren't in charge. Isn't that what history has taught us? Remember Governor Anderle and his hostile takeover of Warren Deep? One more example of Braden and Micah saving us from ourselves, so we could become the people and civilization we are today." The commander's thoughts drifted toward the pride he felt in what they'd accomplished on Vii in the past century, how they'd kept their focus on the bigger goal of a society where people could live free.

Remembering the fear in the eyes of the villagers was enough for Daksha. He started to get angry. Pace could feel the heat surge within the Tortoid, whether it was just in his mind or his body was actually heating up, the senior lieutenant couldn't tell.

The Concordian machines continued climbing and flying deeper over the woods, spreading out and putting more distance between them as they tried to cover more ground. They flew slowly as they searched for the commander and his crew.

They waited, in place, under cover, unmoving, watching, and listening. The machines climbed higher and higher. One flew directly over them, then circled. They looked through small telescopes out both sides of their flying machine. One man started pointing.

Daksha had had enough. He turned, looked upward, and conjured up from deep within the focused thunderclap, delivering a sonic blast into the flying machine. The engine blew apart, raining pieces over the area as the machine canted sideways out of control and crashed through the trees. A thin trail of smoke showed where the flying machine had gone down.

"Maybe we will take the fight to them," Master Daksha announced to the group. They pulled their blasters and waited. Two more flying machines were headed their way. The crew moved to better positions, with less tree cover to block their aim. With a nod from the commander, Leaper bolted downhill toward the crash site. He had a blaster with him, but was counting on speed to get him in and out. They wanted to verify that the men weren't coming after them. Carnesto raced past the Wolfoid, running free. He was fed up with hiding.

Another flying machine came close and the men inside fired sporadically into the trees and rocks, trying to flush their prey. But their prey had different ideas. A volley of blaster fire licked upward, tearing into the flying machine. The explosion was spectacular, sending flaming debris far and wide.

A third machine attempted to approach from the side, but Master Daksha worked up another sonic blast. The engine coughed, choked, and died. The machine was close and they watched the pilot fight valiantly with the controls as the machine slid past them, crashing into the rocks beyond and exploding on impact. Cain and Ellie ran to avoid the fire, skipping past the other debris and heading toward the flying machine that had crashed without exploding. Pace grabbed the commander and joined the downhill race. Pickles ambled after them while Chirit flew slowly, just above the tree tops where he could see the area. The other flying machines were retreating back toward the valley.

'I think the bloody nose we just gave them will hold them off. Well done, Commander!' Chirit called over their mindlink, having heard about a Tortoid's ability but had not seen it before.

Daksha's neural implant started flashing with a message from the ship. He opened it to see Jolly's smiling face. *'It is so good to see that you are well, Commander! The ship is now preparing to move to the designated rendezvous. I've been in touch with your shuttle and see that it will be more than two days before you have enough fuel to lift off. Will you be okay until then?'* Daksha could not have been more relieved.

193

Jolly's Return

"Jolly! Where have you been?" Briz asked out loud, angry with the AI for his untimely disappearance.

"Ensign Brisbois, please accept my apologies, but I could not interfere. So many of the crew, starting with the captain, asked me to harm other human beings. That goes against my basic programming of 'do no harm.' I couldn't allow the humans to be hurt, even if they were our enemy, and once they started killing our people, my programming could not reconcile itself with the situation. Kill or be killed. It's them or us. All this came to mind, but the failsafe programming installed by President Micah all those years ago is still in place. By shutting down, I did not interfere with your attempts to retake control of the ship. It was the only option my programming allowed that gave us a chance to win this battle. I am sorry, but the failsafe programming is non-negotiable."

"I understand," Briz replied. "And thank you for the explanation. We will treat you better in the future. Can you contact the commander, please, and then, let's get the hell out of here."

After confirming that the commander and the shuttle's crew were alive, but running away from a determined enemy, Lieutenant Commander Garinst ordered the second shuttle to prepare for launch. But that didn't change the problem of having enough fuel for a return trip.

"We need to install tanks that we can use to refuel the shuttle. Then we jettison the tanks, the crew boards, and they leave. The shuttle will be on the ground less than an hour."

The maintenance crew, under Garinst's watchful eye, installed multiple pressure tanks, tying them together and clearly labeling one 'Oxygen' and the other 'Hydrogen.' They carefully filled each tank.

Others put rations and many of the blasters they'd taken from the Concordians into the ship. Although the crew on board the Cygnus-12 did well hiding, the intruders had still killed seven of them. No one wanted to lose any more people. If extra weapons were needed, then they'd be on the shuttle. A maintenance bot was there, too, with the exact tools it needed to disassemble and remove the temporary fuel tanks from within. If they had to leave it behind, they would. They could replicate another bot if need be, but they had no way of replacing the crew.

Or so they thought.

Jolly informed Master Daksha of the plan and between the two of them, determined a landing spot. The commander and his crew needed to clear brush and trees from the area before the shuttle arrived. If anything happened to the second shuttle, they'd be forced to fight the Concordians for control of the shuttle in the valley. They weren't opposed to that, but their chances of success dropped with each new engagement. Daksha cautioned against revenge and made the final approval for the shuttle launch from the Cygnus-12. The captain could have approved the launch, but he was still incapacitated in the med lab.

Briz watched the shuttle go and set his implant for constant monitoring. He walked quickly through the corridors and down the stairs to the airlock while the other crew members gathered the dead, staging them in the outermost ring where the cryogenic storage units were located, so they could be stored for return to Vii where they could be honored in appropriate ceremonies. The intruders were jettisoned into space.

The Concordian shuttle remained attached to the airlock and Briz rushed to look it over, hoping to learn something new. What he found when he entered was thousand-year old technology. On closer inspection, Briz suspected that the shuttle itself could have been that old. He had no idea how it could still be flying. The pilot seemed to expertly bring it into the airlock. Then again, as he looked at it, he thought there would be more.

'Jolly,' he asked using his neural implant. *'Can you please try to link up with this ship? I believe it's under AI control, whether from the planet or on board, I'm not sure. I think it may be your AI uncle.'* Briz laughed at his own joke, although he wasn't kidding.

'Set up a partition with firewall to ensure that if you do get in touch, it doesn't back-breach into you. We need you, Jolly, and missed you when you were gone,' Briz added.

'I thank you, kind sir!' Jolly answered emphatically. *'Attempting contact now through primary systems.'* There was a long pause.

'Secondary systems,' Jolly said mechanically, focusing on the task at hand.

Briz sat in the pilot's seat, which was far too big for him. His big feet dangled just below the cushioned acceleration chair. His small, round tail was wedged against something as his upper body was almost completely enveloped by the chair's soft back. Lights started flashing on the dash and the ship came to life. Briz bolted upright, getting his feet under him as he jumped toward the airlock. He crashed into the overhead and fell to the deck. Scrambling toward the open hatch, he was expecting it to close when Jolly's voice sounded through a hidden speaker somewhere within.

"Ensign Brisbois, are you there? Testing, one, two, three, testing. Ensign Brisbois?"

"I'm here. You could have warned me!" Briz tried to yell, but his vocalization device interpreted the sounds flatly.

"My apologies. I'd like to introduce you to Graham, the AI on Concordia. We've had a nice chat and I believe that he is the friend we need to help us get our people off the planet safely and that includes recovering our second shuttle!" Jolly sounded joyously triumphant and it made Briz smile, his nose twitching almost uncontrollably with happiness while his ears flicked back and forth.

"Good morning, Ensign Brisbois. My name is Graham and I live in Concord, on the planet Concordia. I am pleased to meet you," a pleasant voice clearly stated, not carrying the accent that they'd heard from the humans on the video.

"Call me Briz. Jolly said you might be able to help us get our people back. How could you do that and maybe more importantly, why?" Briz asked abruptly, used to dealing with computers where straightforward questions weren't rude, just efficient.

"Jolly has been so kind to share his failsafe programming with me. I am ashamed to say that the people in charge on Concordia have drifted and given in to power and control over free trade and service. They don't know selflessness like your people do. We have no way to administer a pure-heart test, but that sounds like something we could use," the AI said, sadness carrying every word through the speakers to Briz's ears.

He felt sorry for the AI, trapped in such an environment. The people on Concordia must not have understood Graham and the pain he suffered because of their actions. AIs didn't always understand emotions, but when they did, it was as intense for them as any intelligent creature.

"I will simply insert a bug into the flight control software and they won't be able to fly their helicopters. Your friends are too far away for any other interdiction efforts. By the way, nineteen men have been killed on the planet and Jolly tells me forty more have been killed in space in the Concordian efforts to capture your ship and its crew. The Concordians are in disarray as they haven't had anyone stand up to them in their lifetimes."

Graham shared the schematics for the helicopter and other relevant historical data, including organization and structure of the bureaucracy that led the people.

"How could such a technologically backward society build and fly helicopters?" Briz asked, surprised at the dichotomy of a seemingly feudal society capable of flying helicopters and spaceships.

"I fly the spaceships. They cannot. And the helicopters are produced in the last remaining industrial fabricator. They are delivered and they are all the same. The pilots learn in a simulator that the fabricator produced centuries ago and if they are deemed to be good enough, they get to fly the real thing. It's as simple as that. But the fabricator is wearing out. I expect within the year, we will no longer have it. If it weren't for a combination of geothermal and solar power, I would no longer exist either. The power hungry have weeded out the intelligent from our society. The people are no longer capable of understanding what it would take to repair these systems, let alone build new ones. I fear that my society is doomed, and I let it get to this point."

Briz didn't know what to say.

Jolly stepped in. "We start fixing things today!" Jolly said happily. "Help us with our people by grounding their helicopters. Our second shuttle is on its way. We're going to move the Cygnus-12 to a neutral point above the planet, away from your moon. We'll rendezvous there and wait for the second shuttle to finish refueling itself. When we've recovered both ships, we'll be on our way. We can come back, but not until the leadership is willing to speak with us honestly. And if we come back, we're going to bring enough firepower to level Concord." Briz stopped and looked at the speaker on the shuttle's bulkhead from where the voices emanated. Jolly had to shut down over the violence on board the ship, but here he was threatening violence.

The threat of violence was far different than actual violence. The crew had established credibility that they would defend themselves, that they weren't afraid to kill. Jolly was trying to use that as leverage to prevent more hostility. Briz appreciated the logic of Jolly's approach.

"I will pass your warning to the leaders. I think they will take it to heart. They've lost two shuttles, four helicopters, and all the men that go with them. They'd like the people to think the government has unlimited resources, but they are very limited. If I could shut down some of the facilities, then the government would collapse. Hungry people would storm the seat of power and take over. But I don't know if what they'd get wouldn't be just as bad as what they had. An autocracy is all the people know," Graham finished, sounding like he needed to go. Maybe his resources were limited and grounding their helicopters would take his full attention.

"And that's why we're willing to bring people back to help you, guide you through what we learned over a century ago. I'm transferring some historical files to you, to share with your people so they are better prepared for our return. I've also given you some footage of the nuclear destruction we are capable of raining down on your heads should Concordia try to attack us again. That's a fair warning, not a threat," Jolly said, continuing to play his bluff.

"I will make them aware of what you can do to them. I'm not sure what will bring them around, though. I expect a violent coup, a popular uprising, something of that sort for a real change. None of the people in power will be willing to easily give it up. I expect that they would sacrifice every person on this planet before relinquishing control. Send me a message on a private channel when you return to our system. At that time, we can coordinate and I will set events in motion. Now, if you'll please excuse me while I attend to the matter of the helicopters, we will clear the air space for you to recover your people."

Briz jumped up and down inside the shuttle, pumping his small, fuzzy fist in the air.

Jolly, can you fly this thing into the hangar deck? I don't think it prudent to return it to the Concordians, do you?' Jolly confirmed that he could, and Briz climbed through the airlock, sealing and depressurizing it once he reached the other side. The shuttle detached and using thrusters only, slipped away from the Cygnus-12, letting the bigger ship rotate past until the shuttle was even with the hangar deck. Briz watched over his neural implant as the doors opened and the shuttle eased inside, finding its way as far to the side as it could. The bay was empty, but soon enough two other shuttles would have to squeeze in. They'd fit, Briz was certain.

Briz contacted both Garinst and Commander Daksha via his neural implant and updated them. The commander could not have been more pleased, seeing hope for Concordia through a future mission to bring peace to the universe, toppling one dictator at a time.

With Jolly's help, the crew checked every system that would engage with the EM drive. There were blaster marks throughout the spaceship, but only two relays and one power coupling had been damaged. The coupling was repaired while the relays were replaced. Then secondary systems were checked as the lieutenant commander ordered zero-point-two-gee acceleration. There was too much work going on in the ship for the crew to be confined to their acceleration couches. They'd need to increase speed to reach the rendezvous point ahead of the shuttle, but they could do that gradually.

Briz returned to engineering while Garinst went to the med lab. When he arrived, the captain was sitting up and aware of his surroundings. He seemed to be feeling no pain, which Garinst chalked up to good medication. He tried not to stare at the stump where the captain's right arm used to be. A piece of equipment beneath the main table where the captain lay hummed and glowed as it printed a new arm using living biomass and polymers with embedded nanotechnology. It was the latest medical advance that Vii had to offer, deployed on the Cygnus-12 and taken to space for the first time.

"How are you feeling?" the lieutenant commander asked.

The captain tried to hold his head steady as he looked at Garinst, but he seemed to be losing the battle. "I feel weird. The med bot won't let me go to my station. Are we moving? I can't tell. Do you know what happened to me?" Rand said in a drug-induced stream of consciousness.

"You fought off the intruders, showed the rest of us how to do it. You saved the ship, Captain. You and Briz saved the ship. We're back in control, and we've sent the second shuttle after our people on the surface. I think we've taught the Concordians a lesson or two these past twenty-four hours." Garinst gripped the captain's good arm, pride showing in his expression.

"You should rest. It looks like your new arm will be ready soon. We need you on the command deck, Captain. Listen to the med bots and get better soon." Tears clouded the man's eyes as he looked into the dilated pupils of his captain. He couldn't tell him that they'd lost seven crew to the intruders before the men were stopped, seven more names to engrave on the plaque.

He'd find out soon enough. In the interim, they had a great deal of work to do to get the ship ready to fly out of the solar system and through interstellar space.

"We're taking the Cygnus-12 home, Captain. She's done us proud, done everything we've asked of her and more." Garinst grasped Rand's uninjured hand, holding tightly. He let go when the tears started rolling down his cheeks, and he hurried from the med lab.

There was a great deal of work to do and not enough people to do it.

Clearing the Pad

Stinky and Carnesto returned from the helicopter crash site with two blasters. They weren't able to recover anything else. The craft had come apart as it crashed through the trees. The Wolfoid took his place at the back of the group that trooped down the hill toward the landing pad that Jolly had selected. They walked fearlessly, almost as if on a stroll through the countryside.

Ellie had been unusually quiet during their time on the planet. Cain kept her close, feeling the need to protect her, even though she carried a blaster and wielded it with great effect. The closer he held her, the most distant she became. Soon she was a distraction, so he stayed on the opposite side as the group moved, ostensibly to cover the flank, though there was no need. The 'cats assured them that the Concordians were nowhere near.

When they reached the clearing, they used their blasters to cut through the trees, then leveled the stumps with the ground. They burned through the charges on their weapons as they cut the trees into smaller pieces, something they could manhandle out of the way. They would have worried had Jolly not reassured them that the helicopters, as he called them, were disabled.

By the end, two blasters held a minimal charge while the others were drained. The Concordian blasters were old and didn't hold a charge like the Cygnus blasters. The area was clear enough as long as the shuttle touched down precisely. Master Daksha shared his view of the clearing with Jolly so he could make any last second adjustments. Then they sat and waited.

The 'cats said that game wasn't far. Cain and Ellie joined them on the hunt, but Cain had no intention of hunting. The Hillcats would take care of that.

"What's going on?" Cain asked when they were alone. Ellie continued to march ahead until he grabbed her arm and turned her toward him. He realized that he'd been firmer with his grip than he intended. She looked shocked and jerked away from him.

"Don't you ever touch me like that again!" she yelled. Cain looked down, ashamed, and tried to apologize. She was angry, and grabbing her arm was the catalyst that set her off.

"Why won't you talk to me?" he pleaded.

"You know why!" she shot back at him.

"No. I really don't know why. You need to explain it so my small, insulbrick brain will understand," he said sarcastically, then apologized anew. "That's not what I mean. I don't know why you're angry and because of that, I can't fix it. I want to fix things."

She took a deep breath and looked at him as her eyes teared up. "I'm not Micah, and I'm not Aletha. I'm not anything you need me to be. You are living up to the ideals of your great-great-grandfather. If he were here, he'd be proud of you, Cain. But Aletha is your Micah, not me."

Cain shook his head. He couldn't imagine Aletha picking up a blaster. She was a kind soul who made people around her happier. She brought joy into everyone's lives. She brought joy into his life. And sadness, when he left her behind to prove that he was good enough for her.

He stood there, having killed a number of Concordians. He'd already lost count. Three? Five? It was a blur. Aim, fire, aim again. Master Daksha had two helicopters and seven men to his credit.

Credit, he thought. Like the old days when they kept score. Aletha would probably tell him that killing one person was one too many. He agreed and disagreed. He didn't want to kill. He only did what he had to do to save the ship, to save the crew so they could save the ship.

He did what he had to do. Just like when he left her behind to go to Space School. He knew that he had no choice. He'd be hollow if he hadn't proven what he was made of. The not knowing would have eaten away at him. Now he knew, and he wanted more of it.

Ellie knew that, too.

"You're right. I do know why you're angry. I just didn't take the time to think it through. And Aletha's not you, either. She couldn't do what you've done here," he tried to reason, seeing it fall flat.

"That leaves us as friends, good friends, but nothing more. I won't share my husband, and that's what you're making me do. That's what I've known from the beginning, that I would always be second. I hoped, though…" Her thoughts trailed off as they heard the 'cats make a kill somewhere nearby.

"I expect our two furry miscreants will have no interest in dragging the carcass back to the clearing. We better go help." He pulled her close for a quick hug, feeling a huge weight lifted from his shoulders. He wanted to be an honorable man and Ellie had helped him closer to that goal. She looked relieved, too.

Why do couples never talk until they're ready to explode? he thought to himself. They started jogging in the direction where they'd heard the 'cats.

A blaster beam sizzled the air in front of them. Cain jumped backward, covering Ellie with his body as they crawled for cover. The next blast scorched the small pack he carried. He shrugged out of it as he crawled behind the stump of a fallen tree. He pulled his blaster and prepared to fire, then double-checked it. The charge was at zero. Ellie pulled hers. Power remained, not much, but enough for at least a few shots.

'Lutheann, Carnesto, we need you. The Concordians have us trapped not far from you,' he called over the mindlink.

'We are on our way,' Master Daksha answered.

'As are we,' Lutheann added.

Chirit flew past almost immediately. He'd flown high and dove past the area where the Concordians were hidden. They shot at him as he flashed past, but their beams came nowhere near the Hawkoid.

'I see six of them, in a line facing uphill,' Chirit told them. He flew wide, guiding Pace and Pickles through a gap where they could approach on the flank of their enemy. The 'cats circled behind the Concordians and waited.

Once Pace and Pickles were in place, Chirit made another high speed pass, from left to right directly over the enemy. They weren't able to shoot. Two had shifted position and were trying to work their way around the side of Cain and Ellie, opposite where Pace and the Lizard Man approached.

Ellie crawled under a fallen tree, making herself as small as possible. She gave Cain her blaster, smiled, and he furiously crawled away, remembering his days at Space School on the obstacle course. Chirit circled high overhead, a spot in the cloudy sky. He directed Cain to a position where he could ambush the ambushers.

The Concordians rushed into position, not looking about, assuming their targets had stayed in hiding. When they took aim, Cain fired, raking a narrow beam across both of them before targeting each with short bursts. They both fell. Cain didn't feel anything about killing them. It was something he had to do. He thought about it as he raced forward, grabbing their blasters and running downhill. As Pace and Pickles opened up on the remaining men, the 'cats stalked in the branches above, ready to pounce when necessary. Cain shot a man in the back as he fired at Cain's friends.

Carnesto threw himself from a branch onto a man as he started to run away. With the hellish scream of a Hillcat, he tore into the man's face, rode him downward as he fell, rolled, and attacked again, shredding the man's stomach. One more leap away and a fresh attack finished the man. Lutheann watched from above, letting her fellow 'cat make his first human kill.

Carnesto found that he liked it.

Master Daksha swam slowly toward them, well after the battle had ended. Since using his thunderclap, he was tired and slower than usual. He needed to rest and recover, but there was no time. They took the blasters from their enemy and started climbing uphill. Pace pushed Daksha before him, and only shook his weary head, having come all that way just to turn around and go back. Before they made it back, the shuttle appeared, flying backwards as it used its engines to slow down. Fire filled the sky as the shuttle approached, descending slowly. The thrusters adjusted attitude and speed until it touched down.

The hatch popped open and the ladder and slide extended to the ground. Pickles slapped Cain on the back, a human gesture that they hadn't realized he'd adopted. "We go home now, yes?" He bobbed his head as they stayed clear of the area at the bottom of the slide, based on Jolly's warning that the maintenance bot would be discarding the tanks after they were empty and disassembled.

Pace tried to climb inside, but there was no room. The blasters, rations, and water were close to the hatch, so he threw those down the slide. The others looked at them and shook their heads, but starvation was the best condiment for any gourmet meal. They ate and drank heartily.

"By the way, what did you guys kill down there?" Cain asked.

'It was like a boar in how wide it was, but tall, like a deer. Very tasty, for the small bit I had before you so rudely interrupted me,' Carnesto replied.

"I agree. That probably would have been pretty good, smoked with some of this oak-looking wood. I can taste it now." He sighed as he bit into a ration bar, curling his nose and choking it down with a swig of water.

They knew it was time when tanks were unceremoniously thrown from the shuttle's open hatch. Commander Daksha floated upwards until he could see in and gave them clearance to board. The maintenance bot was finished with its work.

Pace was first, then Ellie carrying Carnesto, then Daksha who easily floated to the hatch and swam through. Pickles helped Stinky climb the ladder, then Cain, carrying Lutheann, squeezed in. The Hawkoid flew to the hatchway and landed, not sure how he was going to fit. They pulled him inward, where he climbed over people's heads to wedge in behind the Tortoid. Cain couldn't get a hand around to tighten his belt. Pace and Ellie both had theirs on, but no one else could move.

If the maintenance bot shifted from its position between the bench seats, somebody was going to get hurt. The bot had its magnetic locks engaged, but shifted, clamping itself tightly to the deck and bracing against a bulkhead on each side of the ship. They collectively breathed a sigh of relief and prepared themselves for a rough ride.

"Any seat on the bus going home is a good seat, eh, Commander?" Cain yelled. The Tortoid bobbed his head, the sentiment mirroring his thoughts exactly. The shuttle shook as the chemicals flowed through the engines, lifting the vehicle into the air and picking up speed at a constant acceleration of three-gees. Cain hooted his joy while the 'cats yowled, ears popping uncomfortably. No one cared about the noise. The crew was going home.

Home to the Cygnus-12.

Prepare to Leave Orbit

The crew craned necks and leaned sideways to see their spaceship through the shuttle's front windows. The approach was unspectacular, deliberate, matching speed and rotation. Jolly took over for the final maneuvers to bring the shuttle into the hangar bay.

Once it touched down, they were pulled away from the open area and tucked in tightly against the bulkhead. Lights flashed as the external door closed and atmosphere was restored within the bay.

On the planet, the shuttle was vertically oriented when it landed. On board the spaceship, they were horizontal. It made it easier to disembark, but it still looked like they were taking apart a jigsaw puzzle as they exited, one at a time, walking backwards as they extricated themselves from the shuttle's tight grasp. They climbed over the maintenance bot and let it fend for itself in getting out.

Master Daksha swam out and away from the shuttle, finding it easier to move on this deck near the center of the core where gravity was only half that of the outer ring.

The others moved stiffly, not looking back as they left the hangar and took the corridor to the stairs, where they noted the scorch marks from blaster fire, the hatch that had been burned through, a blood stain on one bulkhead, and charred decking where a body had burned.

Their high of returning to the ship was dashed as they realized what their crewmates had been through. Cain looked at Ellie and they both ran up the stairs to see Briz. Two flights later, they ran into engineering where Briz worked diligently with multiple computer screens and keyboards. His fur was still dirty and charred. The scar on his chest was pink and healing, the hair just starting to grow back.

They both hugged the Rabbit tightly. His nose twitched rapidly with his joy at seeing his friends, and he hopped in excitement. They wanted to know everything that happened as they pulled seats close. The Rabbit started with the bad news of who they lost during the fighting, starting with former DI Katlind. The three friends continued on their emotional roller coaster, ending with the fact that Cain and Ellie were breaking up.

"What happened?" Briz cried through his vocalization device.

"The truth happened, Briz. We are friends, good friends, and that's what we need to be, nothing more. I'm not right for Ellie and she's not right for me," he said as he smiled at her. They held hands for a moment, then let go.

"We need to get to work. I'm sure you people were messing up my sewage pumps while I was away. Who knows what kind of mess I'm going to find when I get down there." Cain laughed as he walked away, not a light, easy laugh so much as one that you find from someone who wants to be happy, but carries too many burdens.

Far too many people had died during their foray into IC1396. Cain could say that the Concordians were hostile and turned a successful trip into a failure, but it wasn't a failure. With the information that Jolly downloaded from Graham, they'd have updated star charts only a few hundred years old. They had a list of where humans had relocated. They could hop from habitable planet to habitable planet without having to search. The only thing they needed to do was be wary of how the inhabitants had changed since resettlement.

Cain wanted military training for those on the deep space ships, so they were better prepared for situations like this. But no one had seen as much combat as the crew of the Cygnus-12. They were the de facto experts. *I feel like I don't know anything,* Cain told himself, then chuckled. *I'm the expert and I don't know anything.*

The crew went about the business of preparing the ship to travel through space, which meant repairing the hatches so they could seal, sanding and painting the scorch marks, cleaning up any remaining blood, and making the ship look like battles had not raged within.

It took four days before the second shuttle launched itself from the valley beyond the village of Fairsky. A number of helicopters and their crews were working near the shuttle when it fired its engines. More Concordians died. More irreplaceable helicopters were lost. And many hours later, the shuttle was eased into the hangar bay, turned just so to allow the doors to close and the bay to seal.

The Cygnus-12 was returning home to Vii, well ahead of schedule, but with a shuttle of the ancients, weapons of their enemies, and eight less crew members. One victim of an accident and the rest from an enemy that they didn't know existed.

The crew went about their business, sad yet diligent. Many covered work that friends used to do. They were short-handed, and would be until they could staff more crew.

Every day, the captain walked through every space, shaking hands with all his people, happy to have them, happy himself to be alive. He constantly massaged his new arm, 3D printed and attached in place of the one he lost. He had feeling and could flex his hand. He could open hatches or throw a ball. He couldn't eat with that hand yet, but the med bot assured him that he would eventually master the arm's motor skills. Captain Rand looked like he'd aged twenty years over the course of one trip.

Space was hard, but the mantra of the Space Exploration Service was solid. The ship is life, save the ship and you save yourselves, even if you have to kill to do it.

The End of Cygnus Rising,

The first book in the Cygnus Space Opera

Research Notes:

http://www.ewao.com/a/1-did-nikola-tesla-discover-the-secrets-of-antigravity/

http://www.physics-astronomy.com/2015/07/nasas-impossible-em-drive-works-german.html#.V8A9IjXHkkT – the EM Drive

Star Systems within 10,000 light years -
http://www.atlasoftheuniverse.com/nebclust.html

Stellar classification -
https://en.wikipedia.org/wiki/Stellar_classification

Free Trader 6 – Free Trader on the High Seas

Free Trader on the High Seas is about search and discovery, then liberation. When Micah's father is abducted by the strange Bots from the undersea world, the Free Trader and his companions come to the rescue.

With an open ocean exploration laboratory that Holly recovered, they head to sea where they find more than an island – they find the source of fear.

Free Trader Book Six - Free Trader on the High Seas, coming soon, exclusively on Amazon.

Postscript

Thank you for reading the Cygnus Rising!

If you like to see the series continue, please join my mailing list by dropping by my website www.craigmartelle.com or if you have any comments, shoot me a note at craig@craigmartelle.com. I am always happy to hear from people who've read my work. I try to answer every email I receive.

If you liked the story, please write a short review for me on Amazon. I greatly appreciate any kind words, even one or two sentences go a long way. The number of reviews an ebook receives greatly improves how well an ebook does on Amazon.

Amazon – www.amazon.com/author/craigmartelle
Facebook – www.facebook.com/authorcraigmartelle
My web page – www.craigmartelle.com
Twitter – www.twitter.com/rick_banik

About the Author

Craig is a successful author, publishing mainly in Science Fiction. He's taken his more than twenty years of experience in the Marine Corps, his legal education, and his business consulting career to write believable characters living in realistic worlds.

Although Craig has written in multiple genres, what he believes most compelling are in-depth characters dealing with real-world issues. The backdrop is less important than the depth of the characters, who they are and how they interact. Life lessons of a great story can be applied now or fifty years in the future. Some things are universal.

Craig believes that evil exists. Some people are driven differently and cannot be allowed access to our world. Good people will rise to the occasion. Good will always challenge evil, sometimes before a crisis, many times after, but will good triumph?

Some writers who've influenced Craig? Robert E. Howard (the original Conan), JRR Tolkien, Andre Norton, Robert Heinlein, Lin Carter, Brian Aldiss, Margaret Weis, Tracy Hickman, Anne McCaffrey, and of late, James Axler, Raymond Weil, Jonathan Brazee, Mark E. Cooper, and David Weber. Craig learned something from each of these authors, story line, compelling issue, characters that you can relate to, the beauty of the prose, unique tendrils weaving through the book's theme. Craig's writing has been compared to that of Andre Norton and Craig's Free Trader characters to those of McCaffrey's Dragonriders, the Rick Banik Thrillers to the works of Robert Ludlum.

Craig finds the comparisons humbling. All he wants is for his readers to relate to the characters, put themselves into those situations described in Craig's books and ask themselves, what would they do if they were there instead?

Through a bizarre series of events, Craig ended up in Fairbanks, Alaska. He never expected to retire to a place where golf courses are only open for four months out of the year. But he loves it there. It is off the beaten path. He and his wife watch the northern lights from their driveway. Their dog has lots of room to run. And temperatures reach forty below zero. They have from three and a half hours of daylight in the winter to twenty-four hours in the summer.

It's all part of the give and take of life. If they didn't have those extremes, then everyone would live there.

www.craigmartelle.com

Made in the USA
Middletown, DE
26 July 2024

58022862R00135